WORLDLY WEALTH AND SPIRITUAL POVERTY

Gloria Sutherland had everything—enviable beauty, a chauffeured limousine, the latest fashions from Europe and a handsome fiancé. But when he was found dead with another woman, she realized that her life had been a sham of emptiness.

Then her search for solace brought her to the quaint country retreat of her ancestors where she met young Murray MacRae. With compassion and wisdom he taught her that there was more beauty to life than money could buy.

But as much as Gloria wished for this new life of peace, she feared she could never be worthy of it or the love of this gentle young man.

Would her past, she wondered, forever be a barrier now that happiness was so close?

Bantam Books by Grace Livingston Hill
Ask your bookseller for the books you have missed

1 WHERE TWO WAYS MET
2 BRIGHT ARROWS
3 A GIRL TO COME HOME TO
4 AMORELLE
6 ALL THROUGH THE NIGHT
7 THE BEST MAN
9 THE GIRL OF THE WOODS
10 CRIMSON ROSES
12 HEAD OF THE HOUSE
13 IN TUNE WITH WEDDING BELLS
14 STRANGER WITHIN THE GATES
15 MARIGOLD
16 RAINBOW COTTAGE
17 MARIS
19 DAPHNE DEANE
20 THE SUBSTITUTE GUEST
22 ROSE GALBRAITH
23 TIME OF THE SINGING OF BIRDS
24 BY WAY OF THE SILVERTHORNS

25 SUNRISE
26 THE SEVENTH HOUR
27 APRIL GOLD
28 WHITE ORCHIDS
29 HOMING
30 MATCHED PEARLS
31 THE STRANGE PROPOSAL
32 COMING THROUGH THE RYE
34 THE PATCH OF BLUE
36 PATRICIA
37 SILVER WINGS
38 SPICE BOX
39 THE SEARCH
40 THE TRYST
41 BLUE RUIN
42 A NEW NAME
43 DAWN OF THE MORNING
44 THE BELOVED STRANGER
45 THE GOLD SHOE
47 THE STREET OF THE CITY
48 BEAUTY FOR ASHES
49 THE ENCHANTED BARN

Beauty for Ashes
Grace Livingston Hill

BANTAM BOOKS
TORONTO · NEW YORK · LONDON

*This low-priced Bantam Book
has been completely reset in a type face
designed for easy reading, and was printed
from new plates. It contains the complete
text of the original hard-cover edition.*
NOT ONE WORD HAS BEEN OMITTED.

BEAUTY FOR ASHES

*A Bantam Book / published by arrangement with
J. B. Lippincott Company*

PRINTING HISTORY
*Lippincott edition published February 1935
Bantam edition / May 1977*
2nd printing .. September 1977   3rd printing .... April 1978
4th printing .... March 1979
5th printing

ISBN 0–553–12846–9

Published simultaneously in the United States and Canada

Bantam Books are published by Bantam Books, Inc. Its trademark, consisting of the words "Bantam Books" and the por-
trayal of a bantam, is Registered in U.S. Patent and Trademark
Office and in other countries. Marca Registrada. Bantam
Books, Inc., 666 Fifth Avenue, New York, New York 10019.

PRINTED IN THE UNITED STATES OF AMERICA

Beauty for Ashes

I

The Sutherland home sat like some royal palace at the top of a grassy eminence, nestled about by dark pines and hemlocks, its lawn sloping softly down to the highway where tall iron grill work girt about the estate, and stone pillars made a stately entrance for the driveway. Thick clustering rhododendrons did their best to hide the place from the casual gazer, and glossy laurel branches filled here and there a space; an avenue of trees gave mystery to the driveway as it disappeared into the thickly shrouded entrance and wound about till it reached the dwelling, which stood, a white gleaming jewel at the top of the rise, not quite hidden from view, tantalizingly beautiful in the morning sun.

Behind the house were terraces down to a blue tiled swimming pool, and a smaller pool where lilies floated lazily, and below that a sunken garden. Beyond, a small native woodland with old forest trees carefully tended gave background to the setting.

Off to the right of the house on another eminence not quite so high, well hidden by trees and shrubbery, and somewhat farther back from the highway, another stone dwelling was fast nearing completion. It was called by the architect and the family "the bungalow" but it might have been but another, somewhat smaller, palace, so complete and wide spreading it was. Gloria Sutherland was to be married next week to Stanwood Asher and this bungalow, a wedding gift from her father, was to be her new home.

The Ashers lived on another hilltop across the town of Roselands, in a mansion of fine old Norman architecture, and were the moving spirits in the social life of the place. What the Ashers and Sutherlands did set the pace for the rest of the set and even the humbler residents of Roselands turned to look when Nancy Asher rode through town on her fine blooded mare, or her brother Stanwood shot by in his fabulous-priced high-powered car; and they stopped to admire when either Gloria or Vanna Sutherland were driven by in the handsome Sutherland limousine. Both Gloria and Vanna were worth a second look besides being the very most charming girls of the younger smart set of Roselands, and wearing clothes straight from the most noted creators of Europe.

It was a bright beautiful morning in Spring. There were daffodils in golden banks here and there along the borders of the driveway, and the terraces behind the house were a marvellous broidery of color in crocuses, hyacinths and tulips. Great forsythia bushes shed brightness against the dark pines effectively, like sudden bursts of sunshine, a flame of red tulips picked out a scallop below the white stone wall, and out on the edge of the woods pink and white dogwood had decked themselves in blossoms. It was a morning that went well in one's mind with the thought of weddings, large priceless weddings where money was lavished without stint.

Gloria Sutherland had arisen at an hour that she called early. It was ten o'clock. She had breakfasted, mainly on orange juice and coffee, in her room, and in her yellow velvet negligee went straight to the sewing room where the fitter awaited who had come up from one of the city shops to make an alteration in an orchid satin evening frock.

She looked like a daffodil herself as she entered the

sewing room and stood by the open window with the sunlight falling on her mop of yellow curls. The yellow velvet gown coming down softly to the little green satin slippers she was wearing completed the illusion of a yellow flower. She stood and basked in the sunshine, and the sunlight on the velvet cast a golden glow over her piquant face. The seamstress who was no longer young and never had been beautiful looked at her with a wistful admiration, and sighed enviously to think what a charmed life this beautiful creature led.

Gloria threw the golden garment aside and allowed herself to be carefully arrayed in the delicate orchid satin. She stood in front of the long pier glass and watched the seamstress as she deftly put in a pin here, smoothed out a pucker there, gave just a little different sweep to the deep flounce that half circled the curiously fashioned skirt and spread out the line of the long train.

"It is a lovely dress, isn't it?" said Gloria childishly, joyously. That was one thing about Gloria that made everybody like her, she was so natural and childlike and happy. Her wealth and beauty had not spoiled her nor made her snobbish.

"She is like her father," the servants whispered among themselves.

After the pinning was complete Gloria gave herself another look, walked the length of the room and back watching the sweep of the train as she walked.

"I want Vanna to see this before I take it off!" she suddenly exclaimed. "I wonder if she has come in yet? I thought I heard a car. She was away at a house party last night, but she said she'd be home early. Just wait a minute and I'll run down and see if she has come yet."

Lightly Gloria caught up the gleaming train, ran down the deeply carpeted stairs to the floor below, then paused to listen. Someone had just come in the door. Yes, that was Vanna's voice. She was talking to Brandon, their younger brother home from school for the week-end. Her tone was wildly excited:

"Oh, Brand! Have you seen the paper?"

"No," growled Brandon, "I just came downstairs. Anything the matter? You look like last year's tax bills. What's happened?"

"Plenty!" said Vanna tragically. "Stan Asher's been killed!"

"Killed!" said Brandon echoing her word stupidly. "How? When?"

"Shot!" said Vanna with a gasp of her breath. "Shot in a night club in New York last night! Shot with a dancing girl he had with him. They're both dead! They've arrested the girl's lover. He didn't make any attempt to get away!"

"Good night!" said Brandon in a shocked voice as if he had suddenly grown up.

"We mustn't tell Gloria!" said Vanna breathlessly. "Not yet! Not till Dad comes! He'll be sure to be here soon. He'll see it in the paper. He'll come to her right away! Better go hide the paper. It says awful things about Stan. She mustn't *ever* see it!"

"She'll havta know pretty soon if Dad doesn't get here!" said the boy gravely. "And if Mother finds out——"

"Is Mother down yet?"

"I don't think so. Her door was shut when I came by. What if we phone down to the office to see if Dad has got in yet! He went to New York yesterday didn't he? You sure he was coming back to-day?"

"No, but you know he'll come when he sees this. And he can't help seeing it. It's in all the papers, great big headlines. 'Stanwood Asher, wealthy heir to millions shot down with chorus girl by jealous lover in notorious night club!' Oh, it's *awful!* To think anything like that could come to our family!"

Vanna caught her breath in a great sob, and then suddenly held her breath and looked up the stairs her eyes large with horror, for there stood Gloria in her lovely orchid dress with her gold hair aflame, and her eyes wide pools of dark blue horror in a white, white face.

"Vanna! What is it? I'm not a child! Tell me everything! *Quick!*"

Vanna gave her young brother a frightened glance and sped up the stairs.

"It's about Stan, dear!" she said trying to make her voice sound steady. "It's bad news!"

"Yes! I heard!" said Gloria. "Tell it over again slowly, just as you said it!"

Vanna gave a little gasp like a sob as she spoke the words: "Stan was killed in a night club in New York last night, dear."

"And the girl?" said Gloria fixing her sister with a keen glance.

Vanna caught another little sob in her throat.

"She was killed too. By a jealous lover!"

Gloria reached out and caught hold of the stair railing.

"Brand!" she called to the brother who lingered in blank horror below. "Bring me that paper! Yes, please———!" as she saw Vanna shake her head. "I've got to know everything right away! Bring it, Brand! Vanna, won't you please help me off with this terrible dress?"

Vanna drew her sister into Gloria's own room and began to unfasten the hooks with fingers that trembled.

"There—couldn't be a mistake, could there Vanna?" asked Gloria casting an imploring glance her way as the dress was lifted over her head.

"No, there couldn't be a mistake," said Vanna sadly. "I telephoned Nance! She said her father went up on the early morning train. He phoned about ten minutes ago. It's all true!"

Vanna looked about for Gloria's negligee.

"No," said Gloria sharply, as her sister brought out a blue silk robe. "No, I've got to have a dress on!"

"You ought to lie down, dear!" soothed Vanna. "You don't realize yet! You need to lie down and take it quietly!"

"No," said Gloria, "I must do something! I don't know what, but there'll be things to do. I must have a dress on and be ready."

Vanna searched helplessly in the closet for something appropriate. What would one wear on an occasion like this? Mourning? If Gloria was dressed people would be likely to see her, and they would criticise whatever she had on. Clothes had always played such a large part in Vanna's life that they seemed important even now.

But Gloria pulled out a drawer and snatched up a brown and tan knitted dress she had worn the day before and flung it on.

"Just anything! It doesn't matter what," she said as her sister looked askance at the dress. "Brand, is that you with the paper? And please, Brand, will you take this orchid dress up to the sewing room and tell the fitter it is perfectly all right just as it is, and she can just hang it up there when she has finished? Tell her I won't be able to come up again to-day."

Vanna looked at her sister in admiration, she seemed so cool, so collected, yet there was something terrifying in her eyes. Vanna put her hand to her throat and tried to still the stifling sensation that threatened to overwhelm her. Oh, it seemed just impossible that this tragedy was really happening in their family. Stan, the handsome brother-in-law dead! Just a week before the wedding!

Then she began to realize.

There would be no wedding!

Over there in the green guest room closet were hanging the bridesmaids' dresses, soft spring pastel shades of chiffon, with silver slippers and lovely big garden hats wreathed in spring blossoms. Back in the apricot guest room the bridal array was waiting and there would be *no wedding!*

Three long connecting rooms to the left were cleared and furnished with long draped tables on which already a goodly array of costly glitter was set out, and the presents were pouring in every hour! And there would be no wedding!

But Gloria went steadily on arranging her dress, smoothing her rumpled curls, putting her brush away as coolly as if nothing had happened. Didn't she realize what it all meant? Why wasn't she lying on her bed sobbing? Why wasn't she breaking her heart? Stan dead, Stan whom Gloria adored, and Gloria going about with a quiet stony look in her eyes! Vanna was frightened.

"Does Mother know?" asked Gloria suddenly in that quiet capable tone that was so new to her, as if she had certain things to go through and just so much strength with which to go through them.

"No," said Vanna, "she hasn't gone downstairs yet."

"Does Mrs. Asher know?"

"Yes, Nance said she was in hysterics. They had sent for the doctor," said Vanna.

"Poor thing!" said Gloria with a terrible trembling sigh!

Vanna stared. She knew Gloria was not especially fond of Stan's mother, and yet here she was without a tear for herself, pitying Stan's mother.

Gloria dropped into a chair and began to read the paper, her white face growing even whiter as she read. Once she groaned aloud, and once she looked up and said, though more as if she were stating a fact to herself than speaking to her sister:

"He'd known that girl for a long time. There had been trouble before. Two years ago! That was before —before we were—engaged!" She looked at the paper again. "No,—it was after! Two months after! Oh——!"

The sound she made was not a sob. It was more like a wounded animal getting to cover.

Vanna was silent, filled with misery for the sister who had always been so much a part of herself. She was feeling what Gloria was going through. Neither of these girls had had any sorrow in their lives before, beyond a broken doll, or a lost kitten. Never any trouble before that money could not mend.

From where she sat Vanna could see the gleam of the tiled roof that was her sister's new home. What would Gloria do now with that house? Would Dad have it torn down? Would they all move or go to Europe or something? How everything had been upheaved and made impossible in a single night! A bullet gone home, a heart stilled, and two families were plunged into dismay, their world collapsed!

Vanna began to think of the young set that made up their social life! How could they bear to go among them again? How could Gloria ever enjoy the crowd and all its gay doings with Stan gone! And gone in such a terrible way!

Suddenly she caught her breath and put her head down on the arm of the chair where she sat, the tears coming like a tempest over which she had no control.

"Vanna! You mustn't!" said Gloria looking at her out of those stony eyes. "We've got to keep up!"

"Why?" said Vanna tempestuously. *"Why?* You ought to cry too, Glory! It'll help you a lot. You'll break down if you don't cry."

"I can't!" said Gloria. "The tears are all locked inside! They can't get out! Vanna, do you think I ought to go and see Mrs. Asher?"

"No," said Vanna vehemently. "Nance said she was wild. They had given her a sleeping powder. She wouldn't see you if you went. Nance said the doctor said they must get her quieted down."

Gloria sank back in her chair again and looked hungrily down at the paper whose flaring headlines had been followed by very little other information concerning the tragedy. Gloria had read every word over twice already, yet she took up the paper and searched earnestly for one more little word. Oh, if there was only so much as a hint of denial that that girl had been anything before to Stan! But there it all was printed out cruelly, just two or three lines, but each word ripe to stimulate the imagination, hints that were worse than the truth could possibly be!

Then suddenly the mother was among them, standing at the door, a look of generalship upon her.

"Gloria! My poor child!" she mourned. "To think that this should have happened to you! And just now before the wedding! It makes it so awkward for you, Petty! But, Child, dear, you should go right to bed; You mustn't think of being up. A trouble like this drains one's strength. Besides, it is so much easier to excuse you to any mistaken friends who might think they had to call if we can just say you are prostrated. Get to bed right away, Honey dear, and conserve your strength."

"No, Mother," said Gloria, "I'm not going to bed. I should go wild in bed!"

Gloria got up and began to pace up and down her room. Her mother watched her with a puzzled look.

"You're a strange girl!" she said almost disapprovingly. "If you take it that way we shall have you sick on our hands before——" she hesitated for the fraction of a second and Gloria shivered as if a cold draught had struck her—"before this is over," the mother finished.

"It will never be over!" said Gloria in a hollow, terrible, young voice.

"Oh, yes, it will!" said her mother quickly. "Of course you can't see that now, but it's a merciful thing that sorrows don't engulf people forever. However, it's much better to just give way naturally to your grief and not try to keep up and hide your feelings."

Gloria looked at her mother as if she did not hear her and went on walking up and down her room.

The mother gave her another hopeless look and turned as if she would go out, then looked back to say:

"We'll all have to have some black clothes of course. What a pity in the Spring of the year! I'll go and call up Sampson's and have them send out some things on approval. That's another reason, Gloria, why you ought to lie down now. You'll have to try on you know, and that's almost as wearing as having to go down town shopping for clothes."

Gloria turned in consternation.

"Mother! I'm not going to try on clothes to-day! No, nor any of these days! One doesn't have to dress for the part to suffer! I'll wear something I've got, anything! But I won't have anything to do with clothes at such a time as this!"

"Now Gloria, do try to be reasonable! You can't just ignore the customs of society that way!"

"Look here, Mother, I'm not going out on exhibition! I shan't probably see anybody at all except the Ashers, and you don't suppose they'll care what clothes I have on, do you?"

"I certainly do!" said the calm voice of the mother. "You must be appropriately dressed. If you're not they would think, and rightly, that you had not the proper respect for their feelings."

"Mother, if they can care about things like that now I don't care what they think! I have plenty of clothes and I'm not going to bother about others!"

"But black, dear! You must wear black!"

"Well, I already have two or three black dresses, if it's got to be black!"

"But they are not mourning, child, and you in your position—, the——"

But suddenly Gloria gave a scream and rushed from the room.

"Don't! Don't! *Don't!*" she cried in a low hurt voice, and fled upstairs to the great attic room which had been the children's play room when they were little and where corners and crannies still held doll houses and baby carriages, and the toys of long ago. Vanna found her there an hour later when she went anxiously in search of her, curled up in a little heap by one of the dormer windows, staring wide-eyed out across the hillside and the woods, down toward the stone bungalow among the trees, the bungalow that was to have been her beautiful home. There was tragedy in her eyes but there was not a trace of a tear yet.

Vanna dropped down beside her and put her arm about her.

"Glory dear," she whispered, "Nance is downstairs. She wants to see you. She says she *must* see you. Do you feel able to speak to her a minute, or shall I tell her you are asleep?"

Gloria was still a minute and then she rose quietly.

"I'll see her," she said, still in that toneless voice that seemed so terrible to her sister. "Where is she?"

"Down in the library. Would you rather I brought her up to your room?"

"No," said Gloria, "I don't know why I should make you do all the work. I'll go down."

Nance was wearing a smart tweed dress of black and white mixture and a black felt hat, and was smoking a cigarette as she stood looking out the long French window to the lovely sloping lawn. She whirled about as Gloria entered, nervously crushing out the cigarette in the ash tray that stood on the little end table by her side.

She fixed hard solemn eyes on the girl who was to have been her sister-in-law so soon and stared. It was as if she were searching her very soul through and through. And Gloria stood there like a thing at bay and took it, with just that quiet inexplicable look on her face. Vanna stood by and watched her, marvelling at her sister.

Then Nance spoke in a hard tired voice.

"I said you'd take it just that way!" she remarked opening her cigarette case and getting out another cigarette. "Mother said you'd be simply crushed, but I knew you had character! I've always said you had character. I've always known you were too good for Stan!"

Gloria winced, caught her breath in as if the words hurt her.

"Oh, don't, Nance, please!" she said pleadingly.

"Well, it's true!" said the sister, her voice sailing up a note or two in the octave, a high shrill, overwrought voice. "Stan was spoiled! I suppose we all helped to do it!"

She took one puff at her cigarette and flung it on the ash tray with the stumps of several others she had played with before the girls came down to her. Then she turned and began to pace up and down the room with long masculine strides.

"My nerves are all shot to pieces!" she remarked bringing up in front of Gloria again and facing her almost defiantly.

"I had no business to come over here this way!" she went on. "I know it! But I couldn't stand Mother groaning and carrying on any longer! And I had to see how you were taking it!"

Gloria gave her a little wistful attempt at a smile, so sad that Vanna over in the windowseat put down her head on the back of a leather chair and sobbed quietly. Gloria put out a gentle hand and touched the other girl on her arm!

"I'm sorry, Nance!" she quavered, "I know—it must be—*terrible*—for you!"

Nance whirled on her fiercely.

"Oh, and isn't it terrible for you, then?" she demanded.

"Oh—!" Gloria drew in her breath with a suffering sound. "Oh—but in a different way!"

"How different I'd like to know?" It was as if Nance had come with a knife to probe the wound in this girl's breast, find the bullet, and rub the wound with salty words.

Gloria was silent for a moment, her face averted, then she answered slowly, hesitatingly.

"The girl, Nance—*you*—don't have to—mind —her! You—don't have—to think—about her at all!"

Nance stared at her averted face.

"Oh, *that!*" she said contemptuously. "That's nothing! You don't mean to say you're bothering about her! They all do things like that to-day. It doesn't mean a thing! I thought you had more sense!"

"Yes, it does mean—a great deal!" said Gloria slowly, her hard sad young eyes looking faraway through the window down the slope of the hill. "It sort of wipes out—a lot—that was—*dear!*" Her words came slower, her eyelids drooped, her lips drooped at their corners and were trembling as she spoke. "It makes it—he doesn't seem—to belong to me—any more!"

Gloria suddenly drooped into a chair and dropped her gaze to the floor, but there came no tears. The tears were all flowing down into her heart. They seemed to drown her inside, but she lifted her eyes and met the cold gaze of Nance, saw the curl of her lip.

"I didn't think you had a *jealous* nature!" The words cut like knives.

Gloria shook her head.

"It's not jealousy!" she said. "It's something wider, more final than jealousy. Jealousy you feel for a day and get over. This is something that puts me out into another sphere, somehow, just makes me feel he never has belonged to me— None of it—has ever—been —real!"

Nance looked into those hopeless, lovely eyes and tried to break their look with her own glance. But Gloria's eyes did not change.

"How absurd!" said Nance. "Stan worshipped the very ground you walked on, Glory. He couldn't say enough about you at home. He was simply crazy about you!"

Gloria looked at her as if she were not looking into her eyes at all, but saw something beyond her, something that outweighed what had been said.

"Yes?" she answered in that strange voice that sounded like a negative. Nance drew her brows together and studied her.

"Oh, Gloria, don't be difficult—now—when all this is happening! Don't be trivial! I own it's hard on you, but don't get notions. Everybody in our set knows how devoted Stan was to you!"

"Yes?" said Gloria again and still looked at that vision of a strange girl in the distance just beyond Nance's head. A girl that was not of her kind. A girl who was no respecter of other people's rights. A girl lying dead beside *her* bridegroom.

"Gloria, you're not going to make more trouble, are you?" Nance spoke sharply, with a kind of hard agony in her voice.

"Make trouble?" said Gloria in a soft amazed voice. "I make trouble? There is no trouble left to make, is there Nance? No, of course I'm not going to make trouble. I'm aching for you now, for the trouble you have already to bear. Is there anything that I can do to help in any way? I have a feeling there is something I should be doing, but I can't seem to think what it is!"

Gloria spoke in her gentle wistful voice out from under the crushing blow that had fallen upon her. There were tears in Vanna's eyes, but there were no tears in Gloria's eyes. There was hard agonizing comprehension in Nance's face, but Gloria kept that stricken smile upon her lips and offered to help. The other two girls watched her, uncomprehending.

"You're a queer girl, Glory!" said Nance at last. "I can see you are making this thing a lot harder for yourself than it has any need to be, a lot harder than it really is. Stan was just a gay boy. You never thought he was an angel, did you? Yet you are taking it farther even than death. You are taking the blow at your spirit instead of just your life. And you don't need to do that. It's hard enough just on the surface, goodness knows! Why should you want to go farther? You can't live in your spirit that way on earth. You just can't. You'd die if you tried to. It isn't being done!"

"I've just been finding out that I can't live if my spirit isn't satisfied!" said Gloria giving her a strange startled look. "That's why I don't know just how I'm going to bear it!"

Nance suddenly gave a great deep awful sob!

"Oh, this is awful! It makes one feel as if there ought to be a God!" said Nance.

"I wonder if that could make any difference?" said Gloria with a longing look.

"Oh, Glory," cried Vanna, "don't talk such awful things! If Dad should hear you what would he think? If you only would sit down and cry as you always do when you feel bad, I am sure it would help you."

"But this isn't just feeling bad, Vanna. And I can't cry. I think I'm bleeding inside. And I'm seeing so many things I never understood before!"

"Sit down, Glory dear, sit down," said Vanna. "I'm sure you oughtn't to be standing up. It takes your strength." She gave a frightened look at Nance.

"Yes, sit down, it takes your strength," said

Nance turning troubled eyes toward Gloria. "Can't you get her something to drink, Vanna? It's the shock. She isn't quite herself."

Gloria dropped into a chair with a wan smile.

"Oh, yes, I'm myself, quite, Nance dear. Don't get that idea," she said quietly, "and I've plenty of strength. You needn't worry about my strength. This isn't anything that has to do with strength. It's something that's away deeper than that. Strength is just your body. This is something that has touched the soul, and I'm not just sure I ever knew before I had a soul. Don't worry, Nance. I'm not out of my head. I wish with all my heart I could do something to help you bear your part of this, Nance, dear!"

Nance stared at her hungrily an instant, and gave a quick meaningful glance toward Vanna. Vanna answered it with another frightened look. Then there came the sound of a car driving up, the sound of a key in the latch of the front door.

"Oh, there's Dad!" said Vanna with relief, brushing away the quick tears, "I'm so glad he's come! He will know what to do. Don't go, Nance! Dad's great when you are in trouble!"

"Oh, I must go! I can't see anyone else to-day. I'll just slip out this back way. No, don't come. I must get back to Mother. I'll let you know when— Father gets back——!"

She ended with a sob and was gone.

II

Gloria's mother had her way. It was a foregone conclusion that she would. She had managed the stage scenery and costuming for her two beautiful daughters since their advent into the world, and she was not one to easily relinquish her rights. If she could not stage a wedding then at least a funeral should have its proper attention. It should never be said that Gloria or any of her family did not do the proper thing, wear the proper clothes.

Also, it appeared presently that this funeral was to be an affair. Gloria had hoped, had supposed of course that whatever ceremonials attended the death of her fiance would at least be private on account of the circumstances. But to her utter dismay she discovered that the Asher family were going to ignore the circumstances and make a hero out of Stan. Whatever fashionable grief could do to make the last rites of the son and heir to their millions a thing to be remembered and respected, that was to be done. Stanwood Asher's mother meant that her son should not be put away in disgrace. He should lie in state and his many friends should assemble and mourn properly at his untimely cutting off from the earth!

So Gloria saw that the awful days ahead of her must be lived through and she set herself to endure.

16

Meekly like a white-faced automaton she submitted to her mother's ordering. She tried on and stood for fittings whenever she was called. There was one thing however they could not get her to do. She would not take an interest in any of the smart black garments they brought for her approval. She would scarcely look at them. She shuddered when she came into the room where they were, and when they tried to get her to make a choice she turned away with a sigh and said: "Oh, I don't care! Whatever you say. Just get the simplest thing there is!"

Then her mother would look hopelessly after her and sigh. "If Gloria would only take things as they come, and be interested, it wouldn't be half so hard for her!" she said hopelessly to the observant fitter. "If we didn't have these practical interests of life like pretty clothes, and social duties, how could we live through trying disappointments?"

The woman looked at her with wondering eyes. Pretty clothes and social duties played very little part in the life of the fitter.

So Glory continued through those endless days with that sweet hopeless look in her eyes, and utter indifference for the things of life.

Sometimes her father would give her a long understanding glance and that helped. She had had very little time with him alone, always someone else was by. Just a low spoken word when he came: "Child, this is going to be hard! Keep steady! You're a brave girl!" Just that and a tender kiss. There never had to be many words between them. They understood each other better than the rest of the family. It seemed to Gloria that her father was the wisest man living.

No one but her father knew how awful it was for Gloria to go and stand beside that dead form of the lover who had been killed with another girl. It was expected of her of course. She had to go. She wasn't sure but she expected it of herself, but she shrank inexpressibly from looking on his face. What she felt was not merely a natural shrinking from death; it was the agony of looking upon a face that had been her lover's, and know that he had never been hers.

Everybody said how wonderful he looked, as if he might open his eyes and call out some gay witticism. As if the merriment that had been on his lips when he was suddenly called away, lingered, ready for expression as soon as he should wake.

But to Gloria it did not seem that way. It was as if a house that had been her welcome abiding place had suddenly closed its doors against her very existence. That face that all her life had been so familiar, so dear, was like a stranger's. The spirit she had thought she loved had fled. Had it ever been what she thought it?

Characteristics she had never seen before stood out on the features. Those closed lips had a selfish petted look, now that they could no longer curve and turn with gay expression.

She closed her eyes and turned away. They thought she was trying to keep back the tears. Her father hoped she would weep. He felt it would relieve the strain. But Gloria had turned away to shut out sights she did not want to see. She had hoped that somehow the sight of Stanwood dead would dispel this awful feeling she had about the way he had died. But instead of that it brought out lacks she had never noticed in his laughter-crowded lifetime.

Gloria was glad that she did not have to sit facing that casket during that long awful service, more thankful than she would have cared to tell anybody that she could hide away upstairs in a darkened room with the family, before the world thronged into the palatial residence to do honor to the son of the house. As she went upstairs, her bright hair shrouded in a heavy veil, she caught glimpses of her young friends huddled in frightened groups, with eyes cast down and gloomy countenances. It was all too evident that they did not want to come here, did not want to be reminded that death was inevitable, did not want to be drawn into this tragedy, yet knew that for very decency they must.

It was like the tolling of a bell for a lost soul when the solemn words of the burial service began. Gloria shivered, and Vanna sobbed silently in her corner. Mrs. Asher swathed in deep black moaned audibly beside her tortured husband, while Nancy sat like a grim specter, her handkerchief to her eyes.

"Man that is born of woman is of few days and full of trouble," began the preacher in a solemn and monotonous voice. "He cometh forth like a flower and is cut down, he fleeth also as a shadow and continueth not. As for man, his days are as grass: as a flower of the field, so he flourisheth. For the wind passeth over it, and it is gone, and the place thereof shall know it no more."

Gloria listened to the desolating statements and shuddered in her soul. How horrible was life! Why did anybody want to live? Stan was gone! In a few hours this place where he had been the life of everything would know him no more! Gloria heard his mother moan and cry out, "Oh, my baby boy!" and there came to her a sudden desire to scream and cry out too in protest. Oh, why did they have such terrible things as funerals? Why put the tortured relatives to any more pain than they had to suffer already? She felt if this thing went on very long she would go stark crazy.

But the monotonous cultured voice of the minister went steadily on through what seemed an endless multiplication of words, statements of facts that they all knew. Death was inevitable of course, but what could one do about it? Why all this harrowing language?

Gloria tried to listen, to catch the reason for all these words. Presumably they were a ritual of the church. She did not know even vaguely that any of them were taken from the Bible. It would not have made any difference to her if she had. There was no hope in the words that were chosen. What hope was there for one in her position? None! All her days she must go with blight on her life. How she was going to do it she knew not. She had not thought one hour beyond this funeral service. Since ever she had heard the awful news she had lived from hour to hour to endure the things that had to be endured until all that she owed to the family of her fiance should be fulfilled. After that chaos! A blank! She did not think of it now except to hope for oblivion in sleep. After that, —well that would have to be dealt with when she came to it.

The monotonous reading ceased at last, followed by a prayer by a retired pastor of the church with which the Ashers were associated. A trembling voice, cultured sentences, becoming more and more personal. Gloria heard herself prayed for as the mourning bride. She grew cold and hot behind her thick veil and trembled again, wondering if this terrible ordeal were not almost over.

But after the prayer the first speaker took up a refrain beginning: "Forasmuch as it hath pleased Almighty God to take out of this world our departed brother—" and Gloria wondered if it had pleased God to do a thing like that, and do it in that way? Had Stan's actions nothing to do with his departure? Had the assassin nothing to do with it? The girl? Was God like that? Was there a God? What made anybody think there was a God in a world like this full of horror?

When she came back from her thoughts to the voice again she beheld a word picture of the young man, a picture that showed him forth almost as a hero! She listened in amaze. Beginning with incidents of his childhood showing forth his kindly temperament and desire to please, the speaker worked his way up through the years, showing what a charming character the young man had possessed, how he had grown in beauty and manly virtues; he told of his merry ways, his popularity, his wonderful prospects in a worldly way. When the discourse was finished Stanwood Asher lived before them as an innocent hero. All else was ignored.

At last the discourse was ended, and a well-paid quartette of well-trained male voices sang:

> "Sunset and evening star,
>   And one clear call for me—"

chanted it exquisitely till it almost seemed there had been a call for Stan, and he had answered it merrily with a cocktail in his hand as he had answered most calls these last few years.

The interment was supposed to be private, and Gloria was glad of that, but it was surprising how many people got in on it for one reason or another. There were cameras ready wherever they went, cameras even, not far from the grave.

By reason of her relation to the deceased Gloria with her father beside her had to stand close to that flower-lined opening into which the casket was lowered, had to watch it slowly go down among the lilies and roses.

Everything about the grave was as lovely as money could make it. There were none of the horrors of an old-fashioned burial. Even the earth which was presently to cover all that was left of her bridegroom, was smothered in a bank of flowers. There was no hint nor suggestion of darkness and the tomb. And yet, as Gloria stood beside that grave she felt as if somehow her own soul was being drawn down into its flowery darkness, to be buried with the man who had so lightly gone from her a few days before, never to return alive.

Her father steadied her to the car when at last everything was over and they turned away home. Gloria felt that if it had lasted one minute longer she could not have gone on. But it was not over yet. Mrs. Asher went weeping aloud from the grave, crying out to go back for one more last look, and there was quite a scene at the car. Mrs. Sutherland went to comfort her and came bustling back hurriedly to their own car.

"She wants you to go home with them, Gloria! She says she has got to have a talk with you."

"No!" said Gloria's father. "She is not able! Can't you see she has borne all she can?"

"But I promised that she would come and stay the night with them. It seems only right since she was his——"

"Get in Adelaide!" said Gloria's father speaking more sternly than was his wont. "We'll drive over there and speak to her at the house a minute, but that is all. There is no point in keeping up this thing indefinitely. Get in, they are waiting for our car to start!"

Gloria's mother got in.

"But I promised," she said firmly.

"I myself will explain!" said the father, and Gloria gave him a grateful look and leaned wearily back in the car.

When Gloria reached home she went up and took off her black dress, putting on a plain old frock of white silk with touches of yellow in the trimming. It was a dress she had often played golf in. Then she sat down at her window and looked out at the sunset light on the lawn, touching the forsythia and the tulips with gold and flaming beauty. She laid her tired head down on her hands on the window sill and wondered how things could go on just the same in spite of pain and shame and sorrow. It was a lovely world, yet she could find no joy in it. She almost envied the unhurt youth of her brother who came to kiss her good-bye before he started back to school.

But when she went downstairs to dinner, where she knew her presence would be required or a fuss would be made about her not eating enough, her mother lifted horrified eyebrows at her garments.

"Why, Gloria! How unseemly! This first night of all times! Suppose somebody should come in! And what will the servants think? Run right back dear, and get on your black dress!"

Gloria looked wearily protesting at her mother's words and once more her father interfered.

"She looks much better in that," he said. "Let her be! She has suffered enough for one day."

"There you go again, Charles!" said his wife haughtily, "trying to decide a question you don't in the least understand."

"That's all right, Adelaide," said the father gravely, "perhaps you don't understand just how little strength this child has left after the ordeal of the day."

"And why wouldn't I understand my child as well as you I would like to know?" said his wife. "I, her mother! You're absurd. You always were sentimental, and you always encouraged her in such ideas. I'd like to know what terrible ordeal there was to-day? It was just a perfect funeral from start to finish. Not a detail went wrong. The flowers were marvellous. Did you see those white orchids? Weren't they the most exquisite things? And not a hitch or mistake anywhere? Not an unsightly moment. Everything just moved on oiled wheels! And Stanwood looked so perfectly natural, just as if he were going to laugh right out at us all! I'm sure I thought it was a lovely funeral!"

"You would!" said Vanna under her breath.

"What did you say, Vanna? I do wish you would stop that habit of talking in such a low tone that no one can hear you? It's very rude indeed!" said her mother.

"Excuse me, Mother!" said Vanna dropping her eyes to hide her indignation. She knew that Gloria was being tortured.

"Couldn't we just forget it for a while, Adelaide?" said her husband with a sigh, "we don't all feel that way about it. We're tired out. It's been a hard strain and we want to eat our dinner now."

"Well, really, am I hindering you from eating your dinner? I'm sorry. But it strikes me that it isn't something we want to forget right away. There's a great deal of satisfaction in knowing that the best people were there, and that there is nothing to regret in the service. I'm sure it must be a great satisfaction to Stanwood's parents to know how their friends honored him. I never saw such quantities of flowers at any funeral anywhere. It seems to me that the time to talk it over is now while it is fresh in our minds, and that reminds me, Charles, did you see the Breckenridges anywhere? I looked all over for them when we came out but couldn't seem to find them. They sent such a perfectly lovely wedding gift, that old English sterling platter you know, that I was sure they'd be at the funeral. It seems queer if they weren't."

But Mrs. Sutherland had her meditations to herself for the family ate in silence for the most part, and Gloria, after a very few bites excused herself and went up to her room, wondering if life was ever going to be bearable again.

But even her mother was startled next morning at her white face with the great dark circles under her eyes.

"We've certainly got to get out of this town right away as soon as we can manage it," she announced when the breakfast was well under way and the servants had withdrawn for the time. "I've been thinking. We'd better go to Europe. There's nothing like Europe for diverting the mind, and getting away from curious people, and of course it's going to be awfully hard on Gloria being in mourning and not being able to go out at all. Charles, couldn't you get away, for a few weeks anyway, right off? You could at least take us over and get us settled in some nice pleasant central place where we could take little trips off here and there, and then you could come back if you had to for awhile. I thought we'd be able to get off by next week if you could. Of course there'll be a few more clothes to buy since we must all go into black at least for awhile."

Gloria looked up most unexpectedly and spoke. She had done very little speaking for the last few days.

"I'm not going into mourning, Mother," she said, "and I'm not going to Europe! The rest of you can go if you want to, but I'm not going!"

"Why, the perfect idea, Gloria, what on earth do you mean? Of course you'll have to go into mourning! And why should you set up to say you won't go? You don't realize what you'll be up against if you try to stay here. Everybody in the town will be watching you and pitying you, and you can't turn around but it will be in the paper. You've got to let this thing die down and be forgotten before you can comfortably live here."

"It doesn't matter!" said Gloria indifferently, "I'm not going to Europe!"

"But don't you realize what you will be doing to your sister if you insist on staying here? Of course we couldn't think of going off and leaving you behind as you suggest. How would that look? And poor Vanna would be as much tied down as you would. She would be under the shadow of your sorrow, don't you see?"

"Why couldn't you and Vanna go to the seashore as you had intended?" said Gloria giving her mother a pleading look.

"And you stay here? What would people think of us for leaving you all alone?"

"I could go somewhere, but not to any places like that!" said the girl determinedly.

Then her father spoke.

"Where would you like to go, child?"

Gloria lifted sorrowful eyes to his face.

"I—hadn't thought—!" she said listlessly.

"H'm! I guess you hadn't!" sniffed her mother. "That's just it! You hadn't thought! You're not used to thinking for yourself, I've always done it for you, and you're not fit to begin planning for yourself now, I'm sure, not in this crisis."

"Wait a minute, Mother," said her husband interrupting. "Daughter tell me, what was your idea? What do you think you would like?"

Gloria looked out the long French window down the terrace to the banks of blue and purple and rose and white hyacinths. Then her eyes brightened wistfully.

"I'd like it if you and I could get in the car together and go somewhere riding for a while, away somewhere in a quiet place where most people don't go. I'd like to go where there's quiet,—and woods, and no crowds nor social duties."

"We'll do it!" said her father earnestly. "When can you be ready to start?"

"Charles!" said his wife reprovingly, "why will you encourage her in her crazy ideas? You know she's not fit to decide now."

But Gloria's eyes were on her father.

"Oh, to-*day!*" she said eagerly. "I could get ready in an hour or so!"

"Gloria! The perfect idea!" said her mother. "You

couldn't possibly go anywhere to-day. You haven't but two black dresses, and your things are not in order for a journey."

"I don't need many things, and I don't want any more new ones!" said the girl. "I've been doing nothing for the last year but buying clothes and trying them on and having them fitted, and this is one thing I don't have to dress for. I'm only going to take along simple old things that I know I'll be comfortable in, and I'm not going to take a single black dress along! It won't take long to pack!"

"Run along then and pack, Glory!" said her father, "I'll phone down to the office and make arrangements to leave. We'll start off somewhere around noon. Get the cook to put up some sandwiches for us and we'll eat them by the roadside."

"Charles! How plebeian!" exclaimed his wife. "Have you forgotten that every newspaper in this region will have Gloria's picture in it? Yes, and yours too if one could judge from the way the cameras were crowded in the offing yesterday. People will recognize you wherever you go and what would they think to see you eating sandwiches by the roadside. A picnic right after a funeral!"

"Nobody is going to recognize us where we're going, Adelaide. Run along child and get ready as soon as you can! Vanna, can you take care of your mother for a while?" There was eagerness in his eyes and voice. His wife looked at him as if he were insane.

"Charles! You simply can't do a thing like that to us all! It is preposterous. Why, you're crazy! Gloria owes a debt to her fellow townspeople! A social debt."

"I don't see for what!" said her husband drinking the last swallow of his coffee and beginning to fold his napkin.

"Why, all those wedding presents for one thing. They'll have to be sent back of course and she'll have to be here to attend to them and write notes and everything."

"Yes? Well, that's all the more reason why I mean to get her away right off this morning. That child is not going through any more harrowing scenes for a while. She'll have a nervous breakdown before another week if she does. Do you know she hasn't cried a tear yet? Do you know that's a dangerous state to be in?"

"Oh, I don't think so," said the mother complacently. "It's just that Gloria is a very self-controlled girl. I brought her up not to cry over things!"

But Gloria was up in her room working fast. She did not even wait for a maid to help her. She was getting out her overnight bag, and suitcase, flinging in a few necessities, toilet articles, accessories, plain sports clothes, rooting out old favorites that she had not been wearing lately since her engagement was announced because her mother had said she was too much in the public eye to go around in clothes that were out of date. She didn't put in a single black dress. White and yellow and brown, a couple of knit dresses for cool days, a coat and a plain little hat.

When her mother, having lost her argument with her husband, and having giving her orders for the day to the cook and her social secretary, finally hurried upstairs to deal with her recalcitrant daughter she found Gloria cloaked and hatted and gloved, sitting by her window with her two bags on the floor at her feet, watching for her father's car to come around.

"Gloria, you're hurting me very much by your strange actions," began her mother sitting down and surveying the rebel.

"I'm sorry, Mother, but I *have* to get away right off. I have to get away from people!"

"You're a strange child! One would suppose you would want to be with your own mother and sister! Now, while you're in trouble, one would suppose you would confide in your own mother!"

Gloria turned despairing eyes on her parent.

"Mother, you just don't understand!" she said desperately. "I've got to get somewhere away from everything. I'll come back sometime when I get my bearings, but I won't go to Europe, nor into society. I've got to get away from those things and find out what it all means!"

"What do you mean, what it all means?"

"I don't know what I mean, but I've got to. I've stood this horror as long as I can. It's been terrible!"

"Gloria, do you think Stan would like you to do a queer thing like this? Wouldn't he expect you to stay here for a few days at least and help comfort his mother and keep up appearances?"

Gloria's eyes narrowed.

"Mother, Stan isn't to be considered anymore! That's over!"

"Why, Gloria, what a terrible thing to say. When you just adored Stan and wanted to do everything you could to please him! Why look how hard you worked on your father to get him to build a bar in your new house just because Stan wanted one."

Gloria's face hardened.

"Yes, and now I wish I hadn't," she said half fiercely. "If Stan hadn't been so fond of drinking he might not be dead to-day!"

"Glory! What a shocking thing to say! Stan never drank to excess. I always felt he was very abstemious. And surely you want to comport yourself as he would want you to do!"

"No," said Gloria, "I don't! I don't think he has any right over my actions now. I think he forfeited his right by going up to New York and taking that dancing girl out to dinner the very week before we were to be married. He has made me feel that nothing he ever said to me was really mine any more."

"Why, you silly child! What a perfectly extravagant idea! You poor child, you take after your father! He's always getting such ridiculous notions in his head! But Gloria, dear, you mustn't make so much of that incident. Even if it were all true what the papers said, which of course it isn't, why that isn't a great thing. Most men have been a little wild before they settled down to get married, and had little affairs with girls that they wouldn't have married for a fortune."

"Mother! You don't mean that! You know Father never was a man like that!"

"Well, no," said the mother with a half contemptuous smile. "Your father of course is an exception. He always had a puritanical conscience, and his bringing up was purely Victorian of course."

Gloria lifted her chin a big haughtily.

"Well, if you don't mind, Mother, I think I'll be Victorian after this like Dad! You know it makes a difference when it really happens to *you,* Mother! You've always had a wonderful husband and lived a sheltered life, Mother, and you don't understand, I —Mother, I *know!* It's happened to me, and it makes all the difference in the world!"

Then Gloria heard her father's voice calling from the hall to know if she was ready and she jumped up and flung her arms around her bewildered indignant mother's neck.

"Dear Mother!" she said kissing her fervently, "I'm dreadfully sorry to hurt you but I really have to go now and find out how to stand things. You don't understand, but I love you!"

"But what shall I tell Stan's mother?" asked the still indignant mother.

"Tell her I was about to get sick and Dad had to take me away for a few days. Good-bye, Mother!" and with a little wave of her hand and a faint attempt at a smile she, without waiting for a servant, seized her two bags and was gone down the stairs and out the door.

Down near the gateway Vanna stepped out of the shrubbery, her face swollen with crying. She stopped them long enough to kiss her sister.

"I understand, Glory darling!" she whispered.

Then they were gone, down the highway, out into a world that the father used to know and hadn't seen for a long long time.

III

Mrs. Sutherland had managed to quash the sandwich idea from the day's scheme of things, so about one o'clock the travellers began to get very hungry, for breakfast had been but a sketchy affair for either of them.

They lunched at a quiet little roadside place the like of which Gloria had never entered before, so plain and quiet that it wasn't even a tea room. It was just a little cottage by the roadside with a sign out by the white gate, "Homemade-bread sandwiches, fried egg or chicken."

It was a revelation to Gloria to enter that tiny cottage. It seemed scarcely big enough to be a bird cage, yet she discovered that it housed five people, a man and his wife, a little girl of eight years, another of three with gold curls almost the color of Gloria's, and a boy of ten who came whistling in from the barn with a basket of eggs.

The cold chicken was delicious, great flaky slices, the bread was a dream. Mr. Sutherland said it tasted just like his mother's, the fried eggs were cooked just right, and the butter was something to be remembered. The little eight year old girl owned that she had helped to churn it. There was a pitcher of creamy milk. It didn't somehow taste like city milk, though the Suth-

erland milk always came from a herd of specially se-
lected cows.

Gloria was hungry for the first time since the
tragedy. Mr. Sutherland talked with the mother. She
told him that they had lived there five years, ever since
her husband had failed in business. He had taken what
little he had left, come up here into the woods, cleared
this land that an uncle had left him, and they were
getting on all right till her husband broke his leg. So
now she had to do something to help out with the doctor's bills. But they were going to get on all right.
The leg was knitting nicely and the doctor was willing
to wait, and the children were selling vegetables in
the next little town. It was only two miles away and
the boy had a small express wagon. Sometimes his
sister went with him. They were doing very well and
were thankful that things were no worse.

Gloria gave a startled look about on the cheap
furnishings of the little front parlor that had been
turned into a wayside inn, caught a glimpse of the
kitchen beyond, and a bedroom opening out of it where
a man lay on the bed with a weight attached to his
foot to keep the leg in position. Could anybody live
in such crowded quarters and really be happy? Thankful that it was no worse? She thought of her own lovely
home which she had known most of her life.

"It isn't as if we had to live in the city," said the
mother happily. "This is a nice healthy place for the
children, and we can raise most everything we really
need to eat, and of course we don't require fine clothing—!" Her voice had a lilt in it, and there was a
dimness in Mr. Sutherland's eyes as he paid the mod-
est bill.

"You don't charge enough for such wonderful
food!" he said and threw down another bill on the
table as he picked up his hat and hurried out.

"Oh, but—" said the mother examining the money. "This is too much! My price covers the cost and
gives us enough—. We really couldn't take this!" She
followed them out to the car.

"It's all right!" said Gloria's father putting his

foot on the starter. "Tell your husband that's just from one brother to another. I used to be a farmer's boy myself once, and I know times can get pretty hard. I'd like to think of you here getting on. Sometime maybe I'll come back again!" and he threw in his clutch and was off, leaving the bewildered little mother standing at the gate clutching the bill and staring after them as if they were a couple of fairies riding in a coach and four.

"Oh, Dad, I'm glad you did that!" said Gloria leaning her cheek lovingly against his shoulder. "They're sweet, aren't they? And they're happy, too, in spite of everything!"

"There are lots worst fates than living in a little cottage in the woods," said the father musingly. "When I was a little tad we had a house as near like that as two peas, and Father and Mother were happy as two clams."

"Oh, Dad, you never told us about that!"

"Well," said her father musingly, "there never was any time to tell about things, not since you were born. We always had so much going on in the house, and you were so governessed, and nurse-ridden, and kindergartened and schooled while you were growing up that I scarcely ever got a chance at you. And then later, you had such a gang of hangers-on at the house! I've always wanted to. But how could I expect you'd want to hear about a little cottage on a big farm where I was born?"

"Oh, tell me now," said Gloria settling back comfortably, "only I'm sorry Vanna isn't along. She would enjoy it too! I guess we should have brought her, only that would have left Mother all alone and she wouldn't have stood for that a minute!"

"No," said the father sadly, "I guess not! But I don't know as there is so much to tell. Perhaps you wouldn't understand it all either. It was different from these days."

"Different? How?" asked Gloria. "Tell me all about it please!"

"Why, we were just a family by ourselves. Of

course there were neighbors who came sometimes to call, but mostly we did things together and were just a family. Outside things weren't always crowding in. And then our ways were different. My people were religious. We always went to church every Sunday twice and sometimes three times, though it was a long ride, and sometimes the ride was a walk when a horse was lame. Father never missed a Sunday if he could help it. But—times have changed—!" He ended with a sigh, almost as if he regretted it.

"It seems queer that you were brought up that way Dad, and now you never go near a church," said his daughter thoughtfully, trying to make her father's tale seem real.

"Yes, I suppose so," said the man looking off into the distance. "I suppose my mother would have felt terribly about it if she had lived to see these days. Why, my father used to ask a blessing at the table before every meal, and we always had family prayers every morning and evening. We've come a long way from such doings."

Their way led now through a lovely woodland with pleasant little villages sprinkled here and there. The father had chosen the back roads purposely to get away from traffic. Everything was new and different from the regular highway to which Gloria was accustomed. Cultivated nature and beautiful scenery was a familiar everyday thing to her since babyhood, but nature in the wild, just nature, and human nature bearing the hardships of life, taking toil and deprivation happily and struggling to overcome the curse that was upon the soil, and humanity, she had not seen that before, or if she had seen it she had not noticed. Now that her eyes were opened by her own first suffering everything seemed different.

They passed some little children going out to a barn with their older brother to feed the pigs. Gloria watched the struggling, snorting, grunting, slimy creatures fighting each other for the best morsels, seeing no connection between them and the great toothsome Virginia hams that came upon the home table succulent and tender, spicy with cloves and wearing rings of pineapple on their velvety brown crust. She wondered why people cared to bother with such loathsome creatures as pigs, till her father suddenly remarked that it used to be his duty to feed the pigs every day when he was a boy, and how proud he was when they grew fat and marketable.

Gloria's eyes got larger as she listened. She was seeing a side of life that she had never before even dreamed of. Her father feeding pigs! She thought of the three stately peacocks that strutted sometimes on the terraces at home, a fancy of her mother's they had been, and suddenly she laughed aloud.

Her father looked down anxiously at her and then joined in, a sudden light of relief in his eyes. Gloria had forgotten her sorrow for the moment and had laughed! He laughed himself at the thought of himself a little barefoot boy going out to the barn with a bucket of refuse for the pigs. It was incongruous. He thought of himself in his bonding office in the city managing affairs of finance that often settled national questions. And yet he had been a barefoot boy feeding pigs and chickens and milking the cow!

"If I had known then that things would change so," he said gravely, and then laughed once more. "If I could have looked forward and seen myself in the office, handling important affairs—!" He paused again and looked down at Gloria.

"Well, what?" said Gloria breathlessly. "What would you have done?"

"Why, I expect," said her father thoughtfully, "I wouldn't have been so conscientious about feeding the pigs! I'm afraid I wouldn't have thought that it was worth while to bother if I was going to be rich in the end."

"And was it?" asked the daughter, drawing her brows together. "Wouldn't it have been better to let someone else who wasn't going to amount to anything afterwards, feed the pigs, and you spend your time in getting ready to be a great business man?"

"No," said her father thoughtfully shaking his

head. "It might be that if I hadn't done my best feeding the pigs and doing all the other duties that were required of me, I wouldn't ever have been in the position I am now!"

"Father! How could you make that out?"

"Why, I had to learn responsibility, and honesty, and diligence, and reliability, and regularity, and conscientiousness somewhere, and I guess in my case feeding the pigs was just as good a way to learn those things as any. Another thing, I had to learn to do things I didn't like to do. You know I never did really like to feed pigs, though I wouldn't have owned it for a farm. It wasn't considered good sportsmanship to give in to one's likes and dislikes!"

Gloria sat quietly considering that for some time.

They changed places after a while, Gloria taking the wheel, and they drove on into the lovely afternoon among the mountains with now a glimmering lake lying silverly in the distance, now a river winding. They did not touch New York, nor anything that could have reminded Gloria of that city. They went by byways, not highways, taking a road when it looked attractive, whether it went in a special direction or not. Deep into the heart of a woods they would wander, and out again plump into a little settlement, so out of the way that the dwellers hadn't even thought to put out a "Tourists" sign, so quiet that it seemed almost like a deserted village.

Many places they passed reminded her father of his childhood, and seeing she enjoyed it he talked on freely. It seemed that he too took pleasure in going back over those old days. It had been so many years since he had anyone to talk to about them. Adelaide his wife had always been restless when he mentioned his early days and upbringing. She had been a Boston girl and considered herself above him, even though he did bring her more wealth than she ever had before.

It was not until the shades of evening began to drop down and seem to wrap them in more cosily to each other, that Gloria after quite a silence, ventured hesitantly:

"Dad, is it true that all men nowadays—that is all *young* men nowadays are,—well—aren't quite true? I mean, do they *all* go after—low-down girls and think nothing of it? Even if—they're—going to be married——?"

Her father gave her a startled look.

"Certainly not!" he said decidedly. Then he stopped short and tried to think what young men of his acquaintance he could be sure of.

"Certainly not," he repeated with satisfaction. "I have in mind several who are not in the least that way."

But he suddenly remembered that they were not young men in Gloria's clique. They were plain hardworking young fellows in his office, and he knew their ways, had had them shadowed before ever he trusted them with important business.

"Whatever put such a question as that into your head?" he asked, turning keen eyes and searching her through the dusk.

"Why, Mother said they all were," said Gloria, struggling to explain. "Mother laughed at me when I said I felt as though Stan had never been mine because of his going up to New York to that girl——" her voice trailed off into silence and she turned her eyes to the woods they were passing through.

"Poor child!" said her father tenderly, reaching out a hand to touch hers softly as it guided the wheel. The tone of his voice made Gloria catch her breath as she went on.

"And Mother said that was silly of me. She said all young men were that way, that they had to sow their wild oats, and then they settled down, and that I was very disloyal to Stan to feel that way, that all young fellows, especially nowadays, thought nothing of a thing like that. Then I asked her if you did that way when you were young and she looked kind of funny and smiled and said no, very sharply, that you were 'different.' But I couldn't quite understand. Dad, I can't *help* feeling that way about Stan, as if I never had really known him, and as if nothing he ever said to me was true!"

The father's hand was still warm on hers, but he was silent for some seconds and when he spoke his voice was husky with feeling.

"I understand, Glory dear," he said, speaking slowly. "You were right in your feeling. It was what I felt for you the most, though I was not sure you fully understood what it all meant. But I felt disgraced and outraged for you, dear child, that one who had undertaken to love, honor and protect you through life should so forget all decency even though he had been drinking. He had no business to be drinking. That was another thing, Gloria. It went sore against me to trust you with a drinker. You know how I feel about that."

"Yes, I know, Dad, and for that reason somehow I never could drink more than a sip or two. Something inside always made me stop. But Stan could stand a lot, Dad. He never seemed to get silly the way some of the others did—. That is one reason why I can't excuse him. Oh, it seems awful for me to be putting this into words even to you. He is dead now, and I suppose I ought to keep still. But Dad, my heart just cried out. I felt as if everything—the very foundations of the earth—were reeling! And then when Mother said I was silly, and it was wicked of me to mind about that girl, and when I think of the way they ignored the whole thing at the funeral, I began to think I was all made up wrong inside, and I had to ask you about it. Is Mother right? Do most of them do such things —nowadays?"

"No!" said her father again earnestly. "No! But if they did, little girl, you'd a thousand times better live out your days alone than marry a man who would be as disloyal to you as Stan has been. It isn't as if there were any question about it you know. I had that looked into," he spoke with a voice of deep sadness, —"and it was all true and more than the paper stated!"

A little sound broke from her white lips but she made no comment.

"That is why,—" went on her father, "that I am hoping you will not grieve too deeply over all this.

The young man was not worthy of it. He was not thinking of you, his promised bride, when he went up there to see that girl. He was pleasing himself."

Then after an instant he went on again, reluctantly, haltingly, almost shyly:

"And you must not think too hardly of your mother, either, Glory. She was brought up in a most careful sheltered way. She really knows little of the evil in the world, and what little she has heard she has chosen to ignore, or not to believe. She has taken up the fashionable way of excusing and condoning the faults of young men and calling them follies rather than sins. Also your mother was not brought up in a religious way as I was, and that makes some difference. I have sometimes thought that she looks down upon me as being rather old-fashioned for holding the views that I do——!"

He paused, thoughtfully, sadly.

"Father, I think I'm old-fashioned too in my thinking," said the girl at last. "And do you know, I think Mother would be too if it were only the fashion now to be old-fashioned again."

Then they both laughed and a tender feeling of sympathy crept into their voices.

Soon after that they came upon a little white farmhouse tucked away under elm trees, winking a friendly light from its windows, and showing a sign inviting travellers to stop all night.

"How would you like to stay here to-night?" asked her father. "Or would you rather go on to a good hotel? There's a small city only about ten miles farther on."

He got out his map and measured the distance with his eye.

"Oh, let's stay here!" said Gloria. "It looks quiet here, and we might meet someone we knew if we went on to the city."

So they went in and found pleasant quarters for the night, and to her surprise Gloria fell asleep almost as soon as her head touched the pillow.

The next day they went on working north and

east, through wooded mountains with narrow dirt roads, deep and dim and silent, where traffic was limited for miles to one farm wagon drawn by an old plow horse, and one ancient flivver. Up and up they climbed till the air grew clearer and colder and the sunshine more crisp and lovely. Gloria began to be interested in all the scenery, a mountain brook rushing musically over great boulders, rambling stone walls that shut in sheep and cows, a glimpse of the sea in the distance, a far city rising picturesquely among the budding spring trees. But they skirted the cities and did not go through them.

And at last Maine.

About the middle of the afternoon Gloria looked up and asked:

"Where are we going Dad?" It seemed to be the first time the thought had occurred to her.

"Home!" said her father.

"Home?" said Gloria, a kind of consternation coming into her eyes and a cloud darkening the brightness of her face from which the gloom had been slowly disappearing ever since they had started.

"To my home," said her father, "where I lived when I was a child!"

"Oh, how wonderful!" said the girl, "I would love that. Have you been back? Are you sure it is there yet?"

"Yes, several times," said the father gravely. "Once I almost took you and Vanna, but your mother had other plans."

"Oh, I wish you had," said Gloria. "Will it be like the little cottage in the woods where we had lunch yesterday?"

"No," said the man thoughtfully, "it is larger. But the little house where I was born is still standing, down in the meadow. It was used for the hired man and his family after we built the big farm house nearer to the road, but they are both standing. Ten years ago I put them in good repair. An old friend of Mother's, Mrs. Weatherby, lives there with her daughter and son-in-law, and another son and his family live in the cottage, but it is all much the same as when I was a child. We are coming to it now. That is the little village in the distance."

Gloria looked up and a white spire showed among the trees, white white houses nestled here and there amid spacious distances, and all about mellow ground lay plowed and ready in various stages for the planting, some were already beginning to show green in symmetrical rows. Out from the wooded road it did not seem so late. The sky was luminous with a fleck of crimson in the west, and there was still a small rim of the red sun left above the horizon. It cast a glow over the fields and made them look like rare merchandise spread out for customers to view. A single star flashed out as they looked, and a light or two from the village, as they neared it, winked at them. Gloria held her breath and watched the little settlement approach, like a picture of the past, her father's past! It seemed wonderful to her.

They had come to the outermost sentinel of the village houses now, white with green blinds and tall plumy pines standing guard. On the right was a cottage quite colonial and tiny. There were lights in some windows of almost every house, though it still did not seem dark in the street.

There were pleasant odors of coffee and frying ham, and something sweet and spicy like gingerbread just out of the oven. The man drew a deep breath and closed his eyes.

The picture-book village opened up, house after house.

"That was where my grandmother lived!" said the man pointing to a small neat house with two wings and a marvellous front door. "She and Grandfather used to sit there on the porch afternoons in the summertime and talk, Grandmother with her knitting, and after Grandfather was gone, Grandmother would sit there and look off at the sunset alone."

"I wish I could have known them!" said Gloria wistfully. "They died before I was born, didn't they? I never heard anything about them."

"Your mother never knew them," said the father evasively. "She didn't like the country and she—never —came up here!"

"How much she has missed!" said the daughter, drinking in the quiet farmer-village scenes.

A cow mooed mournfully at the pasture gate near a big red barn, tinkling the bell around her neck, and off in the pasture there sounded the bleat of a very young lamb, and the baa-aa-a of its mother answering. There were birds twittering in the elms that arched the street, though they must have been chilly for the elms were only just in bud yet.

The glow of the sun was gone, but the night had flung a banner in the east, and a jewel glow of stars rent the sky shining like a halo above the white spire at the end of the village street.

"This is the house!" said the man in a voice that sounded almost breathless with eagerness, as if he had suddenly come young again and was expecting to meet the loved ones who had been gone long years now.

IV

It was a lovely old house, spacious and comfortable, white like all the other houses about, the *whitest* white, Gloria thought, that she had ever seen. It was set about with tall pines, whose dark tassels whispered to each other in the evening breeze. There was a lovely old fanlight over the door and a wide veranda. The road rambled near to the house in a friendly way giving no idea of publicity as the highways at home did, but as if it were only a beaten path from neighbor to neighbor. The house was lighted both upstairs and down, and a welcoming path of light streamed out into the road from the wide open front door. Through one window Gloria caught a glimpse of flames flickering in a spacious fireplace. It seemed like arriving in a new world as they drew up to the front door and stopped. And then almost instantly a sweet old lady came out the door, as if she had been watching for them to come, and a younger man came around one end of the long front veranda and down the path toward the car.

"Well, you got here on time!" was his greeting in a pleased tone. "Emily said we mustn't count on it. She said you'd probably be late, driving up for the first time. But I said you'd make it I was sure!"

"Yes, we made it!" said Gloria's father with satisfaction flinging open the car door. "This is my daughter Gloria, John. Glory, this is Mr. John Hastings."

Gloria found her hand being shaken by a strong rough hearty one, and found her heart warming to this stranger. Keen eyes, a pleasant smile, a genial welcome and nondescript clothes, scrupulously clean and neat, but not at all the right thing for a gentleman to wear at this hour of day, style, material, cut, all wrong, quite out of date, according to the standards she knew, yet strangely she did not think of this at the time.

"And here comes my wife!" he said with a nice ring to his voice as if he were proud of her.

Gloria saw a trim youngish woman in a plain dark blue dress with a ruffled white apron tied around her waist as if she had just come from the kitchen. She had handsome hair, a good deal of it, with a natural wave away from her face, and done in a heavy knot at the back of her head, a bit carelessly as if she had not spent much time or thought upon it, and yet there was something lovely and becoming about the effect. Here was another person Gloria couldn't quite place in her scheme of things. She wouldn't fit into a fashionable picture at all, and yet she had both beauty and dignity. Gloria liked her at once.

But it was the little old lady, Mrs. Weatherby, standing at the top step of the veranda, who took her heart by storm, the one her father had called a friend of his mother's. She was small and frail, her soft gray hair smoothly parted in the middle, but with a natural wilful wave here and there that made it a little like a halo of silver. She wore a simple gray cotton dress without form or comeliness after the manner of long ago, a long white apron, and a little shoulder shawl of gray plaid over her shoulders. She put her hands on Gloria's shoulders, looked for an instant into her beautiful face, then drew her into her arms.

"Oh, my dear!" she said softly. "You look as your grandmother used to look when we were girls together!"

And then Gloria felt somehow that she had got home.

There was stewed chicken for supper on little biscuits, with plenty of gravy. There were mashed potatoes and little white onions smothered in cream dressing, and succotash the like of which Gloria had never tasted before, even though it was made from canned corn and beans, but it was a triumph of home canning. There was quivering currant jelly, home grown celery and pickles, and for dessert a baked Indian pudding, crisp and brown and full of fat raisins.

Up in the big square front room assigned to her, Gloria looked about her. Her father had the other front room across the hall. The bed in her room was a four poster of beautiful old mahogany, rarely kept, and polished by loving hands through the years.

"This was your grandmother's room," said the sweet old lady who had come up to show her about, "and that was her canopy bed. It used to have chintz curtains. It was considered a very fine piece of workmanship. That was her chair by the window, that big rocker. The cushion-covers are the same she had when she was living. Many's the time I've run in and found her sitting there by the window darning stockings, or turning the collar on a shirt, or putting in new risbands. She was a wonderful one with her needle, little fine stitches, the same on an old shirt as on a cambric handkerchief. She did beautiful embroidery too, when she had time, but there were five children, and this was a big house, and what with the washing and churning there wasn't much time for embroidery."

"Oh! Did she do it *all?* Didn't she have any servants?" asked Gloria, wide-eyed.

"Servants?" said the old lady. "Where would she get servants? Sometimes at threshing time or harvest when there were a lot of extra farm hands to feed she would have in a neighbor farmer's daughter to help for a few days, but mostly she was proud and thrifty and did it all herself!"

"Oh!" said Gloria in a small voice, trying to conceive of such circumstances, and failing.

Lying between the sheets that smelled of lavender she tried to visualize that grandmother that she had never known, her father's mother, young and proud and thrifty, doing all that work and living away from the world! She felt a faint vague wish that she might somehow begin over again with things clean and fine and real, things worthwhile doing, and make her life something that could be remembered.

The soft footsteps about the house ceased, the glimmer of the hall light beneath the crack of the door went out. There were only the quiet stars like tall tapers turned low to make the big room luminous, and they were half veiled by the dark pine plumes.

The pines were whispering softly at intervals when a little breeze stirred them, but there were great silences between. Gloria thought she had never heard it so still before anywhere. It seemed as if one might hear even the tread of a passing cloud, it was so very quiet, and there seemed to be so much space everywhere, and such a nearness to the sky.

She stole out of her bed to kneel by the casement and look out. There were only a few dim shapes that might be houses around, somewhat scattered. There were lights in one or two windows. Could that be a mountain off there against the sky, like a soft gray smudge blotting out the starry part, and darkening down into the stretch of what must be meadow across the road? She knelt there a long time looking up into the night and listening to the silence. It fascinated her. The world seemed so wide, and home so far away. She drew a deep breath and was glad she did not have to think about what she had left behind in the last few days. She was too tired and it was all too dreadful. She shuddered, and felt a chill in the spring night air. This north country was colder than the one she had left behind, but it was quiet, oh so quiet! One didn't have to think here. If one dared to think perhaps one's thoughts would be heard in this stillness as if they were a voice shouting.

She slipped back gratefully into the linen sheets, laid her head on the fragrant pillow, and sank into the sweetest sleep she had known for months.

In the morning when she awoke there were

roosters crowing, hens clucking of the eggs they had laid, a lamb bleating, and now and then a cow's low moo. And yet that great silence was all around like a background for these sweet strange queer sounds. She opened her eyes and could not tell for a moment where she was nor what had happened until she heard her father talking to John Hastings outside below her window about the spring planting and the possibilities of the south meadow yield of hay.

There were appetizing odors coming up from downstairs, and cheery voices. It must be late. She sprang up and dressed hastily, her thoughts eager for the day. She glanced eagerly from the window and identified her mountain all hazy pink and purple in the morning sun, lying like a painting on the sky beyond the treetops, and felt a thrill that she had recognized it even in the dark. Then she hurried down to breakfast, trying to imagine herself back in the days when her father was a boy.

After breakfast her father took her over the farm, showing her everything, explaining the ways of farm people, telling her stories of the past, until everywhere she went the way was peopled with the kith and kin she had never known.

She asked her father about those five children of Grandmother's of whom she had never heard until last night, and learned that one was dead in childhood, one had married a European and gone to live abroad, one was in California living on a ranch, and the last lived on another farm only thirty miles away with his wife and family, cousins she had never known.

"And why haven't we known them, Dad?" she asked, wide-eyed. "Why haven't we come up here, and why haven't they visited us?"

A slow dull red came up in her father's cheeks and a cloud came over his happy face.

"Well, Gloria, perhaps I was wrong, but your mother sort of took a dislike to this part of the country when we were first married and didn't seem to want to come up here, and I was too proud to urge her. I figured that some day she would get over it and we'd get together yet, but she never has, and now they are mostly scattered. I don't know how many of George's children are at home now. It's been my fault I guess. I was too busy to write many letters, and when they found we didn't come up here they got rather offended I'm afraid, and I had to let it go at that!" He ended sadly.

"Well, can't we hunt them up?" asked Gloria earnestly. "I'd like to know my cousins."

"Yes," said her father brightening. "We'll do that very thing. It'll make up for a great deal, you wanting to go with me."

It suddenly came to Gloria how much her father would have enjoyed having his children more with him. Why, he was like a boy, going around here in his old haunts and telling her all about it. Her heart thrilled to think how pleased he was to share it with her. And how much she and Vanna had missed in not being more with their father! She reflected that it had been all wrong, going selfishly about their own life, going wildly from one thrill to another, and having such a little to do with their own father! Why, he was interesting and worth cultivating! He could show her a better time that any of the young men with whom she had whiled away her days and evenings sometimes far into the mornings. But somehow she didn't even want to think of those days. She just wanted to enjoy this quiet place and these still beautiful days with her father.

They went fishing in the old trout brook the next day and caught a string of trout. Gloria even caught a couple herself, and went back to the house and stood over her father while he cleaned them, and then stood by while Emily Hastings cooked them. They came on the table a delicious crisp brown, and nothing ever tasted so good as they did, eaten with the white homemade bread and the delicious fresh butter.

There were photograph albums for the evenings, when Gloria got acquainted with a lot of relatives whom she had never heard of before, albums that she pored over again and again, until she felt she knew each one, Aunt Abby, Uncle Abner's wife, and Cousin

Joab and his daughter Kate, little Anne who died just as she was growing into sweet womanhood, and young pretty Aunt Isabella who married the foreigner and went to live abroad in a castle, almost breaking her mother's heart going so far away, that mother who had been her grandmother, who had washed and mended and cooked and lived in this sweet old home. Oh, how could pretty Isabella go away from this home and marry any man? How could any girl? How had she been going to trust herself to Stan and go out of her father's care? Stan who had died with another girl!

She shivered as she turned the pages of the album, and went up to bed to listen to the silence and try to forget.

She learned a number of things in her father's old home. She learned to make her bed, and make it well. Ever since she had come up to her room and found Emily Hastings with deft fingers turning down the sheets smoothly over the candlewick spread, and plumping the pillows into shape, she had made it herself. At first with clumsy fingers that could not get the blankets to spread smooth, nor make the counterpane hang evenly. And finally she had humbly asked to be shown how. Hitherto she had never thought about beds being made. They might spread themselves up as soon as one went out of the room for all the notice she had ever taken of them. Her bed was always made at home and her room in order when she came back after ever so brief an absence. But she discovered that it made a difference to have no servants. It seemed funny to her that she had never thought about it before.

Sunday morning they went to the church with the white spire, the old church which the Sutherlands had attended for years. There was even a tablet up by the pulpit in memory of Great-Grandfather Sutherland, the one who had been taken away from his old wife only a few months before she went herself. The old red cushions on the family pew had faded from red to a deep mulberry, and the ingrain carpet was threadbare in places, and drearily dull in its old black and red pattern. Gloria sat with her toes on the wooden footstool that was covered with ingrain of a later vintage and didn't quite match. She watched the red and purple and green lights from the old stained glass windows fade and travel from the minister's nose, across his forehead, and twinkle on the wall in prisms and patterns, under the solemn sentence done in blue and dead gold, "THE LORD IS IN HIS HOLY TEMPLE. LET ALL THE EARTH KEEP SILENCE BEFORE HIM." It did not seem a happy thought to her. It seemed to her like a challenge from a grim and angry person. She looked about on the shabby little church that so sorely needed refurbishing, and couldn't make it seem a holy temple for a great God to enter. Yet when she looked at her father she realized that there was something sacred here, some memory perhaps, that brought a softened light to his worldly-wise face, and a tenderness to his eyes, and she looked about again less critically.

There was a cabinet organ played by an elderly woman who touched the keys tenderly and dragged the hymns, and the singers were mostly older people with voices whose best days were over, yet she recognized that there was something in it all that held these people to a thought, a standard perhaps, and bound them together in a common aim. Else why should they come here? Why should they keep on coming here Sunday after Sunday, year after year?

She looked about on their faces, old and tired and hardworked; yet they were in a way enjoying this dull service. Gloria puzzled over it and could not understand. There must be something unseen behind it all.

The old minister who preached was closely confined to his notes, and did not get her attention at all. He was to her merely a part of the whole, like the organ and the carpet and the old bell that rang so hard after they were seated in the pew that it shook the floor and the seats, and seemed threatening momently to descend and bring the bell tower with it. Gloria had no feeling of God being there or of anything holy about the place, except when she looked at her father's face and then she wished she knew what it was that reached down so deep into her father's life and was connected with this old building? She decided that it must be the memory of his mother. Such a mother! Her grandmother! She thought she would like to be like that grandmother if she only could.

That afternoon they drove over to call on the uncle's family, and Gloria had a sudden set-back in her enthusiasm for searching out relatives. Uncle George came out to the car to meet them and seemed exceedingly reserved. He didn't smile at all at first until Gloria was introduced, her father stating that she had wanted to come and get acquainted with her relatives.

The uncle turned a quick searching glance on her face, took in all its loveliness, questioned with his eyes its artless smile of eagerness, and finally warmed under its brightness into something like geniality.

"She looks like Mother, doesn't she?" he said unexpectedly, and the pleased color came into the girl's face.

"Oh, that's nice!" said Gloria, "I'd like to be like her! I've been hearing such wonderful things about her, only I'm afraid I never could come up to her standards!"

"She was a great little woman!" said Uncle George with growing approval in his eyes. "You'd be going some to be like her! But I thought all city girls these days were high-flyers." His eyes searched his new niece with surprise.

Gloria laughed.

"What are high-flyers?" she asked with a twinkle in her eyes.

Her uncle twinkled back and said with a half grin:

"Well, if you don't know I won't tell you. I wouldn't want to spoil you, you're too much like Mother! But come on, get out and come in the house. Come see how you like your aunt and cousin."

"Cousin?" said Gloria's father, "aren't they all at home? I hoped we'd catch the whole family, coming on Sunday."

"No," said Uncle George, "the boys are both away out West for good I'm afraid. Only Joan is home, and she goes back to Portland to her school to-morrow. She teaches there now."

"It sounds as if she were probably more like Grandmother Sutherland than I am," said Gloria wistfully as she got out of the car and looked about her at the well kept house and yard.

Uncle George gave a grim grin.

"No," he said with a half sigh, "Joan's more like her mother's side. She never looked like Mother. The youngest boy is the only Sutherland in my flock. Barney. He's out in Chicago now, got a good job. He's not likely to come back unless he gets transferred East. Albert is out in Wisconsin farming. He married a western girl and I guess he's anchored for life. But he's like his mother too. Well, come on in."

In the house the welcome was unsmiling and almost haughty. Aunt Miranda Sutherland was a woman with a prim mouth and gimlet eyes. Gloria could see at the first glance that she disapproved of her at sight, and Joan was only a slightly more modern edition of her mother. She seemed a good deal older than Gloria. They shook hands stiffly and sat down as far from the chair they had given Gloria as the limits of the big parlor would allow. For a few minutes they said little leaving the conversation entirely to the two brothers but when Gloria began to say how charmingly their house was located, and to rave over the view the cousin turned and looked her over critically, and the aunt said with a sharp tinge to her voice:

"How is it you're off up here? The last I heard of you you were going to be married. We got your cards. Wasn't it this week?"

The color suddenly drained out of Gloria's sweet face and pain came into her eyes.

"Yes, I was—" she began haltingly. It hadn't occurred to her that she would meet with that tragic matter up here so far out of her world. It stabbed through her heart like a knife and twisted about cruelly. What to answer, how to explain the terrible thing without making it more tragic? It seemed as if there were no words to go on. But her father had heard and answered for her.

"Gloria has been through a very sorrowful time," he said gravely. "Her fiance is dead. That was why I brought her up here, to get her away from everything for a little while."

An embarrassed instant of silence fell upon the room, and Gloria's eyes were down, but bravely she lifted them and sent a little wan, wistful smile out toward her unknown relatives.

"Oh!" said the aunt obviously curious. "I wondered. We saw a notice in a New York paper. Joan brought it home from Portland. It was the same name as that on the invitation but I thought it might be just a coincidence."

"No," said Gloria quietly, "it wasn't just a coincidence." There was infinite sadness in her tone, but it did not invite further questioning. Her aunt looked at her avidly for a moment, obviously expecting more details, but Gloria remained silent.

"Well, that certainly was too bad!" she said at last, half grudgingly. "There's many a slip, of course, but we aren't always looking for it to happen to folks we know. Did you know the girl he was with when it happened?"

Suddenly Gloria's father arose and stepped forward, his hat in his hand, his voice clear and a bit haughty.

"Well, I guess we must be going," he said offering his hand to his sister-in-law, and then to his niece. "It's quite a drive back to Afton and Mrs. Weatherby is expecting us both to tea. Also, I'm rather expecting a business telegram which may call me back home suddenly. I'm glad to have seen you. It's nice to know you're so pleasantly located. The view certainly is lovely from here. You must enjoy it a lot."

He talked incessantly, keeping between Gloria and her aunt and giving her no opportunity to reply to the question that had been asked her. Gloria managed to keep a semblance of a smile on her face until they were in the car and started off again. She even had the grace—or the courage—to say graciously as they drove away, "Can't you drive over to Afton and see us while we are there? We're going to stay a few days yet I think."

Joan thanked her ungraciously and said:

"I don't think it'll be possible. I go back to Portland in the morning, and Mother doesn't go out much any more."

Gloria, once out of their sight, settled back in the car with a stricken look.

Her father gave her a troubled glance. Finally he said:

"I wouldn't mind so much what she said. I don't think they really meant to be unkind. They're just curious, and perhaps a little hurt that we didn't write and explain, as they are relatives. I think that has been their grievance all along. They think we feel ourselves above them."

"No, I don't mind so much about them," said Gloria with a sorrowful little sigh. "I was just thinking, all the world knows my disgrace. I didn't realize anybody would know it outside of Roseland."

"Why do you call it *your* disgrace? You had nothing to do with shooting Stan."

"No," sighed Gloria again, "but it is a disgrace to have been connected with a man who died in that way. You know that, Dad."

"I always knew he wasn't worthy of you," said her father vehemently.

"After all, Dad, what have I done that should make me worth so much? I've been just a good-for-nothing parasite!" said the girl. "When I hear about Grandmother Sutherland and all that she did I'm ashamed."

"Times have changed," said her father sharply. "You were not required to do so much. Your circumstances were different. If you were back in those times and had the same necessity upon you I'll warrant you would do as well."

"I wonder?" said Gloria thoughtfully.

The telegram that Mr. Sutherland had spoken of so lightly without any real idea one would come, arrived over the telephone as they were coming down to breakfast next morning.

"Your presence in office imperative to-day. Important news from England just arrived."

Gloria's father turned troubled eyes upon her.

"I'm sorry," he said, "I've got to go home at once. I'll have to fly if I can catch a plane in time. Will you stay here? I can probably return to-morrow or next day. Or will you go with me? I could send the chauffeur up on the train to bring down the car."

Gloria's eyes took on a look of panic.

"Oh, I'd rather not go home—yet!" she pleaded. "Would it be all right for me to stay here a little while longer?" Her eyes sought Mrs. Weatherby's face which reassured her.

"Sure, you're welcome as the spring in winter!" exclaimed John Hastings pulling out his chair from the breakfast table. "And Mr. Sutherland, you've time to eat your breakfast." He looked at his watch. "I'll drive you down to the airport. There's a plane that leaves about the time we'll get there. I've gone on it myself."

In ten minutes more they were on their way, for Gloria decided to ride down and see her father off into the sky.

They sat together in the back seat, with the Hastings in front.

"I'm afraid you're going to be mighty lonesome," said the father, taking his distracted mind from his business for a glimpse at his daughter.

"No," said Gloria, "I'll be all right. I've got some thinking to do while you're gone, and I found a lot of old books in the parlor bookcase. I'm going to sit in the hammock on the porch and read between thinks."

She kept up a cheerful front till he had kissed her and gone, even until the plane was a mere speck in the distance. Then suddenly there descended upon her a sick feeling of desolation. Why had she let him go without her? Why had she not gone along with him?

And like a great bird of prey all the burden of her sorrow and the shame of Stan's death came down upon her terror-stricken soul. How was she going to endure the days without her father?

V

All the way back to Afton she was listening to Emily Hastings with her ears, as the kind hearted woman told her who lived here and there and what was what along the road, but her heart was suddenly living over again the tragedy that had come into her life and crying out in horror.

It was as if her father had been a kind of protection that had been about her, wherein she had been able to exist as in a new world, living back in the years of his early life. But now that he was gone the glamour of this place was gone with him, and it became an alien atmosphere wherein she could not breathe aright. She looked into the far bright sky that had swallowed him up a few minutes before, and wished she had gone with him. Going home would not have been any worse than being in a strange world with people who thought they had to entertain her every minute, while all the time she was longing to crawl away in a hole and hide.

Every detail of that terrible funeral lived itself over hour by hour in her mind as the day crawled through its seemingly endless minutes. Every expression on every face she had seen since Stan's death passed before her in review. She shrank again from Nance and her bitter words, her covert sneers at her-

self for caring about that girl. And then her mind
leaped to the cousin Joan, and Aunt Miranda's blunt
questions. She saw again the cold unsympathetic
glances of those two, and knew that they were enjoying
her discomfiture as if she had been a worm on a pin
and they had been watching her squirm. With supernatural insight it came to her that it was not because
those two women were cruel that they had been glad
of her trouble and had tried to rub it in, but because
they had been jealous of her wealth and easy life, and
it helped to assuage some of their pangs of envy to
know that she too had seen disappointment. They had
presumed to think of her as feeling above them, and
now they were glad that she was brought low. She
perceived that it was a state of mind with them rather
than personal enmity.

Yet though she could thus excuse and in a sense
forgive them, her soul groveled in the earth to think
that Stan, her lover whom she had trusted so perfectly,
had laid her open to such pity as this. Doubtless this
was the way everybody thought of her, in spite of
their moden standards, as a girl whose lover had gone
after another girl on the very eve as it were of her
marriage.

She went to her room when they reached the
house saying she must write some letters, but she did
not write letters when she got there. She buried her face
in her pillow and let the whole wretched horror sweep
over her soul and rack it as it would. There was no
one now to interrupt. The tears did not flow down her
face, for still they would not come, but she knew they
were flowing down in a torrent into her heart, tears
of her life's blood, and she wished—oh, how she
wished—that she could cry out her life and be done
with it all.

Then just in the midst of her orgy of sorrow the
dinner bell rang for the hearty midday meal, and she
wondered how she could ever go down and eat. Was
there no place in this wide world where one could get
away and grieve to death?

Then she heard the dear old lady's voice calling her, "Gloria, Gloria dear! Come down to dinner!" and the spirit of her own grandmother seemed to stir in the sweet lavender-scented room and urge her. "Go, dear! Don't grieve my old friend."

Grandmother would never have slunk away and grieved to death. Grandmother would have got up and done her duty.

Gloria arose, washed her face hastily and hurried downstairs.

There was johnnycake, hash and applesauce for dinner. It was the first time Gloria had ever been on intimate terms with any of them and she liked them all. Somehow the good cheer around the table dispelled her gloom. After she had helped with the dinner dishes she hunted out a book from the bookcase, put on a heavy coat, for the spring air was chilly, and curled up in the hammock on the porch to read.

It was a gorgeous day and the very air seemed buoyant, yet her heart was so heavy the sunshine fairly hurt, but after a time she grew interested in the book and managed to while away most of the afternoon.

She tried taking a walk alone but somehow, with her father away, the romance was gone, and when she looked down the aisle of the woods she could only see a long vista of years, her life, with the zest all gone out of it.

Her father called her up on the telephone that night to know if she was all right, and to say he might have to stay a couple of days longer. Did she want the chauffeur to come up after her or could she stand it a little longer without him?

She answered cheerily that she was going beautifully, and though her heart shrank from another day or two of monotony without him she shrank still more from going home, so she told him she was quite all right and he mustn't hurry away from important business just for her.

But when she hung up she had a dreary feeling of being a prisoner in a strange land.

Yet home would have been worse. There would have been Mrs. Asher and her woes, there would have been Nance with her fierce morbidness, and there would have been all the bridesmaids running in to make painful duty calls and bemoan her fate with her. No, a thousand times no, she could not go back home yet. She must get her bearings before she went back, though just how she was to get them was beyond her. She didn't seem to be doing anything about it here, just mooning along through the days, sorrowing through the nights, getting black rings under her eyes, a sorrowful droop to her mouth. How was she ever to bear life again?

For three days, except when she could persuade Emily Hastings to let her help in some household duty, she spent most of her time on the front porch reading.

The second day she heard whistling, and it cheered her a little. It wasn't like any whistling she had ever heard before, not jazzy, nor half crooning as was the crazy music at home. It was clear sweet notes like a bird in the early morning, and sweet quaint tunes that she had never heard before, though occasionally there was a melody which she recognized from some great symphony. The whistler was familiar with fine music, that was evident. Sometimes there was a bit of Scotch melody, and then hymn tunes, whistled with such perfect rhythm that one could almost hear words with the melody.

Whoever was whistling was working just out of sight behind the big white farm house that stood a little back from the road, diagonally across the highway. She heard the sound of a saw, and a hammer,— good strong sturdy blows,—driving a nail of proportions into wood. It made a musical ringing that chimed well with the whistling. Later there came the ring from a heavy roller going over smooth ground, and a little tinkle each time it turned as if some metal fragments were caught within the cylinder and were striking against the iron. Not that she reasoned this out. She was not familiar with saws and hammers and rollers and their work. Such things had not intimately

touched her life. But an inner sense told her that somebody over there was doing something in which he
was interested, and enjoying the work. Without realizing it that cheery whistle comforted her. It was probably that elderly gray haired man that she had seen
working on the farm across the road, though it sounded
like a young whistle.

But Gloria had discovered *Lorna Doone,* and was
deep in the thrills of romance and adventure. She did
not stop to think about the whistler except to be glad
that he was there making cheery noises.

The third day, however, she had come to the end
of her book, and was lying back thinking it over, all
its sweetness and sadness, beauty and tragedy, comparing it with her own life, realizing how different her
lover had been from the lover in the story, feeling those
terrible tears in her heart again, feeling an almost des-
peration.

Her father had not come yet. Instead there was a
letter saying that he was involved in most important
matters in the office which it would be disastrous for
him to leave, and suggesting again that she come home.
Her mother, he said, was interested in getting up a
drive for welfare and very much wanted her home to
help. She sent word that there was much that could be
done quietly, and that no one would criticise her for
going into charitable work. He said that he did not see
how he could get back to her before Sunday, or even
the middle of next week, and it was all owing to some
unexpected turn of affairs in European finance. Gloria
just couldn't have been more down and out than she
was that afternoon. She was looking into a stretch of
endless days ahead of her, wherein the sweet quiet she
had so enjoyed at first, had palled exceedingly upon
her, and yet there was no place in the world to which
she desired to go instead.

It was just when things had reached this stage
that she heard the front gate in the white picket fence
swing open and clang back on its noisy hinges, and
looking up in panic saw a very good looking young

man with a tennis racket under his arm, coming toward her.

She arose precipitately from the hammock to beat a hasty retreat, but he was there before she could get away.

"Please don't go yet," said the young man smiling pleasantly, "I came over to speak to you. I'm Murray MacRae from across the road. I've only been home a few days, but I've seen you sitting out here and I just wondered if you happen to be a tennis player? Because I've been fixing up our tennis court, rolling and marking it, and putting up new wire stop nets, trying to get it finished before my sister Lindsey gets back from her school, and I've just got it done. I wondered if you wouldn't take pity on me and play me a set or two just to try out the court and see if it's all right? I know we haven't been introduced yet, but I guess I can hunt up Mrs. Hastings and remedy that. Won't you come?"

Gloria hesitated, won in spite of herself by the pleasant impersonal smile.

"If you don't play I can teach you," he urged with a grin. "Do come! I don't like to wait a whole week to try out my work."

"Oh, I play, of course," said Gloria wondering at herself that she didn't give him a prompt negative, "but—I haven't any racket here."

"Oh, we have plenty of rackets!" said the young man. "They may not be as good as your own, but they would do for a little exercise I'm sure."

"I'd have to put on my tennis shoes," she said looking down at the trivial high-heeled slippers she was wearing.

"Run along and get them then," he said swinging himself to the porch and the hammock she had deserted. "I'll sit here and see what you've been reading. Then we'll be better acquainted."

Gloria went into the house wondering what she ought to do. In this age of the world of course one didn't stop much on formality, and she liked his looks.

But, was it the right thing for a girl in her position to go out and play tennis in these her days of mourning? Not that it meant anything of course to play tennis with a neighbor of the house where she was staying, but she felt the habit of her mother's formality upon her. Still, what difference did it make. All these people were strangers anyway and didn't know a thing about her. Why not get a little exercise? She was sure her father would approve.

Nevertheless she was relieved to meet Emily Hastings coming downstairs as she went up.

She stopped her with a question.

"There is a person out there who says his name is Murray something, and he wants me to come over across the road and try his tennis court. Should I go?"

"Oh, has Murray MacRae come over? I hoped he would. Why, surely, go. He's a wonderful fellow. I've been hoping his sister would get home while you are here. She's been away all winter teaching. Yes, go by all means. You need exercise and somebody to get you out. I've been worrying about you. I'll come out and introduce you. But Murray's all right. He's wonderful. He's been off all winter too."

So Gloria changed her shoes and felt a pleasant little thrill of excitement at the thought of playing tennis again. At least she wouldn't have to think of Stan's dead face all the time while she was playing.

Emily was out talking to the young man when she came down, in a pretty little green frock that was used to playing tennis.

After the introduction they swung away together down the path and across the road.

It seemed good to Gloria to be out again with some one young, to be going off to play, as if she were still carefree and happy. It was almost like being put back two or three years into her gay girlhood and not having to think of problems and sorrows and tragedies.

"That's a peach of a book you were reading," the young man said as they crossed the road and swung into his gate. "This isn't the first time you've read it of course."

"Why, yes, it is," said Gloria. "I never came on it anywhere. Do you know it?"

"Yes, it's one of my old favorites. I read it several times when I was a kid, and I like to go over it again now and then. There's some fine writing in it, besides being a rare story, and so utterly human and thrilling."

She looked at him surprised. The young men she knew did not discuss books in such a way, especially such books. In fact most of them read very few books and seldom spoke of them. Her friends were a hilarious crowd, always on the move, going somewhere, doing things—— There was never any time to read or to discuss. They would have been bored to discuss a serious book.

"It's—thrilling—" Gloria hesitated for words— "but—it's—so sad. Why do lovely things have to end badly? All life is not that way, is it?"

She was asking the question almost wistfully, hoping he would say it was not.

"Why, yes, I'm afraid life is that way, a lot of sadness mixed with the sweet. Haven't you found it that way? People do die, and sickness and sorrow and trouble do come, sooner or later. Isn't that the way it seems to you?"

"Not until—recently," she answered evasively. "I hoped you would say it wasn't usual. Terrible things do happen once in a great while, but—I can't bear to think they come often."

"Oh, but they do," he said gently. "You can't go among people, especially to-day, and not find tragedy everywhere, all mixed up with the happiness."

"But that's terrible!" said Gloria pitifully. "I never thought until a very short time ago that dreadful things could come to just anybody any time."

"Didn't you?" He turned and looked at her tenderly, as if she were a little child in her first disillusionment. "I learned that when I was just a kid. A very precious older brother died."

"Yes, death," said Gloria. "Of course, but—I don't see why it had to be! It would have been so much nicer if the world was made so that nice things went on always, and there didn't have to be pain and sorrow and death."

He gave her another quick astonished look, and then after a minute spoke again.

"It will be that way someday of course, when the curse is taken away."

The amazement in her eyes showed that she did not at all understand what he meant.

"In the new earth," he explained, "God shall wipe away all tears from their eyes; and there shall be no more death, neither sorrow nor crying, neither shall there be any more pain: for the former things are passed away."

He spoke so earnestly, with such conviction, as if he had authority to give out the words as truth, that suddenly the possibility of such conditions seemed real to Gloria and an unutterable longing welled up in her heart to enter into them. She did not know that in spite of her efforts to hide her deep feeling a heartbreaking yearning showed in her face and voice as she quoted in an attempt at lightness:

" 'Eventually? Why not now?' "

With rare tact the young man responded to her pretense at gaiety:

" 'There's much to be done ere it comes to that'."

"Oh!" The hope seemed to melt out of Gloria's face. "You mean after centuries and centuries people will get better and better and conditions will change, —what good does that do us?" She said it bitterly.

"No, thank God I don't mean that. There is no hope in that. I mean something much better than that, much more certain, much nearer. Say, why not let me come over sometime and tell you about it?"

Gloria brought her gaze from the neat sunny court framed in brilliant green, and gave a long impersonal, searching look to the stranger who had so astonishingly given her a glimpse into another world.

Was it worth while to follow what was probably just a will o' the wisp, an idealist's fancy? But something she saw in the steady, calm eyes, something of assurance and of joyous certainty, brought again that throb of hope and yearning to her sad heart.

"I'd be very glad to hear it," she said. "It sounds like a fairy tale."

"But that's the beauty of it, it isn't a fairy tale, it's true." He gave her a rare smile and she wondered at the light in his eyes. Was this one of those people you called a dreamer? He didn't look fanatical. She had never seen a young man with a look like that in his face.

But just then the side door was opened by a pleasant-faced woman with gray hair. She carried a plate of something in her hand and she had a smile like the young man.

"Here are some cookies just out of the oven, Murray. I thought you might like to nibble at them while you are playing."

"That's great!" said the young man. "And, Mother, let me introduce Miss Sutherland. She's been good enough to take pity on me."

The mother gave a quick keen glance at the beautiful girl and looked apprehensively at her boy, but she gave Gloria a warm welcome and Gloria liked her at once. It amazed her how friendly and home-like these country people were. She felt at home with them at once.

The cookies were delicious and the two young people began their tennis without any feeling that they were strangers.

They were both good players, and Gloria who had in her possession at home a row of silver cups that she had taken in various club tournaments, found that she had an opponent who called forth all her skill and energy. Therefore it was no tame amateurish game but a close quick intensive one, employing not only muscles but brains. Gloria's cheeks began to glow and her gold curls were in lovely confusion. The mother watching occasionally from her kitchen window admired even while she feared for her cherished son. He couldn't help but admire this beautiful girl! And she was no girl for him to become interested in. She was the daughter of a multi-millionaire! She was accustomed to every luxury that money could buy! She was the petted idol of society! And what she was doing up here buried in the country the mother could not understand. She knew enough of the Sutherland family to be sure that this girl was out of her environment, and there must be some unusual reason for it.

She looked at her Murray, tall and straight and fine, and so far as she knew at present heart free, and sighed. Had her boy got to go through the fires of falling in love hopelessly? Those two out there on the tennis court made a wonderful couple as they played together, fine and strong and well matched, but as utterly apart both as concerned wealth, social position and upbringing, as the poles. Why had she been so impulsive and lacking in foresight as to suggest to Murray that he ask the lonesome looking girl on the porch over there to try out his newly finished court with him? If she had had a closer view of her beauty she never would have done it.

They played until suppertime, and John Hastings came over to say that Emily had sent word there was potpie for supper and it must be eaten right away before it fell, so Gloria must come at once.

There was no opportunity for further talk. Gloria was sorry about that. She wanted to ask this strange young man just what he had meant by his talk about a Utopian earth. But she gladly promised to play again the next day, and hurried away with John Hastings to discover what "potpie" might be. It was a dish unknown to the Sutherland cook at Roselands.

Gloria's cheeks were glowing and her eyes were bright. There were no more dark circles under them, and she realized that she hadn't thought of her own sorrows once all the afternoon. Suddenly, as she sat down at the table, it came to her that there was a long empty evening ahead of her. She supposed she would have to hunt up another book to read.

But old Mrs. Weatherby surprisingly provided another entertainment. Of course she had no idea what an utterly strange thing she was asking this daughter of the world to do. It seemed to her a small thing and quite a natural thing to ask.

"I've been wondering, Gloria," she said toward the close of the meal, "if you would mind going over to prayer meeting with me to-night? Emily and John have to go see one of the men that worked on the farm last summer. He's been in an automobile accident. He's in the hospital and may die, and he's sent for them. I do hate to miss my prayer meeting, especially now when our minister's away. Every one counts you know, and it's so discouraging to any leader to have only a handful."

Gloria gasped inwardly. What might a prayer meeting be? Would it be something embarrassing? Would they perhaps expect her to pray? But of course she couldn't refuse an old lady a request like that. So she smiled and said sweetly that she would love to go with her, and hadn't they better go in the car, that would be so much easier for her? And so it was arranged.

Gloria had no idea what sort of costume one was supposed to wear to prayer meeting, but she changed from the gay little sports dress she was wearing into a white dress with a warm white coat and a white beret on her gold head. Old Mrs. Weatherby eyed her approvingly and went off proudly in the five thousand dollar car without an idea what a costly outfit was at her service for the evening.

They were early. There were only five people in the room when they arrived. Gloria had a passing wish that she could stay outside the church and watch the sunset, for it seemed stuffy inside the building and she shrank inexpressibly from the solemn stillness that pervaded the dimly lighted prayer meeting room, where those five people sat with bowed heads. It filled her with an uncomfortable awe, and made her think of Stan's funeral, and his white, handsome face with the selfish lips. Her bridegroom! The knife was in her soul once more turning with a twisted wrench, and she wished she had not come.

She sat down in the wooden chair and bent her head respectfully, her eyes in her lap and her tragedy gripping her by the throat while old Mrs. Weatherby bowed her head in prayer. Here she was in the hands of her life horror again, and here she must remain for at least an hour, or probably more. An hour of horror! Oh, life, life! Why did one ever have to be born into a world like this full of trouble?

Then the big bell in the steeple began to toll, reverberating through the room, and echoing outside and down the street. People came in, by twos and threes. There seemed to be quite a lot of people coming in. Why did they come if they didn't have to, Gloria wondered?

Then suddenly some one walked straight up the middle aisle past her, with quick, springy, purposeful steps, and as he passed her she looked up and recognized the back of the young man she had been playing tennis with that afternoon. So he had come too! Well, he would, perhaps, a man who had a hope in him that this old world was ever going to be rid of its curse. A dreamer, a hoper. A man like that might even be able to go into dreary places like prayer meeting rooms and feel them to be bearable. But somehow the room seemed to be more endurable to her since he entered.

And why was he going away up front? Why! He was even stepping up on the low platform and sitting down behind the table that was there. She watched him startled. He had a soft Bible in his hand, and as he laid it on the table and sat down he put his hand up to his eyes and was praying also. She watched him covertly, noted the fine outline of his head, the thick brown hair that waved away from his forehead, the strength and fineness of the hand that covered his eyes. And his head wasn't bent in prayer as if it were a

formality, either. There was a reverence about him that
showed he was in earnest.

So this then was the explanation! He was a
preacher! What a pity to waste a young man like that!
How well he played tennis! And there wasn't a thing
about him to suggest the smugness that she had always
connected in her mind with the clergy. He was gay and
bright and interesting. But he was different from any of
the young men she knew. She recalled at the moment
the question she had asked her father on their ride,
and it came to her that here was a young man one
could be sure of; he would not have been killed in a
night club on the eve of his marriage, would not have
been the object of a lover's jealous shot!

Sadly she turned her eyes away and caught her
breath with a sharp quick wish that Stan, her Stan,
might have been a young man like this one, a young
man in whom she could have trusted. A wistful yearning came into her heart that even if he had to die and
leave her, he might have left her trusting in him, believing in his love. Even if she had had to go lonely
all her days it would have been something to remember, to hold as her own, to be glad in.

But the meeting began at once with a hymn, and
the young man's voice led off in a strong clear bari-
tone, sweet and full of resonance. She recognized that
it was an unusual voice. It was an old hymn that con-
gregations are used to droning out very often, in the
tone a dying swan might use, but it was new to Gloria and it was not droned. The vital young voice that
led made sure of that.

> "Sweet hour of prayer, sweet hour of prayer,
> That calls me from a world of care,
> And bids me, at my Father's throne,
> Make all my wants and wishes known!"

And he sang it as if the hour were sweet to him.
He was not here merely because he had to lead this
meeting, merely because his profession obliged him to

come and go through certain forms and ceremonies. He was here because he wanted to be. He was here to worship, to meet a God who was in this church, this little old-fashioned country church, with an ingrain carpet, and a cabinet organ, and hard wooden chairs. He looked as if he were glad to be here, and were enjoying it.

And the prayer that followed kept up that impression. He began to talk to God as if he knew Him, as if He were a personal friend.

The subject was prayer. The scripture reading was on prayer. Murray MacRae's talk was on the conditions of prayer which ensure answer. Gloria had never prayed in her life! She had never thought about prayer. The whole matter was a revelation to her. The hour sped away on winged feet, the hour that she had been dreading. She had been interested every minute!

"Isn't he wonderful?" she heard the people about her saying to one another after the meeting was over.

"It was nice to have you here," said Murray Mac-Rae as he came down the aisle and passed near her at the end of the row of seats where she waited for Mrs. Weatherby to speak to a woman about the missionary society.

His eyes had a smile in them as he passed on to speak to others, men and women who had known him all his life, and who were waiting to tell him how much they had enjoyed his talk.

Her eyes followed him down to the door. What an extraordinary young man! What kind of impression would he make among her crowd of intimates at home? Would they respect him, or would they laugh at him? They would stare, surely. But they wouldn't understand. She didn't understand either. He was a phenomenon.

Yet when she got back to the house that night and answered her father's nightly telephone call her voice was much more cheerful than it had been other evenings when he called. He recognized it at once. He had been greatly troubled that he still had to put her off. But he was reassured when she told him that she had been playing tennis that afternoon. She left it exceedingly vague who she had played with, and he didn't think to wonder about that until afterward, but she made him understand that she was all right and didn't want to come home yet.

She was still wondering about Murray MacRae when she fell asleep that night, and the morrow didn't seem, in prospect, nearly so drab and monotonous as it had the night before.

VI

Murray MacRae was suddenly called away the next morning on business he said, stopping a moment at the Sutherland house to explain, and he put off the tennis until Saturday afternoon when he expected to be back. Gloria as she turned back to the breakfast table felt the day go blank again. She had been looking forward to the exercise, and most of all to asking that strange young man a lot of questions, and now they would have to wait. She was disappointed.

"Has Mr. MacRae a church somewhere?" she asked as she sat down again to her interrupted breakfast.

"A church?" said Emily Hastings, pouring more cream into her coffee. "Why no, he isn't a minister. He's just a young business man. They say he has a very fine business opening offered him and I suppose he has had to go to New York and look after something, although he isn't going to start in regularly until fall I believe."

"Why, I thought he was a minister of course. He had charge of the meeting last night."

"Oh, did Murray lead the meeting? My, I'm sorry I had to miss it. We got in so late last night Mother didn't have a chance to tell me yet. He's fine, isn't he? No, he isn't a minister, but he might as well have been, only he thinks we need more Christian business men who understand the Bible. You know he's just graduated from some kind of theological college down south somewhere. He went down there and took a regular ministerial course just as if he had been going to preach. He said he thought it was up to all Christians to-day to understand their Bibles, and if they were going to be business men they needed it all the more."

"He's—" Gloria hesitated for a word, *"different,* isn't he?" she finished lamely. "At least he's different from any young man I know."

"Yes, I suppose he would be," said Emily thoughtfully, "but I like to hear him. He had the Sunday night services all last summer when he was home on vacation, and the church was just packed. People came from over the other side of the state line after it got known he was to speak. They say he is a smart business fellow too. They say it's a wonderful position he's going into this fall. I don't know just what the business is. I haven't heard his mother say. His sister Lindsey will be home next week. She's lovely. You'll like her too. She is registrar in a girl's school. She is older than her brother but a very charming young woman."

"Her brother spoke of her," said Gloria politely trying to keep up a conversation.

"We have several nice young people around here you would enjoy knowing," said Emily. "There's Bob Carroll down beyond Ripley. He's Murray's friend. Everybody thought he was going to be a college professor, but instead he surprised his friends by taking a course in agriculture, and now he's gone in for intensive farming, developing some land his uncle left him."

"How interesting!" said Gloria wonderingly, trying to fancy any one of the group of gay young men who had constituted her "set" at home going in for anything that required manual labor. "You don't mean that he does the actual work himself, do you? He just directs his laborers I suppose?"

"Not a bit of it!" spoke up John Hastings a flush on his own face, although he could see that Gloria hadn't an idea that she was casting a little slur at himself. She hadn't been there long enough to see him in overalls plowing, or out by the stream shearing sheep. "Bob Carroll is right on the job all the time. Last summer he had only one helper, though I hear this spring he's hired a couple more hands. He's *real,* that fellow is. He and Murray are two of a kind. Not a lazy hair on their heads. He's no slouch either. He's called awfully good-looking by most people, and he was an honor man at college, and a Phi Beta Kappa man, and had no end of athletic letters. Football captain and all that. He's just two years out of college! Wait till you see him."

Gloria found it impossible to stretch her imagination enough to take in such a person. In her secret heart she was sure she would find something more to be desired in this farmer paragon.

During the next two days Gloria devoured three more books and found herself wondering if Murray MacRae had read them, found herself thinking deeply over the questions they raised in her mind, wondering why these old books were so different from the literature which had hitherto come under her notice. There was scarcely a hint in any of them of the present day triangular love theme, though there were plenty of sweet love stories woven into their fascinating pages. Murder, mystery, crime there was in some proportion but it did not constitute the main theme of any of these books. Pride, hatred, selfishness, impurity, unscrupulousness were there, but not exalted nor victorious. Love and fineness and chivalry were stressed as she had never heard them stressed by anyone except her father.

As Saturday drew near she found herself anticipating the coming of Murray MacRae. She found herself most eager to ask him questions, and determined to open the way at once for him to give that explanation he had promised.

But of course, her common sense told her, it would turn out to be some mystic thing connected with religion, and nothing she would be able to comprehend, nothing from which to get any real help in her trouble. There wasn't any help for such trouble as hers. Her life was just blasted that was all.

Yet after all her resolves, when Saturday afternoon came and he came over after her, wearing a white sweater that made his eyes look young and blue, and escorted her over to the tennis court, she grew suddenly shy before him, shy about asking questions such as she wanted to ask. She kept thinking of him as almost a minister, and dreading to bring out her crude thoughts which only had reference to her own personal troubles. She shrank from having his keen knowing eyes look deep into hers and read her life. She found she didn't want him to suspect that the man she had been going to marry had been a man who frequented night clubs and had been shot by a chorus girl's lover. So she walked beside him across the road and around to the tennis court talking of most indifferent matters, what a lovely day it was and how the spring was getting almost as advanced here as it had been in her home when she came away.

Yet there was something exhilarating in it, just to be walking beside a pleasant young person, acting like a carefree girl again, forgetting the dark cloud on her life.

The air was crisp and clear, the sunshine bright, the court in the pink of perfection, for Murray had been working on it all the morning, and they played like two old hands who had been playing together for years. Gloria wondered why it was so pleasant to be playing with this stranger of whom she had been just the least little bit afraid when she was walking across the street with him.

They had played two sets and were well on into the third when John Hastings came around the corner of the house and signaled for their attention.

"Sorry to have to take the lady away," he said with a grin, "but she has callers over at the house."

Gloria's face went blank. Calling on her? There must be a mistake. Who would call on her away up here? It couldn't be that some of her friends from home had hunted her out and mistakenly come to see her! She shuddered at the thought and the sunlight went out of her eyes as if a cloud had suddenly passed across them.

"Perhaps it's some one you want to see very much!" suggested Murray with a grin, but that didn't seem to help.

"Perhaps they won't stay long and we can finish this afterward. It's three all and the last was a love game, remember."

Her eyes lighted.

"Here's hoping!" he said with another grin that seemed to make him her comrade and friend.

So she hurried across the street ahead of John Hastings who had lingered to talk to Murray about his garden. She forgot that she had carried the racket with her, forgot that it was not her own, and remembered too late, as she came within recognition of her callers, realizing that a racket was the wrong thing for her to be carrying. She felt their disapproval by the very set of their shoulders, as they sat in Emily Hastings porch rockers awaiting her. It was her aunt Miranda and her cousin Joan! Of all people the least expected! And they would think a game of tennis a waste of time. She was sure they would. If she had only left that racket behind they might have thought she had been over to call on Mrs. MacRae.

But there was nothing for it now but to walk up, racket and all. They had seen her. She could not well cast it in the road. And anyway, why should Gloria Sutherland cringe before a disagreeable pair of relatives? It really didn't matter whether they thought that tennis was a waste of time or not.

So she walked coolly up to the porch and greeted her relatives as if they were welcome, laying her racket aside on a table as calmly as if she had not seen two pairs of eyes fasten upon it just as her intuition had foreseen they would do.

"We heard that you were still here," said Aunt

Miranda fixing her cold eyes upon Gloria, "and Joan seemed to think we ought to come and call, since you asked us."

"That was nice of you," said Gloria trying to smile into the hostile eyes of her cousin.

"We thought perhaps you were lonesome," said Joan, her eyes giving a significant glance at the racket, "but it seems you have found other friends."

"People have been very kind," said Gloria looking her cousin in the eye and trying not to change color. "I've just been having a little much-needed exercise. Since father had to go back home I have just stayed around the house and read, and I really needed to get some good hard exercise."

"Don't they have any extra housework here they could let you do?" asked her aunt, looking about on the immaculate porch with its neatly painted chairs in a row, each chair back covered whitely with a clean linen cover. In her glance Gloria read for the first time that even a row of porch rockers wearing white linen covers, required labor to make and keep them that way. It was a revelation but Gloria did not let her callers know it. She suddenly realized that there must have been other ways she might have helped besides just making her bed and drying the dishes now and then. She tucked that away in her mind for future reference.

"Oh, they let me do a little now and then," she smiled pleasantly. "Are you home every Saturday, Joan? How nice that must be!"

"Yes," said her mother grimly, "she manages to get a good deal done Saturdays. She's always been one to help at home. My Joan never was one to shy at work."

"I suppose you play games a good deal, don't you?" remarked Joan with another glance at the tennis racket.

"Oh, I do almost anything that's going," laughed Gloria.

"I shouldn't suppose you'd feel much like games,

now, though; not under the circumstances," remarked her aunt grimly with a thin disapproving set of her lips.

Gloria's eyes suddenly grew dark with surprise and pain and her color went white.

"One doesn't always do just what one feels like," she said slowly, with down-drooping eyes.

"Well, I should suppose almost anybody would excuse you now from engaging in frivolity," said Aunt Miranda. "I shouldn't suppose they'd *expect* you to go playing around *now!*"

"I think perhaps," said Gloria, feeling around for words, "that it's just as easy to go ahead and do things. It sometimes helps you to forget the hard things."

"I've always thought good hard work was the best panacea for trouble," said her aunt severely. "I'm sure I've found it so in my own case. When my little boy was killed by a tree falling on him, I just went downstairs and cleaned the cellar. That was the only way I could stand it. Get at something hard that has to be done and do it! That's my way!"

"We don't all have cellars to clean," smiled Gloria faintly, "and I don't suppose everybody bears trouble in the same way."

"But wasn't this to have been your wedding day?" asked the cousin sharply with another hostile glance at the tennis racket.

Gloria felt as if she should scream. She wondered if she did what effect it would have? Would Emily come and help her out? Would her callers take their leave? But she answered quietly, her eyes down-drooped.

"No, it was last week!"

"Oh!" said Joan, "a week ago! *Only* a week ago!"

Gloria felt that she had stood all that she could stand. She suddenly lifted up her head with some of the old hauteur wherewith she had always been able to subdue enemies, and looking at her cousin with a lovely smile she said:

"Oh, there are some darling little new kittens down behind the barn. Wouldn't you like to come around and look at them? They are the darlingest things!"

"No, thanks," said Joan with a look of disgust, "I can't bear cats, either new or old. They give me the shivers."

"We came over, Gloria," said her aunt ignoring the interlude, "to suggest that perhaps you would like to come over and spend a few days with us while your father is away. How long is he going to be gone?"

Gloria barely suppressed an exclamation of distress at this suggestion, but she managed an icy little smile.

"Oh, that's sweet of you," she said, controlling a shiver of dislike, "but I think I'll just stay here where Father left me."

"But it doesn't look right for you not to come to us for part of the time," urged the aunt severely with a tilt of offense to her chin and nose. "The whole countryside will think it's queer."

"Why bother?" said Gloria. "It doesn't matter so much what people think."

"It certainly does!" said Joan with a toss of her head. "We have to live here, you know."

"I'm sorry," said Gloria sobering thoughtfully. "It hadn't occurred to me that the countryside had anything to do with it. But in this case I guess you'll just have to explain that I'm staying here where Father can call me on the telephone at any time. He expects me to stay here. He calls me up every day sometime."

"He calls you on the long distance telephone *every day!*" exclaimed the two in unison.

"But isn't that terribly expensive?" asked the aunt severely.

"Why, I really don't know," said Gloria, "I never thought of it in that way. But anyhow, Dad does it and he expects me to be here! Thank you for your kindness, and I do appreciate your thinking of me, but at present I'm staying right here. And after all, it's in a sense my own home. Dad owns this house you know!"

A quick startled look passed between the mother and daughter.

"No, I didn't know that!" said the mother. "I

understood it passed out of the family years ago. I don't see why your father should have any more right to it than the rest of the children."

Gloria looked at them puzzled.

"Why Dad bought it back again several years ago. Didn't you know that?"

"No, I didn't know it," said her aunt, as if she thought it an extremely doubtful statement.

Gloria looked at her in despair. She didn't seem to be getting anywhere with any kind of a conversation. She turned to her cousin and took a fresh start.

"Did you have a pleasant week in your school?" she asked courteously.

"Pleasant? Teaching school? Well, no, I should say not! I don't teach school exactly for pleasure!"

Gloria laughed.

"Well, I should think it would be interesting at least," she said, determined to make this girl unbend from her stiffness. "I think children are darling!"

"H'm! Well, I *don't*. I think they are little devils!" said Joan. "If you don't believe it come and visit us some day."

"I'd love to," said Gloria, "could I?"

The other girl's face hardened.

"You wouldn't like it," she said sourly, "and you wouldn't find out just visiting anyway. They'd be on their good behavior, they always are when there are visitors. You'd have to be a teacher and sit there day in and day out keeping those thirty wild young ones in order, and beating a little knowledge into their heads, whether your feet ached and your back ached and your head ached or not. Whether the children were impudent and stupid and full of the old Nick or not. Having eyes in the back of your head to find out what's going on out in the hall, or in the back of the room. Having mothers come and complain because you didn't give Johnny as good a mark as some other boy. Having the superintendent call you down for something you didn't do. Oh, yes, you'd love to teach, I'm sure. It's well enough for you who don't have to earn your living to talk that way. You'll get married to somebody pretty soon again, and you won't do a thing but play bridge and ride around in different cars and go to parties. Yes, you know a lot about it!"

Gloria caught her breath as the tempestuous words swept on, and then a kind of pity grew in her eyes.

"I'm dreadfully sorry you've had such a hard time," she said gently, "and you certainly make a good-for-nothing picture out of me. I didn't realize I was such a lazy selfish little brute before. But I would gladly have shared my good times with you if I'd known. It's quite true I haven't had to earn my living," she went on thoughtfully, "but I've always hoped I'd be brave about it if I had to, and I can't help thinking one of the ways I'd choose to try and earn it, if I knew enough to get the job, would be to teach little children."

"Well, it's not so hot when you get to doing it," said the cousin dryly, "and as for sharing your good times, I'm not asking anything of anybody. I've got my life to live and I'll live it, but I'm not going to pretend it's all velvet. Ma, isn't it time we were starting home? If Gloria thinks she can't go with us there's no reason why we should wait any longer."

"Oh, but," said Emily Hastings, appearing at the door just then with a tray, "you're going to have a cup of tea before you go. Yes, you are. I've got it all ready. Gloria, pull out that little table by Mrs. Sutherland so I can set the tray down. It's all poured out so it won't take you long. Do you like cream or lemon in your tea?"

"Neither!" said Mrs. Sutherland severely, "I take mine straight. Just one lump of sugar. And I never did hold with such heathenish customs as putting lemon in tea. What would lemon have to do with a good plain straightforward thing like tea?"

Emily Hastings smiled.

"Well, isn't it strange what different tastes we have? Now I drink the tea merely for the lemon."

"I don't call it tastes, I call it a slavish adherence to fashion!" said the caller helping herself to the largest piece of cinnamon toast on the plate.

"Oh, do you?" said Emily peaceably. "Well, now I hadn't thought of that! By the way, how is your garden? Have you got any peas up yet?"

A garden seemed a safe enough topic, but there were presently caustic sentences being launched about different methods of planting peas and Emily had to think up some other neutral subject.

When at last the callers took their departure Emily sighed.

"Poor thing!" she said, "she's never quite happy unless she thinks she's making somebody else unhappy. She's always been that way ever since I knew her. We used to go to school together, and nobody liked her because she had everybody mad in about five minutes after she arrived. Her daughter's growing just like her too! It's too bad! And her husband is so nice and kind. I don't see how he ever stands it!"

"He is nice, isn't he?" said Gloria. "It's the first time I ever saw any of them you know."

"Yes, I know," smiled Emily, "everybody in the countryside knows. She takes pains that they shall, and you can't do a thing about it. But don't worry. She must have liked you or she wouldn't have taken the trouble to drive over and see you."

"That makes it nice, doesn't it?" laughed Gloria. Then catching sight of the tennis racket she glanced at her watch.

"I was supposed to go back and finish that set," she said, "but I guess it's almost supper time, isn't it?"

"No, run along. I haven't got the supper started yet. Besides to-morrow is Sunday and you can't finish it then."

Gloria gave her a quick astonished look but she said nothing. It hadn't occurred to her that Sunday would be any different from any other day as regarded tennis. But Emily didn't even see her surprise.

The twilight almost caught them before they had

finished the set, for they both came to it with renewed vigor, and it stretched itself out with exciting fluctuations, till finally with one last smashing blow Murray landed the ball over the net close to Gloria's feet, and the set was won.

"I'd like to come over and talk awhile to-night," said Murray as he escorted her across the road in response to the supper bell, "but I find I've got to do something else this evening. I wonder how about Monday evening?"

Gloria felt a little disappointment as she turned to go in. She had been meaning to ask him to come over to-night and answer her questions, and now she must wait until Monday night. A long dismal Sunday between! Sunday! Why couldn't they play tennis on Sunday? She began to perceive that standards were different, and she sighed as she vaguely visioned other equally perplexing questions that made a great wall of separation between her world and this one where she was staying for a little while. Why, at home, a tennis tournament would have gone on with more vigor than ever on Sunday because the crowd of observers would be all the greater.

Well, there would be nothing to do but go to church probably and listen to that droney old preacher she had heard last Sunday, unless she took a lonely walk in the woods, and she shrank from that. The last time she had attempted to walk by herself in the woods she had come upon a man who looked like an old tramp, with shaggy hair and ragged garments, sitting on a log cleaning up a fierce looking gun. She had been fairly petrified with fright, and had stolen back to the road in haste and run almost all the way home. She had not spoken to anybody about it, because of a secret fear that perhaps he wasn't a tramp at all, but a well known character in the neighborhood, even a fond relative of someone. She had discovered already that you could not always judge a man by his garments and haircut. But she did not care to take any more such chances, so she went to church.

But there, to her surprise and relief was Murray

MacRae again in the pulpit, and her heart was lifted up with hope. Now she would hear some more of his strange doctrines, and perhaps inadvertently some of her questions would be answered without her having to ask them. She dreaded asking any of her questions, lest her tragedy would be revealed and her heart laid bare. It seemed so dreadful to have him know what she had just been through.

The sermon was about the coming of the Lord Jesus for His church, a thing she had never even heard of before, and it filled her with a fine frenzy of fear. She watched the young speaker's face glow with joy over the thought that sometime, perhaps in the glow of early morning, or possibly in the solemn hush of night, Christ, his Christ was coming, and it might be soon.

It might be all very beautiful for people like Murray MacRae to be glad over a catastrophe like that, but what of a poor lost, unshriven soul like herself? There were not likely many people like himself in the world, perhaps a few more than she dreamed. She looked about speculatively on the quiet group of elderly people, interspersed with earnest young people, and wondered if they all knew and understood what the preacher was talking about, and if they believed it too, and were looking forward to a rapture in the air with Jesus Christ. But what would happen to a world left behind with all such true believers taken away? She shuddered almost visibly and Emily looked over and offered her light shawl she had brought with her, thinking Gloria was cold. Gloria accepted it and threw it around her shoulders, but it did not warm her soul. That was still cold and lonely. Death and horror seemed imminent. Sin and darkness and curse all about! Oh, she hoped such a thing couldn't be true. She hoped it was only the vision of a dreamer. It would be so much better to have a perfect earth and let it go at that. Why did anyone want anything better? The earth without pain and sorrow. She would ask him all about it to-morrow night. And she would not go to church any more and hear these unsettling things,

things which spoke of another world, and made the death of Stan come back so vividly.

Yet when evening came and she heard the old church bell give the half hour warning for service she went upstairs and put on her hat and coat again. Just from very torture of her own thoughts she must go out and hear more. Perchance there would be something comforting, or clarifying to-night.

And there was! It was made quite plain. She was told that she was a sinner, with no hope throughout eternity, until God sent His own Son to bear the consequences of her sin and die on the cross in her stead. She learned about the shed blood so clearly that she would never be in doubt again what part it played in man's salvation, and she was made to see what was meant by eternal separation from God, the fate of the unbeliever.

Most unhappy she sat and found tears going down her cheeks. She had not cried a tear yet for all the tragedy through which she had passed, but now the tears were breaking through and she felt that they would soon be beyond her control.

They introduced her to Robert Carroll after church, and winking back the tears that still stood brightly on her lashes she looked into his clear true eyes and saw the same radiance in his face that she had noticed in the face of Murray MacRae. Then there were two such men in the world! And if there were two, perhaps there were more! Why had she never met any of them before? Why had her world contained not even one who seemed to have found that look of peace? There were plenty who were hilariously gay, but none with a depth of peace in their eyes like these two.

She heard talk of the coming of Lindsey, references to her Sunday School class who were anxious to have her back again after her long absence, references to the man she was to marry. Bright, eager interested talk. These people were not gloomy nor dull. They were as interested in their lives and church activities as ever her home group had been in parties and gaiety.

They were not in the least discontented. What was the secret? That thing they spoke of as being saved? Was that it?

She felt exceedingly small and lonely and left out, and was glad when they went home. And that night she wept into her pillow, hot tears that had been rending her soul all these days, and wondered if the God of Murray MacRae had ever really thought about her, and knew what she was suffering?

And now the ice in her heart seemed to be melting and taking away some of the terrible cold and horror, and making her from a cold frozen girl who never could go on living again, into a warm human being once more, who was suffering keenly, and needed terribly to be comforted. She wished for her father and decided that if he telephoned the next day she would tell him she was coming home. At once. Only she would have to wait until after Monday night, for she must first have that talk with Murray MacRae. She knew that she would never forgive herself if she went away from here without understanding what he had meant that first day when he said that a time was coming when all the sin and pain and sorrow would be taken away from this earth and it was to be full of perfect joy that nothing could dim. She simply must know what he meant. If there was anything in it but a dream she must know and understand it. Only—it would be too late now, for Stan was dead!

And so she fell asleep, with the haunting tune of a lovely song that had been sung at the close of the service, sung with wonderful effect by Robert Carroll, the gentleman farmer she had heard so much about:

> "Oft me-thinks I hear His footsteps,
>   Stealing down the paths of time;
> And the future dark with shadows,
>   Brightens with this hope sublime.
> Sound the soul-inspiring anthem;
>   Angel hosts your harps attune;
> Earth's long night is almost over,
>   Christ is coming—coming soon!"

VII

Murray MacRae kept his promise Monday evening. He came breezing into the kitchen where Gloria was wiping the dishes, took another dish towel from the little line that hung behind the stove and went to work.

"This isn't the first time I've wiped dishes in this house is it, Mrs. Hastings?" he said as he saw Gloria's astonished look. "I grew up running over here to play with whoever happened to be living here," he explained to Gloria.

After the dishes were put away Murray took Gloria up the road a little way to a spot where the sunset could be better seen than anywhere else in the neighborhood, and they stood a long time watching the great ball of crimson slip briefly down behind a purple mountain, then watching the tatters of crimson and gold it had left behind, till the crimson faded into coral, a pale clear green stole up and spread into the sky, and was met by a rosy glow above, turning the mountains and the hills below into deep dark greens and browns. They watched while the twilight dropped down, shutting them into a great world of wondrous color, and a single star shot out and twinkled at them.

"When I consider Thy heavens, the work of Thy fingers, the moon and the stars which Thou has ordained," quoted Murray in a hushed voice, "what is man?"

"Yes, what *is* man," broke in Gloria. "What are we here for? If there is a God that made us and put us here as you believe, why did He do it?"

"Thou madest him to have dominion over the works of Thy hands," answered Murray seriously. "Once when I was a little boy my father made a boat. He was wonderfully clever with his hands and it was like a real motorboat, every part perfect, and the marvelous thing about it was that it actually had a tiny motor in it and it would go! It was an exquisite bit of workmanship, even as a child I think I recognized that. I believe he could have sold it for an astonishing amount, but what do you suppose he did with it? He *gave it to me!* We had a good sized pool in the yard —you saw it there beyond the tennis court—and the boat was mine to sail in the pool. I was delighted with it of course, but childlike, instead of letting my father show me how to run the boat, I deliberately disobeyed him and took it out myself. And in a very short time the whole thing was a wreck! I have it yet, I keep it to remind me."

He was still for a moment, a humble, wistful look upon his face that seemed beautiful to Gloria. She had never seen that look upon a man's face before, except the time last week when her father was telling stories of his childhood. She was utterly bewildered by what this man was saying, but she recognized that he was not through yet, and she remained silent, waiting.

"God made the earth," went on Murray, indicating the sweep of horizon they had been watching, "and He gave it to man to rule! But instead of letting God direct him in everything man deliberately rebelled and disobeyed God. That was sin and it resulted in the wreckage of the earth,—pain, and sorrow, and hatred, and death ruled the world."

As he spoke it seemed as if all the unutterable anguish of the whole world of centuries was spread out before them in a ghastly panorama, and Gloria saw her own sorrow there as part of it all.

"When my father came home and saw the boat wrecked, I think it nearly broke his heart, although I believe now that he knew it would surely happen," went on Murray. "I shall never forget his face as he looked at me and then looked back at the boat. He didn't scold me, but he took me up to my own room and without a word he cleared everything off the shelf at the foot of my bed and there he placed the wreck of the beautiful thing he had made. You can imagine how I felt. I knew he wanted me to have to see it every day. It is there yet," Murray said sadly.

"Then father turned to me and spoke very sternly. His disappointment in me and his love for me together made him say what he did. 'Son,' he said, 'you've ruined this boat, but I'm going to make another boat, it'll be a real boat,—this other was the little model of it. This one cost me something, my hands had to work hard to make it, but that one will cost much more,—more than you can possibly understand now. And I'm going to give you the real one, but—that will be *when you are a different boy!*' My father said that with such a confident glad ring to his voice that I have never forgotten it. And, friend,— my father did just that thing! May I tell you about it?"

Fascinated, Gloria nodded.

Murray was still again for a moment, as if the thing he was about to tell about his own life moved him deeply.

"I had a wonderful brother once," he said huskily. "He was a good deal older than I. He went to work for my father when I was just a boy,—you know my father used to be a shipbuilder, and at one time he was pretty well-to-do. He made some of the finest ships that are afloat to-day. As he told me, it was his plan to build a yacht for me when I should grow old enough to use it. The men used to work on it when business was slack. It was my brother's dearest pleasure to go over to the ways and work on it himself,—he and my father spent hours together doing actually hard labor on it. One night,—my brother was working there alone, and—he fell from a scaffolding! My father found him

in the morning!" It was hard for Murray to speak.
"He was—very dear—to us all—but that made me a
different boy."

Gloria found the tears brimming over again as she
looked with awe into the heart of this strange young
man.

"You wonder, I suppose, why I've told you all
this. It's not easy for me to talk about it. But I think it
all happened for a very wonderful reason,—that I
might understand a little of what God did when He
gave His beloved Son to die for me that I might become
'a different boy', and that He might make a new heaven
and a new earth for His 'new boy'. You may not
understand *how* God can make you and me righteous
because Christ died, nor *how* He is going to make a
new happy earth because Christ died, but it you choose
to believe it because God says it, you will have the
truth of it proven over and over to your heart. And if
you had looked at the wreck of that boat every day as
I did for twenty years you would understand why God
is waiting a while before He makes over the earth and
does away with pain and sorrow."

"That is all very beautiful," said Gloria after a
moment's silence, "but I don't understand how you
know that this is so about the earth. Where is there
any authority for such a supposition?"

He looked at her with surprise but answered
quickly:

"In the Word of God. It is all there, plainly told.
God has not left us without knowledge. When He gave
us the Bible He meant it to be a full revelation of
Himself and His works."

It was Gloria's turn to be astonished now.

"You don't mean that there is any such thing in
the Bible as you have been telling me!" she exclaimed.

"Yes, the whole story. Of course, not the story of
my boat, but the story of the world that God created,
which was ruined by the sin of Adam, the first man.
When Jesus Christ, as man's representative, died and
rose again, he rose as the head of a new race, who shall

rule with Him over a new earth when God's appointed time comes. Accepting His death as mine and His life as mine makes me a member of the new race,—a 'new boy'."

Gloria was silent, thoughtful, for some minutes as they walked along together in the twilight.

"I never knew anything about the Bible," she said with a sigh. "We studied it a little in school, of course, but only as literature. My teachers thought it absurd to believe in it as more than fine literature."

"There is a curious thing about the Bible," said Murray, "you have to enter it with belief. Belief is the only key that will unlock its wonders."

"But how could you believe it if you had not read it?"

"I do not mean belief in the sense of being intellectually convinced that it is true. I mean the willingness to accept it as God's truth. Then it proves itself to you as you read it and obey what it says. People who presume to teach the Bible without believing from the heart its statements cannot possibly understand it."

There was another long pause and their footsteps grew slower as they walked along in the twilight. Then Gloria spoke again.

"You make life a very solemn thing," she said gravely.

"Isn't it?" answered Murray.

"I suppose it is," she said with a sigh. "I would like to understand your Bible. I would like to see if it has a solution for my own personal difficulties."

"It certainly has," said Murray with a ring of delight to his voice. "There is a solution in the Bible for every human difficulty. I'd love to introduce you to the Bible if you will let me," he added eagerly.

"Will you?" she asked giving him a wistful look. "I would be so grateful!"

Then, just as they came around a bend in the road, they saw a car drawn up in front of the MacRae home, and a tall figure coming out of the gate and striding across the road to the Sutherland house.

"That's Bob Carroll!" said Murray. "I wonder what he wants? They've likely told him I was over seeing you."

They hastened their steps and arrived just as Carroll was knocking on the door.

"Oh, hello, Murray!" he said, "Glad I found you. Good evening Miss Sutherland. I hope I'm not intruding, rushing over this way after Murray, but I had a message for him. They want you to speak over at Ripley to-morrow night at a Young People's Rally, Murray. Can you make it? The fellow they had engaged has to go away to a funeral. I told them you would if you could I was sure."

"Of course," said Murray. "When you promise for me what else can I do? Or suppose I make a bargain. I'll speak if you'll sing at the close of my message. How's that?"

"They've already asked me," said Carroll with a deprecatory shrug.

"Oh, well, you can sing twice then," said Murray with a twinkle. "That suits me still better."

"I don't mind singing, but they have a terrible accompanist over there. I came over hoping I'd find Lindsey home and I could inveigle her into coming down with me. If I had my own accompanist they couldn't feel hurt, you know."

"Sorry, she isn't back yet," said Murray, "though we're expecting her Friday or Saturday. But how about asking Miss Sutherland? I shouldn't be in the least surprised if she played, and if she plays the piano just half as well as she plays tennis she's a winner!"

Carroll turned eager eyes upon Gloria.

"Why, I could try. Of course I play some. But I wish Vanna was here. She can really *play!*"

"And who is Vanna?" asked the young man. "What an interesting name!"

"Vanna is my sister. Her name is Evangeline of course, but we've always called her Vanna," said Gloria.

"Lovely!" said young Carroll. "But since Vanna-

Evangeline is not here might I be so presumptuous as to ask you to accompany your humble servant?"

"I'll be delighted," said Gloria, wondering what she was letting herself in for now, "that is if I can do it. I'd have to see the music."

"Well, I guess we can manage that," said Carroll. "Murray, you've got one of our books over at your house, haven't you? And I've got a new one along I'd like awfully well to try if you don't mind. I brought it along hoping Lindsey would be here."

"Well, you'd better come over to our house. There's no piano in the Sutherland house."

"Yes, I've missed having a piano about," said Gloria. "I don't play nearly as well or as much as my sister, but I do like to sit down now and then and amuse myself."

"Well, I certainly am in luck finding you," said Robert Carroll. "Why don't you and your sister come up here and live, and then we'd always have one or the other about when we needed music?"

It was good to get among young people again even if they were strangers. It was good to hear their pleasant banter and jokes. Yet she wondered as she went up the MacRae steps between the two young men, what some of her gay friends at home would think of her if they could see her now, and know that she had actually promised to help in a religious service. She wondered what Vanna would think. She wondered most of all what Vanna would think about the two young men. Vanna had never seen any like them. Would Vanna laugh at them and say they had too religious a complex if she were to see them? Well, it wasn't in the least likely that Vanna would ever see them. In a few days now she herself would be gone away from here, and there would be little likelihood that she would ever come again, unless Father wanted to run up for something.

Yet the thought gave her a pang. She wasn't sure she never wanted to see these young men any more, especially Murray MacRae. He had promised to tell her more about such wonderful things. He had promised to lead her where her perplexities would be solved, and her heart hungered for such knowledge.

It was a big pleasant room where the old fashioned square piano stood, with touches here and there that showed a modern girl had been here, a picture here, a book there, a lovely cushion on the rare old davenport. And there on the piano was a framed photograph of a beautiful girl with one of the sweetest faces Gloria had ever seen. She had eyes like Murray's. Gloria went to it at once and stood before it.

"That's my sister, Lindsey," said Murray with a smile, "I do want you to know her."

"She is lovely!" said Gloria studying the face.

"We think she is," said Murray modestly.

"She's all that and then some!" said Robert Carroll. "I'm terribly jealous of that professor of hers that she's going to marry. And the worst of it is that I'm convinced that there isn't another girl like Lindsey on the face of the earth."

"Why didn't you tell Lindsey so before she went off and found her professor?" laughed Murray. "There isn't another fellow on the face of the earth I'd like half so well for a brother-in-law I'm sure."

Gloria as she heard the laughter thought how lovely was the friendship between these two.

She turned away at last from the picture of Lindsey MacRae and her eye was caught by another picture on the mantel, a man's face this time, with a look in the eyes like Lindsey and Murray, yet something deeper, something so strong and noble and tender that instinctively Gloria turned to Murray and said in a low tone,

"This was—your brother——?"

Murray had been following her glance and he was beside her now. "My brother Cameron, yes!" he answered her, though his eyes had answered for him first. "This was the brother of whom I told you."

Gloria had no words ready to express the emotion that picture stirred in her heart. It was too deep for words. But at last she turned away.

"Why should a man like that be taken away from the earth when there are so many men who could be spared so easily?" she said, almost as if she were thinking aloud.

"God's purposes are often served best in ways that seem to us inscrutable," answered Murray, "and sometimes it is just to save some poor worthless sinner like me!" And he drew a deep breath that was almost a sigh.

Then Gloria looking up suddenly saw his face and understood, and the story she had heard a little while before went even deeper into her own soul.

They gathered around the piano presently, and Gloria shyly attempted the music they put before her. She was not very familiar with sacred music, and hymns and gospel songs had never been in her repertoire at all. She found them very different in character from the jazzy stuff she had been wont to rattle off, and much harder to play, though they looked so simple at first sight, but she stumbled on and with the help of the two young men presently swung into the right rhythm and was able to follow on after the singing, if she did not exactly lead it.

Murray MacRae was singing now, too, and the two voices blended beautifully. In spite of her blundering playing Gloria felt a part of a lovely whole, and found a thrill in listening to those two voices as they sang hymn after hymn making the words as well as the music live for her.

When they finally said good night to Robert Carroll promising him to drive over to Ripley the next evening for the meeting, and saw him drive away, Gloria suddenly realized that she had had a wonderful evening. She had enjoyed every minute of it.

"Are you all tired out?" asked Murray solicitously looking down at her anxiously. "Did we bore you to death?"

"I've enjoyed every minute of it!" she said earnestly. "It is something entirely new for me, but I've loved it. Only I do wish you had had a better accompanist. Vanna plays beautifully. I really am more at home on the violin!"

"Wonderful!" said Murray. "I'll have to rustle us a violin. And wouldn't there be some way to get your sister up here? Say! That would be great! But may I ask why you didn't bring your violin along?"

Then suddenly plunk! down came her tragedy upon her! She caught her breath. Perhaps she ought to tell this young man all about herself! But why break this brief pleasant fellowship that could not possibly last more than a few days longer any way? Why have to explain, and endure commiseration? It would only make embarrassment for them both.

"I—why—I came away—in a hurry——!" she evaded. "I don't usually take it with me. In fact I've played very little—these last few months. I'm—quite—out of—practice."

"It certainly is time you got into practice again," laughed the young man happily.

When Gloria went into the house she was dismayed to find that her father had called on the telephone.

"How dreadful!" she exclaimed. "What will he think of me? He told me last night he would call again to-night. I ought to have come back sooner! I ought not to have gone!"

"No, it's all right," said Emily Hastings, "I told him you were just across the road at MacRae's and I would call you, but he said no, he was in a hurry. A man was waiting for him. He said tell you it would be another day or two yet before he could possibly come up and if you should want to start home before that to call his office at ten in the morning."

Gloria went up to her room but her thoughts were troubled. She had had a rare evening and enjoyed it, and it didn't seem the right thing. If her mother were here she would be all the time asking her, "What will people think? You in your position?" If her Aunt Miranda should hear that she had spent the evening playing the piano for two young men she would gloat over the news and probably spread it over the country-side. Yet it had been such a pleasant simple little thing to do whereby to while away the time, and the fact remained that she had enjoyed it. Was there anything wrong in that? In fact, she asked herself, wide-eyed, staring out into the darkness of her room long after the other members of the household were asleep, had she anything tangible to be loyal to? Did a bridegroom who died with another girl deserve loyalty? And even if he did what had she done but play a few accompaniments? And anyhow she was committed to the meeting to-morrow night. She couldn't go back on her word now. And she owned to herself in the secret of her heart that she really wanted to go to that meeting and hear Murray MacRae speak again. There was something in his words that brought hope. Dim, far hope it was perhaps, but hope, and she wanted to hear more. She could not go home till she understood how to read the Bible for herself and get something out of it. She was sure the brief Bible lessons she had had in school had not had hope in them, and if hope was anywhere to be found she must find it.

The meeting the next evening was unlike anything she had ever attended before. A church full of eager young people come together for religious worship. It hadn't occurred to Gloria that young people ever went into religion, except in a musical or social way. In fact before she met Murray MacRae the word Christian in her vocabulary simply meant the opposite of Jew or heathen, and her vague idea of a heathen was a cannibal who worshipped idols. A Christian therefore would be a good, respectable, possibly moral, person who lived in a civilized land.

There was a new phrase which was introduced to her that evening during the course of the meeting. It figured in the prayers, the singing, and several times in the address of the evening. That was the word "saved." "Is he saved?" she heard a young man ask of another concerning some one else, and "She's only been saved about two months, but she's growing fast," she heard a young girl on the front seat say to Robert Carroll. But later when Murray began his address she learned that the strange new phrase meant saved from sin, made fit to be with God eternally.

Gloria had never had any sense of sin herself. She did not know that she was a sinner. But as the address went on she learned that she was, for Murray held up Jesus Christ and the Bible like a mirror in which they all might look, and see themselves as Christ saw them.

The service of prayer that preceded the address amazed her. She had never heard young people pray before, and there were so many of them that took part, so freely, so eagerly, sometimes two beginning at once, and so simply, just speaking their hearts to the great God! Gloria found herself wishing that she dared speak out and say: "Oh God show me how I can go on living!" but her lips seemed to be sealed, and she had a shy feeling that she was not one of these young people, she was an alien and therefore had no right to come boldly and make her petition. These young people must have passed through some strange initiation or preparation that she had never known that gave them a right to fellowship with heaven. She found her heart hungry to have this same privilege.

She was seated on the platform of the ornate small-town church. It appeared that the usual pianist was not present, and Robert Carroll begged that she play for the general singing as well as for his solos. Gloria did not feel at all happy about it for she did not feel confident when it came to hymn playing. But this strange company of young people under the leadership of Robert Carroll and Murray MacRae took up the tune at the first note and bore it above her playing until confidence returned to her and she began to really enjoy being a part of this great tide of song.

Right in the midst of it all it came to her suddenly to think how amused her family would be if they could see her. How her friends at home would jeer and laugh at the idea of her playing in a religious meeting. Then something fierce and loyal rose up in her and resented the attitude of her world. There was something wonderful about this new world she was in now, that lured her. She was glad to be here. She was not just enduring it. It was like eating hash and johnny cake and apple sauce in place of the constant ices and pastries and confectionery she had been used to all her life. There was something deeply satisfying in it that did not cloy like rich sweets.

There was a testimony meeting after the prayers and that was another amazing thing. So many of these young people were ready to testify what the Lord Jesus had been to them since they had accepted Him as their Savior. Gloria did not know what to make of it and watched them jump up all over the house, one after another, with brief messages that sounded sincere. This certainly was a new world! Perhaps she might have laughed at it before she knew Murray MacRae, for some of the messages were exceedingly crude, and the people who gave them both plain and uncultured, but she did not laugh now. She had had a glimpse of what all this meant. She knew her own world would neither understand nor appreciate what was going on. She was not sure she did herself, but she respected it.

She was deeply stirred by Murray's address. It seemed to go right on from where he had been talking to her last, and to convict her own soul, so that she could scarcely keep back the tears.

And then at the close of the meeting a strange thing occurred. She remained in her seat by the piano awaiting her escorts, while the young people surged about the platform, when suddenly a group of girls came toward her.

"Oh, I do think you play so beautifully!" said a girl with blue eyes and a dress the same color. "I just loved to watch you up here playing!"

"Yes," said another girl in brown, "it was so nice of you to come and play for us. Jennie usually plays, but she's sick to-night. Have you come to live in Afton?"

"Oh, no," said Gloria much amused, "I'm only here for a short time."

"Oh, I'm sorry," said the brown girl, "I hoped we'd have you to play for us again."

"That's nice of you," said Gloria, feeling shy herself at so much evident admiration, "I don't consider myself much of a player."

"Oh, won't you write your name in my Bible," asked the one with blue eyes. "I've got Mr. MacRae's name and Mr. Carroll's name and I'd like so much to have yours."

"In your Bible?" said Gloria puzzled. "Why, I'm nobody to have my name in a Bible."

"Oh, yes, you are," laughed the girl. "I want to keep it to remember this meeting by. Hasn't it been a wonderful meeting?"

"Why, yes, it has," said Gloria.

She accepted the offered fountain pen and the shabby little Bible and wrote her name under Murray MacRae's feeling that somehow she was inscribing herself within a charmed circle where she did not at all belong, and wondering if this was not presumption.

"Oh, what a pretty name!" said the blue-eyed one. "It sounds just as you look! I just know you're a wonderful Christian!"

"Oh, but I'm not," said Gloria full of dismay.

But other girls were surging up now for autographs. Other Bibles were forthcoming, hymn books, programs, scraps of paper. Gloria gave a little hysterical laugh, protested that she was nobody and they didn't want her name, but the rush around her continued and she wrote on, half ashamed of herself that she didn't frankly tell them she wasn't a Christian at all, that she didn't even know what it was all about.

But somehow when it was all over she felt that in some way she had identified herself with tremendous things, and a glow was about her heart as she received the warm thanks of the pastor of the church for her part in the evening.

It was a strange experience. Gloria had never felt half so thrilled at praise she had received from her fashionable friends when she had played at one of their social "Benefits" for some cause they had taken up. Although she recognized that the autograph craze was merely silly hero-worship, she felt she had been a part of a meeting that had impressed itself upon her as dealing with tremendous issues, and somehow she was glad all through her being that she had been allowed to help.

Gloria was very quiet all the way home, listening to the talk between the two young men.

"I am sure Sam Skelton made a decision tonight," Robert was saying, and Murray's "Praise the Lord!" spoken in low reverent undertone brought a thrill to Gloria's heart which she didn't in the least understand. What was the decision that was so important, and why should she care? Was it just because Murray MacRae cared? She didn't know. She looked at the outline of his strong fine face as he sat beside her and felt how wonderful he was. Not just different from others, as she had judged him at first, but "wonderful!"

VIII

The next morning about ten o'clock Vanna arrived in a taxi!

Gloria saw her from the window and flew down to receive her with open arms.

"You darling old thing!" she cried eagerly, and enclosed her with a bear hug.

"Dad said you'd be glad to see me!" said Vanna gazing at her sister with satisfaction. "But you don't look as if you were moping yourself to death at all. Mother thought you would be in the last stages of decline. She insisted I should come up and make you come home!"

"I'm not moping!" said Gloria with a smile and a sudden realization that she didn't want to go home because she was getting interested in things that were going on in Afton. There was a sudden wild clutching of her heart strings lest Vanna wouldn't understand and would make fun and jeer. She couldn't stand it if Vanna got that way about things.

"It's a peachy view," said Vanna looking across the meadows toward the mountains, "but aren't you bored sick? What on earth do you do all the time?"

"No," said Gloria gravely, "I'm not bored. I like it here. It's different. It's restful. It's— Oh, I don't suppose you'll like it, but I really enjoy it!"

"H'm!" said Vanna looking at her keenly. "You don't look so bad, but how do you get this way? I can't understand."

"No, I'm afraid you won't!" said Gloria with a troubled look. "I'm all kinds of glad to see you. But I wish they hadn't sent you. I really do, Vanna. You'll be bored to death! I know you will, and I'm all right. I just couldn't come home yet."

There was shrinking, pleading in Gloria's eyes, and her sister saw it.

"Don't worry, Kid, I don't blame you. It's been infernal, that's the truth. Everybody weeping on our shoulders, making moan for you. It would have been twice as bad if you had been there. And Mrs. Asher has been the limit. You'd have thought that we as a family were personally responsible for Stan's death! It's been simply awful! But she's gone to a sanitarium now. Thank goodness that's over!"

"A sanitarium!" said Gloria, her bright face suddenly overspread with new gloom.

"There! I suppose I shouldn't have told you that!" said Vanna.

"Yes, you must tell me everything," said Gloria insistently, "I want to know everything. You needn't think I am a baby you know. I've had a chance to get my bearings to some extent at least, and eventually I've got to know."

"I suppose so!" sighed Vanna sympathetically, "but let's forget it now for a while and let me get cleaned up. I'm simply a sight travelling all night on the cars. I'd forgotten what a lot of dirt one accumulates on a train."

They went into the house and Emily in her tidy little bright cotton dress came out with a smudge of flour on one cheek to greet the newcomer.

Vanna gave her a quick scrutinizing look, wondering if she was some superior kind of a servant. Gloria sensing the situation hastened to introduce her.

"This is Mrs. Hastings, Vanna. She's been awfully good to me, and so has her mother, Mrs. Weatherby. I suppose Dad will have told you all about them. This is my sister Evangeline, Mrs. Hastings. She came up to surprise me."

Vanna was quick to take a hint and smiled sweetly at the hostess.

"I have hardly had two words with Dad since he came home till yesterday when he called me on the phone and asked me to come up here and stay with you awhile or bring you home, because he couldn't," she explained. "Dad has been at the office every blessed minute, except perhaps an hour or two in the night, but he came after I was gone and departed before I was up. There's been a lot to bother him I guess, for we've scarcely seen him since he came back."

Emily Hastings went upstairs with them carrying one of the largest of the suitcases. Gloria seized another bag, and Vanna, looking a trifle surprised, picked up the third one and followed. Vanna had never had to carry her own luggage before. Not that she minded. But it seemed a bit odd to her.

Vanna looked around the big comfortable rooms in surprise, took in the four poster, and the fine old chests of drawers, the desk, the highboy, the deep winged chair, with approval, watched Emily hurry away for clean towels and turned to Gloria.

"I see what you mean," she said significantly, just as if Gloria had been saying how lovely it was. "It's really sweet here. What nifty old furniture! Is it ours or theirs? I mean does it belong in the family, or did they bring it here?"

"It's ours I think," said Gloria. "The house was left furnished just as it was when Grandmother died. Father bought out the other heirs' shares I think, house and furniture and everything."

"Then it's really ancestral," said Vanna with glowing eyes. "That does make it interesting."

"Yes," said Gloria, "it does. For instance my bed belonged to Father's mother. She seems to have been rather a wonderful grandmother. She had five children, did all her own work including washing, ironing, cooking and housecleaning, and even cooked for farm hands at harvesting times. She did the family sewing too, made shirts and everything. Mrs. Weatherby, Emily's mother and Grandmother's best friend, has been telling me. She was some grandmother! Made preserves enough to stock a wholesale grocery. I've seen the closet that they say she used to fill every year. And with it all she did beautiful embroidery."

"Heaven preserve us!" said Vanna, "how did she get time to play bridge and go to her clubs?"

Gloria laughed.

"I haven't heard of any clubs, and I don't believe there was anybody up here to play bridge with in those days. The Weatherbys lived five miles away then on another farm and the MacRaes hadn't come yet. There was only a store and a postoffice down in Afton village and most neighbors lived several miles away!"

"I wonder how that would be?" said Vanna dreamily. "I feel as if I were in a foreign country, don't you?"

"No," said Gloria thoughtfully, "I feel as if I were back in the past century. I've had the strangest feeling about it ever since I came. It's that that has helped me to endure life. It seemed somehow as if I had just been taken out of the time that I lived in and put back into a simple restful place where I didn't have to think about anything, only go around and look at the old things and places and try to realize how it must have been. It's just as quaint as can be. It's been only now and then I've been jerked back into now, and I remember all that happened and it's just as if somebody had struck me over the heart."

"You poor kid!" said Vanna pityingly. "It's been an awful comedown for you and you have taken it like a soldier. I'm proud as I can be of you."

"I haven't been brave," said Gloria shaking her head, "not at all. I've been a shirker. I ran away from it all. I just felt as if I couldn't bear it there where everybody knew about it. But, do you know, Van, the hardest thing about it was the way everybody tried to camouflage what Stan had done, and act as if it was nothing at all. Why, that made me feel as if nobody could understand what I was suffering, and I felt just humiliated as if I, too, was pretending that nothing was the matter but death. Why, Vanna, if Stan had just died in some ordinary way, like crashing in an airplane, or being in a smash-up or having pneumonia, it would have been a decent death, and one could have mourned and borne, and felt some self-respect. But the way it was I couldn't mourn! I was just shocked! I was shocked almost to death! I don't know if you understand or not, Vanna, but you always used to understand me when we were children."

"Sure, I understand," said Vanna getting up and going to the window to look out across the meadows abstractedly. "It isn't according to the code of our crowd of course to mind things like that, and it wouldn't be considered good form to let it be seen that you felt that way, but—there's something fine about you, Gloria,—perhaps I might say about— well, our family. At least in our feelings. We don't go quite as far as the rest. Mother of course talks a lot about doing what we're expected to do, but even Mother really has a pretty conventional way of thinking, and I'm sure she was terribly upset about what was in the paper. That was why she wanted everything done to cover it up."

"I know," said Gloria sadly, drooping down on the foot of the bed.

"But here," said Vanna wheeling around, "this is no way to be talking to you, dwelling on things like this. I was sent up here to cheer you up. Let's talk about something else."

"No, Vanna," said Gloria, "I want to talk about this a little yet. There are some things that simply have to be said, and you and I have got to understand each other. In the first place I do feel that part about the girl awfully, and I always will. In the second place there are some things I'm done with forever, and drinking's one of them. If Stan hadn't been drinking a lot he never would have put himself in a situation where he would have been shot. As I've been thinking back I'm disgusted at the way our crowd carries on."

"Maybe you're right," said Vanna looking serious.

"And when I go back," went on Gloria, "—if I've got to go back—I'm not going back to the old ways in lots of things."

Her sister eyed her gravely.

"Father feels the way you do," said Vanna irrelevantly. Gloria looked up quickly.

"Has Dad been talking to you?"

"No, but I overheard a few words he said to Mother the other day. I've always known Dad's quietness covered a lot of thoughts. He told Mother he wished we could be done with playing up to the multitude."

There was silence in the room while both girls thought this over.

"There's another thing," said Gloria slowly, "I want you to understand. I don't think I'll ever marry anybody, no matter how rich or popular they are, but if I do, it'll not be anybody who trains in a crowd like ours, or has that kind of standards."

Vanna looked at her sadly.

"I don't blame you, Glory, but where would you find anybody else? There aren't any men who don't do that kind of thing!"

"Yes, there are!" said Gloria decidedly. "I've found out there are! Father says there are and I've found he's right. I've met a couple that I'm sure about!"

Her sister brought her eyes about and surveyed her piercingly.

"Lead me to 'em!" she said at last. "I don't believe it but I'd like to see one just to say it was true."

"Well," said Gloria, "maybe you wouldn't understand. Maybe you wouldn't like their type, but I know they are decent and fine and clean."

"Hicks, I suppose?" said Vanna half contemptuously.

"No, not hicks either," said Gloria. "Now, Vanna, please tell me about the Ashers. I suppose I have a duty there. I ought to write to them. Somehow I couldn't before, but I feel as if your coming had cleared the atmosphere a little."

Vanna laughed.

"I'm glad I've done some good, but I don't know that it's good for you to discuss the Ashers."

"Yes, it is. It's something that must be done. Is Mrs. Asher really very sick, or just gone away to rest?"

"Well, I guess she's sick all right. She had the highstrikes so continuously that Nance was almost insane herself, and then they took her away to a sanitarium for nervous cases. She's really off her head I guess. They don't let even the family see her, and Nance is staying home looking after her father. He's had a stroke and may not recover."

"Oh, Vanna! How terrible!"

"Yes, isn't it? Poor Nance is so bitter and hard! It makes me shudder to hear her talk. She's been going a lot with Ad Harrison. She doesn't seem to care what she does any more. You might write to her when you feel able, but I don't know what you could say."

"Oh, I don't either!" groaned Gloria. "Nor what to say if I write to her mother either. She was the one who spoiled Stan. She taught him to drink and gave him everything he wanted."

"I know," said Vanna, "but you won't have to write to her. She's nuts and she won't know whether you've written or not. Besides, I went up the day after you left while she still could understand what was said to her, and I told her that you were in a pretty bad way yourself and had to get away, and for a wonder she seemed to expect it, and to be a little sorry for you, but then she started wailing again and wailed for you too, and I couldn't stand it. I had to leave!"

"Poor Vanna! I ran away and left you to do my duties!"

"Nonsense!" said Vanna winking back the tears. "You had no duty toward her. She has always encouraged Stan in all his wildness. Besides, I was glad if you could escape any disagreeableness."

"Dear Vanna!" said Gloria getting up and standing beside her sister's chair. "You've been wonderful.

It must have been awful for you. And Mother doing a welfare drive! I'm so sorry! Tell me, what have you been doing? Wasn't there *anything* nice to break the dreadfulness of it all."

"Oh, well, Emory Zane has been rushing me a lot since you've been gone, if you call that nice. I don't know whether I do or not. I came up here to find out."

"Emory Zane!" said Gloria in dismay. "Oh, Vanna! Not *Emory Zane!*"

"Well, what's the matter with Emory Zane?" asked Vanna crossly. "He's rich and awfully good looking. He's full of pep and it would never be monotonous around him. Of course I haven't been going out. Mother wouldn't have thought that was proper so soon. But he's been at the house almost every night. He took me up to his apartment one day. It's perfectly fascinating. He has things there from all over the world where he's traveled."

"Vanna! You went to his apartment alone with him?"

"Well, I didn't know where he was taking me. I thought we were going to a roof garden, but it seems he'd planned a little surprise dinner for me in his own apartment, and I couldn't very well get out of it when we got there, could I? But really it was quite proper. He knows I won't stand for any nonsense. He says that's why he admires me. He says I'm so sweet and innocent."

"Oh, Vanna! He's so old! So much older than you! And so—well I don't know what to call it. Worldly I suppose is the word, but it's something more than that that I mean. It's sort of—well, he has really wicked black eyes. I've always hated to have him look at me. I never thought that you would fall for him!"

"Well, I haven't fallen for him yet, have I? Only there is something rather thrilling in having a man of the world fall at your feet that way. You can't help feeling flattered. And after all, perhaps he's as good as anybody I'd ever know."

"Oh, Vanna! Why what has become of Reagan Moore and Halstead Camp and Teddy Stansbury? They were all crazy about you!"

"Well, they're all around of course, sending flowers and trying to make quiet dates that will be suitable to my circumstances, but what are they but three more Stan Ashers? Just a lot of kids making whoopee like the rest. After all if one has to stand that sort of thing why not go in for a man who is really interesting?"

"Oh, but not Emory Zane, Vanna! Why he has a son who is nearly as old as you are, and what about that story of his first wife?"

Vanna shrugged her shoulders.

"I'm sure I don't know, it may be true. If I married him I shouldn't expect him to be an angel of light of course. But would I be any worse off than you are?"

Gloria gave a little shiver and then answered steadily.

"Yes, Vanna, I think you would. I've been thinking sometimes that perhaps I was saved from something else more terrible."

"Well, I don't see it," said Vanna, "and anyway if I married a man like that I'd have my own private fortune, and there is always divorce if the worst comes. It's all a gamble anyway."

"Oh, Vanna! You mustn't! You *mustn't!*" cried Gloria the tears starting into her eyes. "Oh, why, when we've been so happy, must everything awful come at once? Vanna, have you thought of Mother and Father? Do they know you went to Mr. Zane's apartment?"

"No, and don't you dare to tell them!" said Vanna flashing her eyes angrily at her sister. "I don't intend to do it again, at least not until I marry him, if I ever do, and what Dad and Mother don't know won't hurt them."

"No, I won't tell them—not now, anyway. Not unless you do something terrible! Not unless you decide to marry him. Then I'd have to do something! I couldn't have that go on!"

"Well, I'm not married yet!" said Vanna sharply, "and I'm not at all sure that I'll ever marry anybody. Why should we have to if we don't want to? You and I can go and live together somewhere and just have a good time."

"Of course we can," said Gloria slipping her arm around her sister and nestling up to her. "You're unhappy, Vanna, aren't you? I've been so taken up with my own affairs that I didn't know it. I'm sorry dear. We'll both of us think of something better to do than get married."

They were laughing now, though there was a bright sparkle of tears on their lashes. They had not been given to showing much emotion, and were half shamefaced about it.

Then suddenly the bell for the midday dinner pealed out and Vanna gave her sister a startled look.

"What on earth is that?" she asked.

"That's the dinner bell, old dear, and we must wash our faces and go right downstairs. There is usually something good that needs to be eaten while hot."

So Vanna went down to her first farm dinner.

Emily had not been idle. There was fried chicken, new potatoes and peas, with hot biscuits and honey for dessert. Vanna was enthusiastic about everything.

"I begin to see why my sister wasn't willing to come home," she said as she accepted a second helping of peas. "There's a taste about this dinner that we don't get at home in spite of our French cooks."

Vanna did full justice to the hearty dinner, and made herself most friendly with the Hastings and Mrs. Weatherby who told Vanna she looked like her grandfather Sutherland.

Vanna laughed, tossed back her dark head with a gay little motion all her own and declared:

"Well, since I cannot look like the wonderful grandmother I've been hearing such great things about, it's nice I can look like Grandfather."

"Your grandfather was a very fine looking man," said the old lady, "and a very noble gentleman," and she went off into one of her interesting tales of the olden days that fascinated Gloria so much. She sat watching her sister half fearfully. Would Vanna see the beauty in it all or would it bore her?

But if Vanna was bored she certainly concealed it well. She led the old lady on and asked many questions, often throwing in a bright comment that made them all laugh. It was most evident that the Hastings and Mrs. Weatherby approved of her, and Gloria drew a breath of relief.

When the meal was concluded Gloria began to pick up the plates to carry them out to the kitchen as she had been doing of late, but Emily put up a deprecating hand.

"Don't bother about helping to-day, Gloria," she said in a low tone, "you run along and have a good time with your sister. I can get on very well alone."

"Helping?" said Vanna turning a quick ear to the furtive conversation. "Let me help too. How does one do it?" And Vanna sprang into action and began picking up the silver.

"I've never done this before so I'll be awkward," she declared laughing, "but I'll confess that it's been a secret ambition since I was a child to clear off the table and wash the dishes. I used to play it with my dolls hour upon hour. It must have been a little of Grandmother Sutherland stirring in my soul!"

So both girls helped with the dishes and had a gay time together.

"This is fun!" said Vanna. "I'd like to have a house of my own and do all the work myself!"

"I guess you have more of Grandmother in you than I have," said Gloria. "I rather enjoy doing a little work, but when I see all Mrs. Hastings accomplishes in a day I'm just appalled. I couldn't ever do it all. And see, Vanna, Grandmother had to cook in that great old fireplace over there at first, with that crane to swing her kettles on and a funny old oven to bake in!"

Vanna was intrigued. She went around asking questions and entering into everything as if she had come to stay, begging to be taught how to do this and that.

"But you would never have a chance to use it even if you did learn how to make biscuits. Fancy Mother letting you go into the kitchen and cook!" said Gloria a little later when they had gone upstairs together. "Fancy you as the wife of some millionaire like Emory Zane, being allowed to *cook!*" There was a note of contempt in Gloria's tone.

"That's the worst of it," said Vanna thoughtfully. "I'd have to surrender what little independence I was born with, and in our family even that isn't much, for Mother has always ruled us with a rod of iron. Of course we've had nearly everything we've asked for, and been terribly spoiled, but it's beginning to pall on me."

Gloria laughed.

"My, it's good to get you back again, Vanna! There is something about the way you say things that goes right to the spot. I certainly have been missing you and I didn't know just what was the matter!"

But Vanna was looking out the window.

"Mercy!" she suddenly exclaimed. "There come two of the best looking men I've ever laid eyes on, and they're coming in this gate! Who on earth could they be? Come here quick, Gloria, before they get up on the porch out of sight. They don't look like agents, and it must be too early for tourists. Besides, they haven't any hats on."

"Only a couple of hicks!" said Gloria with a covert smile in the corners of her mouth as she flung herself indifferently on the bed and yawned.

"Glory! But they're not! They're stunning! I don't see why you have to be utterly indifferent to all mankind just because you've been through trouble!"

"But I'm not indifferent," said Gloria. "I told you there were some men that were worth respecting."

"Well, why can't you come here and look at these two? They're talking with Mr. Hastings out by the fence. You can see them from behind the curtain without being seen. Come, Glory dear! It is perfectly thrilling to find two good looking men out in the wilds like this. They have very interesting faces!"

"Yes, haven't they?" said Gloria grinning impishly.

Vanna turned around upon her, and caught the grin upon her lips.

"Gloria, what is the matter with you? Do you know who they are? Have you seen them before?"

"I have a pretty good idea who they are," said Gloria still smiling, "but they really are hicks you know. You said so. You said all the people up here were."

"Well, who are they then?" asked Vanna impatiently. "One is very tall. He must be over six feet, and well built. How well he manages his height!"

"That's Robert Carroll," explained Gloria in a slow tantalizing tone. "He's a young farmer down near Ripley, three or four miles away."

"A *farmer!*" said Vanna incredulously, "but he doesn't look like a farmer. You must have made a mistake. This man is a gentleman!"

Gloria laughed.

"You'll have to learn as I did that it is possible to be both a farmer and a gentleman. Vanna dear, I've met some farmers up here that are more surely real gentlemen than any millionaire in our crowd at home. They're *real* gentlemen. I've found out that a man's occupation doesn't have anything to do with whether he is a gentleman or not."

"Oh, I suppose this one then is a millionaire who plays at farming," said Vanna, watching the men out the window with a critical eye. "This man never really does manual labor. Why, Glory, he's well dressed!"

"Yes," said Gloria, "always well dressed, even when he wears overalls I understand. But he's not playing at farming. He works himself, and he's been to college and then taken a post graduate agricultural course. They say he's some farmer."

"Well, I like his looks," said Vanna doubtfully, "but he certainly isn't my idea of a farmer."

"Well, you'll find a good many of your ideas will get upset up here if you stay long enough," said Gloria. "Mine have."

"All right, maybe I will," said Vanna, "and who is the other man? I don't know which I think is the better looking."

"I do!" said Gloria, "but I'm not telling. The other man is Murray MacRae. His people live across the road there in that big white farm house. He has a sister Lindsey who is engaged to a college professor. They say she is lovely. She is coming home the end of this week and I'm crazy to see her. Her picture is lovely!"

"Yes, but what about the young man? Is he a farmer too?"

"No, he is in business in New York, or is about to be. His father was a famous shipbuilder. He built the Columbia and several other big boats. Murray is a dear. He is just up here on a visit."

"You've met him, haven't you?" Vanna gave a swift glance at her sister and then turned back to the window.

"Yes, I've met him," said Gloria trying to make her tone quite casual.

"Just met him? Is that all?" queried Vanna.

"Oh, I've played tennis with him a couple of times."

"Oh! I see why you're so willing to stay up here now! Does Father know about him?"

"No, he didn't arrive until after Father left. But he's quite all right. The Hastings have known him all his life and they say he is wonderful!"

"I wasn't asking whether he had a recommendation or not," said Vanna dryly. "One would trust him even from this distance. He looks that way. I was just wondering."

It was quiet in the room for a moment and then Vanna spoke again in a lower tone.

"They're coming into the house, Gloria, what do you suppose they want?"

"Well, if you ask me, they've probably come to get you to play for them. They both have gorgeous voices."

"*Me* to play for them!" Vanna turned around and gave her sister a wondering stare. "Why how on earth would they know anything about me, you silly?"

"They don't, only that you can play. I told them that."

"But you didn't know I was coming," said Vanna.

"No, and they don't know you are here, but when they find out they will ask you to play because I've told them you can play so much better than I can."

Vanna turned and rushed upon her sister to give her a good shaking, but Gloria laughing slid out from under her grasp.

"But really, Van, they're awfully nice. I haven't seen much of them of course, but you'll like their voices and they're real gentlemen if they are hicks."

Then came Emily Hastings' voice calling:

"Gloria! Can you girls come down? The boys are here and want to see you. I've got my hands in the dough and can't leave!"

"All right!" carolled Gloria. "We'll be right down!"

Vanna looked at her sister curiously.

"This certainly is a place of informalities!" she said, but she followed her sister down the stairs, curious to see these two young men at closer range.

"My sister Vanna has come!"

There was a real lilt in Gloria's voice, as she came flying down to the two who stood in the front hall, but it was Murray MacRae's eyes that her eyes met, Vanna noticed, and who looked gladly into hers. It was left for the other tall stranger to welcome Vanna. Their glances met and locked for an instant, a long inquiring glance, growing almost intimate before Robert Carroll broke the silence.

"I've been wondering what you would be like," he said in that rich husky tone of his, "I'm glad you've come!" and then he reached out a big warm hand and clasped hers for a moment, and Vanna found herself glad also that she had come.

And yet Gloria had said that this man was a farmer! It was incredible!

IX

All the time they were talking in the hall, while Murray MacRae was being introduced to her, and they were planning what they were going to do, Vanna was only conscious of Robert Carroll watching her. She had the strangest feeling that she was in a dream and had met a dream man, and would presently wake up and find he was not real.

She answered when they spoke to her, she laughed with the rest, she was conscious that Murray MacRae was interesting and spoke like the gentleman he looked to be, but she kept looking at Robert Carroll and wondering. She kept thinking that the look in his eyes was so clean and strong. She kept comparing it with Emory Zane's world-weary look, his deep meaningful glance.

When they walked across the road to MacRaes' house it was Robert Carroll who fitted his step to hers and walked beside her, pointing out the mountain in the distance that was the show mountain of the locality, telling her about the cowslips that he had found in bloom that morning, and when she asked what was a cowslip, describing it to her in all its delicacy of tiny golden scallops and rough grayish-green leaves, promising to bring her some the next time he came up.

The girl who had been the recipient many times of the costliest orchids and roses and gardenias that money could buy felt a breathless desire to see and know cowslips.

They entered the dim old parlor at MacRaes' and Vanna took in its quaint beauties and wondered just as her sister had done, recognizing something intrinsically lovely that made up a thing called home, the kind of home the white stone palace at Roselands had never been in spite of all its luxury.

Vanna saw a likeness between the pictured daughter on the piano and the sweet plain woman who came in presently to greet them. She wondered if all the women in this part of the world looked as if they came out of other days.

They made her play of course, though she demurred. But when Carroll looked at her and smiled, something beyond her own control made her sit down at the piano and play a Chopin Prelude that she had scarcely looked at since her days of taking lessons from her great and expensive teacher, who had loved such things as this. Somehow it was the only thing she knew that came to her as appropriate, and she wondered at herself as her fingers felt their way among the yellow old keys.

She had thought when she first saw the old square piano with its mother-of-pearl decoration that it would be quite impossible to play on, but to her surprise it was in perfect tune.

"I hope it's all right," said Murray anxiously hovering round. "We just had it tuned last week for Lindsey's coming. She's very particular about it."

"It's lovely!" said Vanna, noticing what clear beautiful eyes the young man had, astonished again that there should be two such young men in this out-of-the-way place.

The little audience settled down in the big company room, while Murray tiptoed around to raise the shades and let the sunlight in till a long bright ray rested on Gloria's golden head.

Murray's mother came softly in again to listen,

sitting in a dim corner with a pleased tender look upon her face. Later, when they spoke of trying to borrow a violin for Gloria to use she slipped quietly out of the room, returning presently with something wrapped in a soft silk cloth, and walking over to where Gloria sat she unwrapped it and laid it gently in Gloria's lap.

"It was my son's," she said softly. "I'd like to hear you play on it. I don't know whether it is in shape to play or not, but Lindsey had it put in good order last summer and it has been wrapped away from dampness and cold. Perhaps it will need some fixing. Murray will know."

The little company were silent as she laid one of her treasures down for their pleasure. Gloria was deeply touched, and even Vanna who had not heard the story of the brother who had died in such a tragic way, brushed her hand across her eyes and thought what tender unusual people these were. Again she had that feeling of being in a dream and expecting to wake up pretty soon and find it all a mirage, everything was so different from all her experience heretofore.

Gloria took up the instrument and touched it tenderly.

"It looks like a very fine one," she said looking carefully at it. "It looks—why it looks like a Stradivarius!"

"Yes, it's a Strad," said Murray coming over to point out an inscription inside, which could be dimly read if turned in a certain way.

Gloria drew her fingers over it softly.

"But I'm not a great enough player to play on an instrument like this!" she said softly, bending her head lovingly over it and touching the strings.

"The G string is broken," she said regretfully.

"I think there are some strings," said the mother. "The case is on the chair in the hall, Murray."

Presently they had the violin supplied with strings, and Gloria tuned it and played a chord or two.

"Ah!" said Murray drawing in a breath of

pleasure as he realized that Gloria was bringing a great tone from the old instrument.

Then together the girls played snatches of old masters they had learned when they were studying intensively, and the mother sat and wiped a furtive tear away now and then and thought of how her boy used to play for her.

After they had played for some time Gloria laid the violin down and turned to Murray.

"Now, you will please sing! It's quite your turn to perform, and I've been telling Vanna about your voices."

"Voice, you mean," said Murray. "I'm not much of a singer."

"Now, just for that we'll make you sing first!" said Carroll.

But it finally ended in Murray selecting some music from the music cabinet and making his friend sing it alone.

Vanna was thrilled to find such a voice, just as she had been astonished to find such a man so far from sophistication. She accompanied him as one who recognizes a truly good singer, and his voice rang out deep and true until it filled the big parlor. Gloria, able to sit and listen now without having to think about her playing was rejoiced to see that her first impression of his singing had not been exaggerated. He really sang wonderfully.

"Now," said Carroll as he finished the last long note of his solo, "come Murray! We'll give them a jolly one first, and then 'What Did He Do?' "

Without bothering to hunt any music the two young men stood together, their arms across one another's shoulders and sang a funny little melody, only a jingle really, where the words tumbled over one another so rapidly that one wondered how mortal tongue could speak them and not trip up.

Then while their audience were still laughing over this, and still without accompaniment, the two sounded a soft note and broke into another song:

"Oh, listen to our wondrous story,
        Counted once among the lost,
Yet, one came down from Heaven's glory,
        Saving us at awful cost!
                Who saved us from eternal loss?
                Who but God's Son upon the cross?
                What did He do?
                He died for you!
                Where is He now?
                Believe it thou,
        In Heaven, interceding!"

From the first note Gloria had fixed her eyes upon
their faces, recalling the story Murray had told her
of the ship and the lost brother. The meaning he had
meant to teach her came more clearly to her now,
and it was as if the message came straight to her own
heart. "He died for you!" She had heard enough in the
meeting last night to understand what that meant and
the message sank deep, taking on a personal insistence
that she knew sometime she had to meet and answer.

When the second verse began, as the two voices
blended so exquisitely, the enunciation being so perfect as to seem like but one person speaking the words,
she glanced toward her sister to see what she thought
of this, and found Vanna's eyes fixed upon the singers, a look of utter astonishment and bewilderment
upon her face.

"No angel could our place have taken,
        Highest of the high, though He;
The loved One on the cross forsaken,
        Was one of the Godhead three."

Again that striking chorus, those questions and
answers! Gloria looked at Vanna again and saw she
wore the same almost frightened look that had been on
her face at Stan's funeral. It was getting Vanna too! She
didn't understand this strange thing that these young
men had, that made them so different from other
young men, but it was getting her!

But when the last verse was reached it seemed to

Gloria as if it were personal, just for herself, and she sat with down-drooped eyes throughout.

> "Will you surrender to this Saviour?
>   To His sceptre humbly bow?
> You, too, shall come to know His favor,
>   He will save you, save you now!
>   Who saved us from eternal loss?
>   Who but God's Son upon the cross?
>   What did He do?
>   He died for you!
>   Where is He now?
>   Believe it thou,
> In Heaven, interceding!"

The room was very still as they finished, and the two stood with arms still about one another's shoulders, heads slightly bowed for an instant, almost as if a prayer were going up from their hearts.

Then, suddenly they dropped their arms, and smiled on their guests.

"How about getting out for a little tennis now, and then perhaps we'll come in later, or maybe this evening and do some real practicing together?" suggested Murray.

Out into the bright sunshine they trooped, to the tennis court, where a meadow lark was trilling off in the distance, and lazy little spring clouds were drifting over a blue June sky, but there was a hush over the two girls, a diffidence that at first they could not overcome. The impression of that last song was still upon them, and Vanna at least, felt very much like a fish out of water.

Murray and Gloria played against the other two and found their antagonists were well matched. Almost at once it became obvious that this was going to be a lively set.

Vanna was alert and ready with her play, but she was watching her partner with even more interest than the game. This amazing man who was a farmer and a scholar and a singer, yet could take part in a song like the one that had just been sung and get away with it.

Religion! And yet a kind of religion that Vanna had never met with before! What did it all mean? Or was that song just a bit of good music that gave a good dramatic effect and showed off their voices? Somehow the way they had spoken those words, earnest, tender, grave, did not seem like an attempt at dramatic effect. Vanna could not make out what it was all about, but she was fascinated as she could now see Gloria had been fascinated.

Well, what was the harm since it took Gloria's mind off her own troubles? At least it was interesting.

And so Vanna played on, every now and then meeting the eyes of her partner, in one of those long, interested, searching looks, lit with a smile that took her into his friendship and comradeship in such a pleasant way. She felt more intrigued by it than by anything that had come her way in many a long hectic month.

They had just sat down on the long bench to rest a bit from the third set when Mrs. MacRae came out to tell them that they were all to stay there to supper. She had arranged it with Emily Hastings and supper would be served on the side porch where they could watch the sunset while they ate.

There was a great scurrying to wash up, and brush back untidy hair, and they all came laughing gaily back to find their places at the white-spread table. Vanna slipped into her seat and was about to make a gay remark, when she felt a sudden hush come over the table.

"You ask the blessing, won't you Robert?" asked Mrs. MacRae, and Vanna, bowing her head a trifle tardily because she had never before been at a table where a blessing was asked, heard her recent partner ask a blessing on the food and on them all in such a beautiful tender way that all her shyness returned to her once more, and the gay remark died on her lips. Who were these people who took their religion with their daily food, and as a matter of course, and were happy over it? How did they get that way?

There was a big brown bean pot standing on a

little side table. It was steaming and rich with molasses, and had been simmering in the oven all the afternoon and now was sending out most delicious fragrance. There were big thin pink slices of cold ham, delicious fried potatoes with a tang of onion in them, puffy hot raised biscuit, baked apples with the thickest richest cream imaginable and squares of golden sponge cake for dessert.

The side porch was wide and spacious and turned a corner of the house, so that the space allotted to the table was large enough for a room. The outlook was over meadows to the mountains, and as they sat down the sun was just touching its ruby rim to the top of a mountain, a great ball of fire, sliding down the west in a chariot of glory. It was the most magnificent banqueting hall that one could desire and the sun seemed here to meet one on intimate terms.

"One feels almost embarrassed, certainly privileged," said Vanna suddenly as she gazed, "to be looking in on the sun in his private life this way. I don't think I was ever so near to a sun before!"

Robert Carroll looked up and smiled.

"It is privilege indeed to be where one can watch him, isn't it? That's one reason why I decided on living in the country. I always feel so sorry for the folks who live in the city and never see a sunset!"

"And it is so still here!" said Gloria watching the red ball slip slowly down. "One can almost hear the sun slipping away. That was the first thing that impressed me when I got here. Did you notice it, Vanna, how very quiet it is?"

"Why, yes that must be it," said Vanna laughing. "I noticed there was something big missing. It must be the noise. But really you know, we've kept things pretty lively ever since I came. I haven't had much chance to hear the quiet!"

Then they all laughed and began to be busy about the supper, passing the delicious viands, and eating as if they were hungry little children.

"I don't know why it is," said Vanna, "but I don't remember that food ever tasted so good before!"

"Yes, isn't that so!" said Gloria.

The sun slid swiftly out of sight but waved a flag behind it, a panorama of color. Everybody kept still for a moment watching the last red gleam of the sun disappear. Suddenly Vanna spoke.

"I hear it!" she said, her eyes large with wonder.

"What?" they asked her.

"The silence!" she said. "Listen! I never heard anything like that before, and didn't the sun seem to make a little sliding noise as it slipped over?"

They laughed together over this, but Gloria turning back caught the look in Robert Carroll's eyes as they rested on Vanna, and she felt suddenly glad that her sister was making a good impression. But she wondered what Vanna thought of these people who so interested herself? She was playing up to them of course. Vanna was like that, adaptable. It was a part of her training. But what did she really think of them in her heart? Would she rave about them, or laugh at them, when she got back where they were alone together? Something within Gloria shrank from the thought. She did not want these people misunderstood.

The tennis court presently receded into twilight and the supper table had to be provided with candles before they had finished.

"We must have some more tennis together," said Murray as they rose from the table at last.

"Yes," said Vanna. "It was gorgeous! I haven't enjoyed a tennis game so much in ages, and it's awfully good for Gloria."

"Well, how about to-morrow then?" asked Murray. "Can you come, Bob? Why not stay over here to-night and be ready to play early?"

"Sorry," said Carroll, "but you know I'm a working man. I'm planning to plant corn to-morrow. My men are coming early and I'll have to be on hand."

"Corn?" said Vanna wonderingly, "do you plant it yourself? How I'd like to see you do it! Could Gloria and I drive over and see you, or is it a secret ceremony?"

"No," laughed Carroll with slightly heightened color. "There isn't anything secret about it, but I'm afraid there isn't much to watch. And—one doesn't wear full dress to do it you know."

"I'll put on the plainest thing I have with me," said Vanna earnestly. "May I plant one corn myself if I'm good?"

Gloria watched her sister and wondered. Was Vanna trying to mortify Robert Carroll, or was she really interested? Gloria couldn't tell. She was almost vexed with her for suggesting this thing. But Robert Carroll was looking at her with that keen questioning glance again, and then grinning at her suggestion.

"Murray, will you bring them over in the morning?" he asked.

"I surely will," said Murray with satisfaction. "Maybe I'll plant a corn or two myself."

"All right, then come over about ten-thirty," said Carroll, "and when we lay off at noon we'll have a picnic lunch under the trees. I warn you it won't be much, but I can rustle some bacon sandwiches and we can build a fire out of doors and toast them. There'll be strawberries too, eaten from their stems. That's about all I can promise you."

"Oh, we don't want to make you all that trouble," said Gloria earnestly, "we'll hinder your work. We don't need to stay but five minutes just to see what you do." She was beginning to be really vexed with her sister. Did Vanna think this young man was just another one to be conquered? Or did she think because he was a farmer she could just wind him around her finger for awhile and then toss him aside?

But Vanna spoke up.

"Indeed five minutes will not be long enough. I want to know just how planting corn is done. And I adore toasted sandwiches made out in the open."

"We could put you up a lunch," suggested Mrs. MacRae.

"No," said Robert Carroll lifting his chin in a pleasant but firm smile, "if I'm going to be favored with guests I prefer to entertain them myself in my own style. Of course I can't compete with any lunch you would fix my dear Mrs. MacRae, but this is my party and they'll have to put up with what I can give them."

They had more music before they went home, singing with both instruments, and Vanna playing tender little interludes as if she were thoroughly in the spirit of things, yet Gloria watched her furtively and wondered. She had never seen her sister in this mood before.

Back in their rooms at last, the girls were both quiet. Vanna was occupying the room just back of her sister's and there was a communicating door between. Gloria could hear Vanna going about the room putting away her things, putting on slippers and negligee, and finally she came and stood in the doorway.

"Well," she said her face gravely sober, "what do you make of them? You've seen them longer than I have. Are they real?"

"Real?" said Gloria wheeling about upon her sister, "why, of course they're *real!* Had you any question of it?"

"I wanted to get your reaction," said the older sister. "You've had more chance to study them."

"One doesn't have to study them. One has to adjust oneself to a new point of view!" said Gloria thoughtfully.

"Perhaps you're right," said Vanna gravely, "but, why bother? There surely can't be any more like them in the whole universe, can there? And if one should really get adjusted, wouldn't it make one dissatisfied with the rest of the world?"

"Maybe!" said Gloria with a sigh, sitting down slowly on the edge of her bed, "I guess that's about what it does do."

Vanna gave her sister a sharp glance.

"Don't you think we had better pack up and go home in the morning?" she asked after studying Gloria for a moment.

Gloria sat up sharply.

"I thought you were so keen to learn to plant corn," she said.

Vanna looked down and tapped her toe on the old-fashioned carpet.

"Well, I thought it would be interesting to see a man like that in his own environment once," she said. "That ought to be a test of his genuineness, oughtn't it?"

"Yes," said Gloria dreamily, "if that were his real environment. That's only a side-issue with him. He earns his living by it. But I've seen him in his real environment, his spiritual environment, where he's working out what he was put into this world for, and I don't need any convincing for I *know!*"

Vanna looked at her in wonder, and a kind of wistfulness.

"What is his real environment?" she asked curiously.

Gloria was still a long time and then she answered:

"I'm not going to tell you, Vanna. If you stay here long enough you'll probably see for yourself. Vanna Sutherland, if you're going to try any of your tricks on either of those two men, believe me I'll do something about it! They're not like the men we've known. They're not game to be shot and hung at our belts. They're men, and they're real! If you're going to make fun of them I won't stand for it."

Vanna surveyed her sister in stern amazement.

"What do you think I am, Gloria Sutherland? Do you think I'm going around collecting scalps or something? Don't you think I can appreciate true worth when I see it, even if I don't belong in the same class?"

"Well," said Gloria only half appeased, "anybody that is willing to go around with Emory Zane when you know what he is——"

"I haven't said I was willing, have I? Didn't I come off here in the wilds to get away from him, where

I could think it over and find out just what I do think? And now because I'm trying to get your reaction to these two who are so different from anything I've ever even heard of before you accuse me of making fun of them."

"I'm sorry, Van, only I didn't know just where you stood. And I don't know what I think about them, only I won't have them made fun of."

"Well, I'm convinced from all you say that it's rather dangerous to be in their company long. Perhaps we'd better give up planting corn, stick around here and read the classics out of that old bookcase downstairs," said Vanna solemnly.

"Don't be a fool, Van! I'm learning things, and you can too if you'll take it in the right way. Our father was brought up to lots of things we've never had and I think we ought to understand them a little at least. These men have somehow mysteriously got the secret Dad knew once and I want to know it too."

"Exactly!" said Vanna. "Interesting but dangerous! However I'll stick around and take care of you Glory. I know my duty when I see it!"

"Oh, stop talking about it, Van, and go to bed. We've had a pleasant afternoon and evening, anyway, haven't we?"

"Too pleasant for one's peace of mind," said Vanna half laughing. "Really, darling, it's been gorgeous. I never dreamed anything so simple could be so nice. Now get to bed and don't look so troubled. I'll say this, anyhow, I'm glad you came up here! —And I'm glad I came too! Good night!"

X

Vanna came home from the corn planting sweetly thoughtful and spoke no more of insincerity or doubtful questionings.

They had had a glorious time. The day had been perfect. Each of them had ridden the corn planter once around the field and had the thrill of watching it perform its intricate function with celerity and accuracy. They asked questions that would have astonished a scientist and made an old farmer laugh, but they were tremendously interested, and had an immense respect when they came away for a young man who was willing to give up a city career, bury himself in the wilderness, and get down to hard work.

They had gone through the old farm house, only a small wing of which Robert Carroll was using for himself, the rest being entirely empty, and had admired the spacious rooms and the pleasant outlook. Vanna had stood for a long moment alone at one of the upstairs windows looking off to the bright hills and wondering how it would seem to be the mistress of that house and live there with none of the gaieties in her life which she had always had. Then Robert Carroll came over to the window and smiled down upon her and the drab outlook suddenly grew bright.

"You know it isn't really just a game I'm playing," he said, and his tone was strangely deep and significant.

She looked up startled as if he had read her thoughts.

"We don't have picnics under the trees every day, nor strawberries and a group of friends. There are cold days and dark days and lonely days and a year's round of work whether one feels like it or not."

Was he trying to make her understand the difference between her world and his? Vanna looked off to the quiet hills and felt a wrenching of her heart. What was there about this young man that so intrigued her? It was powerful. She must get away from it. She did not belong in this world and it was casting a spell over her.

Yet she lingered a long time at the window talking, trying to find out the secret of the peace in this young man's life, while down on the front porch Gloria and Murray MacRae were poring over a small limp Bible that Murray carried in his pocket.

It was a bright simple day, full of wholesome activity and restful talk, but its result was far reaching.

A few days later Mrs. Sutherland at the dinner table demanded the attention of her abstracted husband to a letter than Vanna had written her.

"Charles, there's something I must speak to you about at once. Do give me your attention for a few minutes. I'm worried nearly to death," she said in a tone that her husband knew meant business.

"Worried?" he said vaguely lifting questioning eyes across the table, just as though he was not worrying himself these days and nights all the time. "What is the matter now?"

"Why, I've had a letter from Vanna," she announced, unfolding one of Vanna's brief scrawls, two-words-to-a-line, three-lines-to-a-page. "It's high time those girls came home and we three can go off to some really respectable place for the rest of the summer. If you can't go with us at least we three can go. Listen!"

She lifted Vanna's letter and began to read:

" 'You don't need to worry about Gloria. She is looking well, and seems more rested than I have seen her for months. We are leading the simple life and really enjoying it. Yesterday what do you think we did? Learned how to plant corn. We each tried a round on the corn planter. And, Mother, it was fun! We both enjoyed it!' "

The indignant mother lifted her eyes to her husband's face. "There, Charles, what do you think of that? It seems to me the limit has been reached! Your daughters, reared to refinement, riding on a farm machine for planting corn. Gloria and Evangeline Sutherland planting corn!"

"Well, what is the matter with that?" asked the annoyed head of the house with his mind eager to return to a knotty problem of the morrow. "They've ridden on bicycles, and wild horses, and even tried airplanes a little, why shouldn't they do so simple a thing as to plant corn? I'm sure I am glad if they can get down to simple healthful things for a little while and learn how the world lives and grows."

"Charles!" fairly snorted his wife, if one can use so plebeian a word for a cultured Bostonian wife. "How pitiful that you cannot understand! It only goes to show that one never overcomes the initial environment! You cannot see the difference between riding on fine horses at the riding club, or hunt, and driving a corn planting machine through a muddy field! Oh," she moaned, "what a sight they will be when they get back!"

"My dear, one doesn't plant corn in the mud," informed her husband quietly, "your agricultural knowledge is somewhat at fault."

"No!" said the comely matron sighing deeply, "thank goodness I wasn't brought up on a farm! It's something one doesn't get over. And that is the very reason why I think the girls should come home at once! I want you to call them up this evening and order them home immediately! As carefully as we have brought them up, to have them exposed to such common things at this impressionable time of their lives! Those girls are both like you, Charles, and I'm afraid they're reverting to type. I couldn't stand it to have that happen to them after all their brilliant prospects! To think of Gloria just on the eve of a splendid marriage——!"

"Mother! Can you say that, after what happened?"

"Now Charles, don't be absurd. You know the Asher family is beyond reproach and socially about as high as one can get around here. No family is more respected, and everybody counted that a brilliant marriage. It's absurd to hold a moment of weakness against poor Stan. It wasn't Stan's fault that he got shot by some low-down creature that wasn't fit to live on the same earth with him. Poor Stan!"

"Adelaide! Stop that sentimental patter!" said her husband indignantly. "It was Stan's fault that he was shot in the company he was in, and you know it! I feel that Gloria was providentially saved from a life of sorrow. If you can bewail her fate when you know all the circumstances, then I cannot understand a mother's heart."

"No, you can't understand a mother's heart, Charles!" said his wife furiously. "You think it is pleasant to plan and work and sacrifice to put children into their proper sphere in life and then see everything upset by a whim. Gloria sent off to play childishly in the fields, making mud pies to forget her trouble that she ought to sit up and face like a woman and get over as quickly as she can; and Vanna sacrificing her whole summer, and perhaps her life's fortune to be with her! It is absurd. It is unspeakable. I don't suppose that you know that Vanna was probably on the eve of making a brilliant engagement, did you, when you ordered her off to that outlandish farm town to care for her sister?"

"No," said the father wearily, "what brilliant marriage was Vanna meditating?"

"Well," said his wife preening herself reproachfully, and turning her head so that the long jet and pearl eardrops twinkled and one of them drooped on her white shoulder, "you've been so absorbed in business lately that you haven't paid the slightest attention to what was going on in the heart of your family, but Vanna has made a brilliant conquest. A really distinguished man of the world has been deeply devoted to her ever since Gloria went away. It's strange you haven't noticed, even abstracted as you are! He has been here almost constantly, until she went away, and it really was very impolitic for her to have gone. I am sure only stern duty would have allowed her to accede to your request! I don't suppose you in the least realized, but a girl doesn't have a devoted lover like this one often. Rich, distinguished, cultured, traveled! They say he has been all over the world, and visited intimately with the nobility of Europe. He———!"

Mr. Sutherland raised his hand in protest.

"Who is this paragon of a lover, may I ask?"

His wife pronounced the name impressively.

"Mr. Emory Jarvis Zane!"

"You don't mean that hound of an Emory Zane?" roared the incensed father.

"Now, Charles, if you are going to start being abusive!" said his wife offendedly. "Every time I speak of somebody you take a dislike to him at once. Just because I tell you how wonderful he is!"

"Look here, Adelaide! You don't know what you are talking about! Emory Zane isn't fit for Vanna to wipe her feet on! Why, he isn't respectable! Every man in town knows what he is. Did you know that he has been divorced twice? And the wife he now has is seeking a divorce from him?"

"Oh, you're mistaken, Charles," said his wife in a superior tone, "his first wife died when they had only been married a few months, and his second wife ran off with another man. This third wife is really insane. She has been in the asylum for two years and escaped and he has had an awful time with her. Poor man, he is so misunderstood. He has been telling me all about it. He says our Vanna is so sweet and unspoiled and sympathetic———"

"Adelaide!" roared the man of the house exasperated beyond measure. "Don't ever let him come near her again! He's the offscouring of the earth! All that line he has been giving you is a downright lie! I happen to know the truth. His first wife left him the first week they were married, sued for a divorce at once and got it some weeks before her death. Her child is almost as old as Vanna now. The second wife was another like himself and went off with the next man who interested her, knowing that her husband was already tired of her. The third wife was *put* in the insane asylum by Emory Zane and kept there two years because he was interested in another woman and wanted to get rid of her. She was told that she was going to a rest cure when she was committed, but found that she was in the state asylum and had to run away to get free. She has never been insane, though she has had plenty to make her so, and the whole thing was a frame-up between Zane and two doctors who were well paid. Is that the kind of mess you want your daughter to be mixed up in?"

"Oh, no, Charles, that's all wrong. That's what that poor insane woman is telling around among his acquaintances, and it isn't true in the least. Why the authorities don't put her right back under sufficient guard so she can't run away again, I don't know—! But I didn't think you were one to listen to gossip!"

"Adelaide!" said her husband sternly, "I know what I'm talking about! I've been in the confidence of that woman's family for some time, and have used all the influence I had to help them. She is no more insane than you or I, and has suffered terribly. She was a beautiful young girl when he married her, she is not much older than Vanna now, and yet her hair has turned perfectly white with trouble! I insist that you shall have nothing more to do with that man! I insist that he shall not be allowed in the house, and that neither you nor my children shall have any further communication with him!"

"Now, Charles! How absurd! You can't give me orders that way you know!"

"I certainly can, and I will! This is one matter in which I will be obeyed!"

"But Charles! What can I say to him when he comes? I can't insult him!"

"No, you're right in that Adelaide! It wouldn't be possible to insult a man like that because he has no quality good enough to insult! He is entirely beyond insult. The worst that you could say to him is not as bad as he is. Adelaide, I insist!"

"Now, look here, Charles, just because you have listened to a lot of gossip I can't treat any man that way! I have been friendly and sympathetic with him. I would have to give some explanation————"

"Tell him your husband has forbidden his presence in the house!" thundered the man who was usually so quiescent regarding the matters of the household. "He is a viper! He is a fiend!"

"Now, Charles," soothed his astonished wife, "don't talk so loud, the servants will hear you! Of course if you feel that way————!"

"I do feel that way! And, furthermore, I cannot understand why you don't feel that way also! You who are afraid of a little manual labor for the girls!"

"Well, but, Charles, that certainly is the limit, girls like that going out on a farm machine! It isn't respectable! I suppose of course they only did it for fun, but really, if it should get back to Roseland I don't know what would be thought of them. It is such a queer freak, anyway, going off up there to that forsaken place and being around with farm people! When they might be having their own congenial friends about them."

"If you ask me I think they will find a lot more congenial friends up in the country than down here in Roseland. At least the young people up there aren't going around all night from one speakeasy to another, trying to see how much liquor they can carry, and how many wild crimes they can get away with under the name of fun, or 'whoopee', or whatever crazy name they may happen to call it!"

"Charles! You oughtn't to talk that way. As if the girls went with lowdown company."

"Well, they do, don't they? Didn't they just escape being caught in a lowdown place in lowdown company last winter when Madden's Road House was raided? They hadn't been away from it five minutes when it happened, and it's a miracle they didn't have to come up in court to testify at that murder trial. They were in the place when the quarrel began, weren't they? Oh, I tell you there are a lot worse things they can do than plant corn! There are a lot worse places they can go than back to my old home in the country. If you would only go up there once and see for yourself you wouldn't be so prejudiced!"

There was a wistfulness in his tone as he spoke the last sentence and his wife jumped up from the table sharply.

"Well, I'm not going," she said. "I don't like the country. Let's not talk any more about it." Then she left the room.

Mr. Sutherland left his coffee unfinished and slowly, sadly retreated to the library which was considered his special province, and there he plunged into business perplexities, working at his desk until far into the night. Occasionally, though, he was haunted by the vision of the man whom he considered a fiend incarnate, and he would sit back in his big chair and drop his face into his hands and groan at the thought of his two beloved girls. Vanna and Emory Zane! It was unthinkable. He must get off and go up and have a talk with Vanna. He couldn't trust his wife, she was too easily influenced by wealth and public opinion and a desire for brilliant marriages for her daughters. She wished to be known as a mother who achieved big things.

But Roseland was not the only place to which the corn planting episode brought disturbance. Back on the outskirts of Ripley Township there stood a little old farmhouse, up on a hillside overlooking the cornfield owned by Robert Carroll. The woman who lived in that farmhouse had the reputation of being up to date in all the news of the county, especially such as came under her own observation. Having no children and being somewhat isolated from neighbors, she had much time hanging heavily on her hands, and she made the most of the few advantages that were left her in life. She could still see out her end windows, down across the rich valley of farm lands, to the highway that ran to Ripley, and because her eyes were beginning to fail her, and one could scarcely hope anyway even with good eyes to recognize people and cars at such a distance, she kept a pair of fine field glasses close beside the window on her little sewing table. Afternoons when her work was done, mornings too, sometimes, she amused herself by studying the landscape and watchings all comers and goers on that highway. It was often thus she picked up many a juicy item of news that helped out the village paper news editor. And so Mrs. Coulter had come to be known in the locality as one who knew a thing or two about almost everything that was going on.

On the morning of the corn planting Robert Carroll and his two men were out in the field early with their team and machine, and Mrs. Coulter got out her glasses and laid them handy, knowing that she was sure of something going on nearby that day. When she had washed up her dishes and set her bread to rise she went out on her side porch with a basket of mending and her field glasses, and prepared to enjoy herself. She liked to watch the mellow ground being turned in furrows, liked to look at the straight rows and smooth lines where the machine had passed. It was to her an art.

But it was not long before a car going by on the highway, turned in at the opening in the fence where the bars were down and drove slowly around the border of plowed ground till it came to a halt not far from the big elm tree that made a wide shade near the back of the lot.

Matilda Coulter raised her glasses and leveled them at the strange car, thrilled with joy as it drew nearer, straight into her line of vision. She did not often find her traveling shows coming so near.

It was a big car, not any car that she knew hereabouts. She studied its peculiarities, and made up her mind it must be one of two very expensive makes. She wasn't sure which because not many fine cars came her way. But it had an opulent look and it might even be one of those priceless foreign makes that one heard about now and then but never saw nearby.

As it came on she noted that there were two girls and a man in the car, though she couldn't see the girls very well until they got out. Then she saw that one had yellow hair and one was dark. Ah! That must be the yellow-haired Sutherland girl who was staying at the Weatherbys, and the other was no doubt her sister. She had heard that her sister had arrived the morning before. Tom Batty the taxi driver had stopped to beg for gingerbread on his way back from taking her up, and he had told her. Tom always knew he could get gingerbread in exchange for the news, and many were the choice morsels that found their way into his capacious mouth as he taxied here and there by Matilda Coulter's door. Yes, the Sutherlands! And of course that was their car. They would bring a nifty thing like that up there in the country to astonish the natives! But who was the young man? She had heard they had a brother, but had always thought of him as a child.

Then Murray MacRae got out and stood where she could get a glimpse of his face and she recognized him. Ah! Murray MacRae and the Sutherlands! Of course. And Robert Carroll! She licked her lips and drew a breath of pleased surprise! Right at her own door. It didn't often happen that way!

Her active mind began to get out and display in orderly manner all that she knew about the young people out there in the field below her. Gloria Sutherland. That was the girl with the yellow hair. And her lover had just been shot in a row in a New York night club. Kind of disgraceful doings. She was supposed by the neighbors up here to have come to her father's old home to mourn her bridegroom and get out of the public eye, but here she was coming in the company of an attractive young man—rather soon if one were really mourning—to the home of another young man during his working hours! Rather queer doings! One who mourned did not disport herself in public, thought Matilda Coulter as she watched the young people with avid eye.

All through the morning she watched, even catching their expressions with her far reaching glasses, noticing how much they laughed, and how little sadness was in the face of the yellow-haired girl who ought by good rights to have been dressed in black, but who was gay in a bright little scarlet cap and jacket over a white thin dress. Matilda could tell it was thin because of the way it blew in the breeze.

Then the other girl, the one in bright green, went out in the field with Robert Carroll, right into the plowed ground and got up on the seat of the planting machine. The bold hussy! And Robert Carroll almost had his arm around her, helping her up into the seat!

Matilda Coulter caught her breath and watched with all her eyes, forgetting the yellow-haired girl for the moment, but then when she turned her glass back to the place where she had left her, there she was sitting down on the grass shoulder to shoulder with Murray MacRae, looking at something he held. What was it? A book! A little book! But of course the book was only an excuse for sitting close together! A flirtation that was what it was. So! That was the kind of girls Charles Sutherland had for daughters! Well, that was what one might expect from people who went off to the city and got rich and never came back to see their own kith and kin!

All through the morning she kept tab on them, and when they built a fire and began to get their lunch ready she hurried into the telephone which was conveniently placed so that she could see out the window while she was talking, and called up her best friend who lived on another mountain. She reported what was going on, together with her surmises and interpretations, until a fairly thrilling story was evolved.

"Why, isn't that the Sutherland girl who was engaged to the man that was shot in a speakeasy in New York by the lover of the girl he had with him?" contributed the friend who was listening.

"Of course it is!" Isn't that awful!" said Matilda Coulter. "Well, she certainly isn't doing much mourning to-day!"

Now this friend had a daughter who taught in the same school in Portland with Joan Sutherland, and in due time the story with embellishments reached Portland and was discussed and turned over and exclaimed over. And not many days hence, on a Saturday afternoon to be exact, and just after the noon dinner hour, Joan, driving the family flivver, arrived at the Sutherland house in Afton and asked for her cousin Gloria.

Gloria was getting on her tennis shoes for an afternoon over on the MacRae court, and Vanna was changing into a pretty little sport dress that made her look like a full blown rose when Emily Hastings came up to say that Joan was downstairs.

Gloria's face went stormy in an instant and she sat down on the edge of the bed and let out a stifled groan.

"Now, what's the matter?" said Vanna, whirling from the looking glass where she was brushing her brown hair.

"Oh, that awful cousin of ours is downstairs!" moaned Gloria softly. "Now our afternoon is all in hash."

"Nonsense!" said Vanna, "tell her you're sorry but you have an engagement!"

"You can't, Vanna, not here! People don't do things like that! It's all wrong. Everybody in the state would know it before to-morrow and you would be hurting everybody else who had been kind to you!"

"Folly!" said Vanna. "Leave her to me then!"

"No," said Emily laughing, "she particularly asked for Glory, said she wanted to see her alone. She seemed very secretive about it."

"Well, tell her you can't spare her but five minutes," said Vanna. "Then I'll come down and rescue you. That'll divert her. She doesn't likely know I'm here."

"The dickens she doesn't!" said Gloria glumly, "she knows everything in the most uncanny way. Well, good-bye, I'll have to go down, but don't you bother to come after me. Just slip down the back stairs and out the back door, and go around the barn over to Mac-Raes', then she won't see you. Tell them to go on playing without me. Tell Murray to play the two of you till I come."

"Well, can't you bring her along?" asked Vanna anxiously. "No telling how long she'll stay."

"No, I can't bring her along," said Gloria, "she'd have all of us down under a wet blanket before three minutes had passed. Good-bye if I don't see you till night."

Gloria hurried down and found Joan ensconced in the darkest corner of the big parlor attired so drably that she had trouble in discovering her.

"Well, you see I'm here bothering you again," greeted Joan grimly. "I'm sorry to trouble you. I suppose I'm likely interrupting some of your plans, but I couldn't help it. I thought I ought to come whether you like it or not. I thought it was my duty."

"Duty?" said Gloria settling down near a window where she could catch a glimpse of the road. "Why make it a duty to come and see your cousin?"

"Oh, yes, that cousin stuff is all right for talk!" said Joan, "but it isn't so pleasant when we're expected to answer for the actions of one's relatives."

"Do we have to do that?" asked Gloria innocently.

"Well, that's what it amounts to!"

"Why, I always supposed each one of us had to answer for our own actions," said Gloria.

"It seems we can't live to ourselves!" said Joan severely. "Anyhow, I felt it my duty to come and tell you what people are saying about you."

"What people are saying about *me!*" exclaimed Gloria. "Why what could they possibly say about me that could make any difference? Why should they know anything about me, or think anything about me? I know very few people around here."

"No, that's just it, and you're taking the very best way not to know anybody. When a girl comes into a community and picks out one man and specializes on him morning, noon, and night, and gets herself into questionable situations with him, then people don't want to know such a girl. Not right-minded people!" Joan leveled her cold eyes at her cousin severely.

"Have I done that?" asked Gloria with an amused light in her eyes.

"You certainly have!" said Joan firmly. "It would have been bad enough under ordinary circumstances, but for you, practically a newly-made widow, to carry on that way is unforgivable."

"Do you mean that you consider it wrong for a girl who has been through recent sorrow to have any friends?" asked Gloria, that amused light still in her eyes.

"She doesn't need to have *men* friends," said Joan bluntly. "There are plenty of women around. She could keep in the background for a while at least for decency's sake, and not get herself talked about. I thought I ought to come and tell you that people are saying terrible things about you." Joan drew a breath as if she had just thrown a powerful bomb at her cousin and expected it to blow her up immediately.

"Well," said Gloria, considering her cousin gravely now, "that was kind of you I suppose, but, just why should it matter to me that people were talking about me? I'm not conscious of doing anything wrong according to the standards I was brought up on, and if I am violating some local code here without knowing it, why bother to tell me about it? It really won't make any difference a hundred years hence will it?"

Joan's cheeks grew angrily red.

"It certainly makes a difference to the people who are unfortunate enough to be related to you," she said sharply. "I've had to defend you all this week and I'm about sick of it. I'm ashamed. I thought of course if you knew you'd do something about it!" There was a desperate sound in Joan's voice as if there were almost tears behind her words.

"But I don't understand, Joan," said Gloria more gently, "what could people possibly say about me that could worry you or make you ashamed? I can't see what they would say or why they should want to say anything."

"Well they do. They say you are a bold girl. They call you a hussy! They say you have made a dead set for Murray MacRae and that you spend all your days and evenings in his company. People see you driving off with him, and it is said that you've been seen openly making love to each other in public places. They're telling how you go out in open fields and eat meals together, and you were seen with two other people, some say one was your sister, going into an empty lonely farm house and that you stayed there an hour or more before you came out again! They say—Oh, a lot worse things about you——! I'm ashamed to tell you everything. But Mother thought I ought to come and let you know. She said if the things weren't true and you were an honest girl you'd put a stop to all this talk!"

"What's all this?" said a voice from the doorway and looking up they saw Vanna standing there in her soft pink frock like a lovely summer rose. "Put a stop to all what talk?"

"Oh," said Gloria, looking up with relief, "Joan, this is my sister Vanna. Vanna this is our cousin Joan. She's come over to tell me that people are talking about us because we went over to Robert Carroll's and learned how to plant corn, and because I've been playing tennis with Murray MacRae so soon after a death in our circle."

"Yes?" said Vanna coolly. "Well, now suppose we forget it. You know, Joan, Gloria has been through a terrible time, and we brought her up here to get her mind off of it, not for her to sit down and mourn. Murray MacRae has been very kind and thoughtful and has helped a lot to pass the time away. He seems from what I have seen of him to be a fine, clean, moral young man, and so far our whole association with him has been entirely decent and open for anybody to see. If you don't believe that come on over with us now. We are due to play tennis at MacRaes' this minute, and Murray's sister Lindsey is expected in an hour. Perhaps you know her. I am sure they will be glad to have us bring you over. Then you can go back and tell your friends who have been talking about my sister, just how much foundation there is for the talk, that is if you care to defend us. It really would be immaterial to us whether you did or not. People who will get up lying tales about strangers are really not people I would care to know, so it doesn't matter what they say. Now, will you come with us?"

"No, indeed!" said Joan, getting up sharply, her face growing red with indignation. "I wouldn't think of going there. Murray MacRae is not one of my friends, and I shouldn't like to be mixed in with gossip. Besides, I have a lot of work at home to do and I only took time from other duties because I felt you ought to know the truth."

"But it isn't the truth!" said Gloria indignantly. "They've been telling lies if they've said anything such as you suggest about us. It's most amusing to think such talk could start on so little foundation and go so far as to reach you in Portland."

"Even a child is known by his doings!" quoted Joan primly and significantly.

"Yes, well, Gloria is not a child, Joan," said Vanna coldly, "and people have no right to talk of things they know nothing about."

"But people have seen her!" insisted Joan.

"Well, if they have, they have seen nothing indecorous," said Vanna, "or else they are lying."

"But you were seen entering that farm house where a young man lives alone!" said Joan in a high key facing down the two sisters as if she meant to fight to the last ditch. "Did you or did you not go there?"

"Why, certainly, we went in at Mr. Carroll's invitation to see the quaint old fireplaces," said Vanna,

"but there were four of us, besides one of the farm
boys, and it is really nobody's business whether we
went in or not. If people are so evil minded as to
make gossip out of that they will have to do it. Don't
bother any more about it please. It doesn't bother us
in the least, and it will soon pass away and be forgotten. The young men are certainly so respectable that it
can't hurt them, and we shall soon be away from here
again."

"But what am I to say when people tell me these
things?"

"Say nothing," advised Vanna, "or better still,
tell them it is none of their business. You know the
least said is soonest mended. I wouldn't answer such
talk. Just laugh. It really can't live without fresh fuel
you know, no fire can, and most of all the fire of gossip. Come on now, go with us over to MacRaes'. We
are already late."

"No, I must go home!" said Joan offendedly, and
marched straight out to her car without further words
and drove rapidly out of sight.

"Well, and that's that!" laughed Vanna, casting a
quick anxious glance toward Gloria. "Come on! She's
some swell cousin, isn't she?"

"I think perhaps she meant to be kind," said Gloria thoughtfully. "But can you imagine it, making
talk over that little picnic? And how on earth did it all
get started? There wasn't a sign of a person in sight,
except those two hired hands and they were mere boys,
and one of them was along with us when we went in.
He opened the shutters ahead of us to go through the
rooms. Well, forget it, dear. It's just funny, that's all."

"You don't suppose that it will hurt Murray and
Robert, here in their own home locality do you?" asked
Gloria anxiously.

"Hurt them? How could it?" asked Vanna. "They
are too big to be bothered by a little gossip. Tell them
about it and see how they'll laugh! My word! What
would these dear people do if they lived in Roseland
and had some really wild parties to report and enlarge
upon?"

Then they swung back the MacRae gate and saw Murray and Robert coming to meet them, and the cloud on the horizon vanished.

But a little later when they were sitting together resting between sets and watching for the car that was to bring Lindsey and her professor, Vanna told of the visit of Joan.

There was great merriment over the story but Robert suddenly sobered down.

"That's Tilly Coulter's doing, the whole thing!" he said gravely. "I ought to have remembered her prying eyes and her powerful field glasses. I might have known she'd make ten mountains out of a little mole hill. However, I know a way to straighten things out. I'll just go up and have a frank talk with Tilly, and let her know I understand all about it, and I'll make her eat her own words over the telephone to a few loquacious friends of hers. It doesn't matter, of course, only it's just as well to clear the name of our friends when we can. It makes a better witness in the world."

Then a car was heard at the front of the house and they all rushed around to greet Lindsey MacRae and her professor.

XI

Three more delightful weeks passed in Afton and Joan came no more to trouble them with idle tales of gossip. The gossip had somehow taken a turn for the better, and kindly eyes turned curiously toward the girls as they went about in the little village, or attended the church where their father used to be as a boy. Vanna reflected one day on this and decided that Robert Carroll's method for stopping gossip must have been effective.

Vanna had seen Robert Carroll and Murray MacRae in what Gloria had called their "real" environment now. She had attended several meetings with them, indeed played for them, and had watched the response of young people to the preaching of the gospel. She knew now what her sister had meant by a spiritual environment, and yet she had not said anything more about it to Gloria. She had just gone on from day to day having a good time, watching Robert Carroll, listening to him sometimes when he talked of the things of another world, yet taking no stand, only listening. But Gloria felt no longer worried lest she would make fun of their two new friends, no fear lest she would intentionally try to win the heart of either of these young men just to throw it away when she went from them. Vanna was thinking deeply, that

149

was apparent, but what she was thinking she did not say. Only one thing, she had not mentioned again the name of Emory Zane.

And then one day just after lunch a great cream-colored car bright with chromium and noisy with trumpets came blaring up to the quiet old door of the Sutherland house, and there was Emory Zane, come to find Vanna!

Mrs. Sutherland had been most discreet in her further talks with Emory Zane, following the conversation she had had with her husband about him. For he came again as she had known he would, to see what news there was of Vanna, to see if she had returned yet. And when he came Vanna's mother received him with a purring tone and discoursed discreetly about Vanna's father, "poor man," being so distracted with business that they really didn't like to cross him in his whims, and one of his latest whims had been to send Gloria and Vanna off to his old home town and have them stay a while among rural surroundings.

"And of course it isn't so bad for Gloria," added her mother with a pensive tone, "poor child! She really is just as well away from things for a while. But poor Vanna! It is terribly hard on her to be stuck away in that isolated hole with nothing on earth to do from morning till night. It was so sweet of her to be willing to give up her own life here and go up there to try and help her sister out."

"Where are they, Mrs. Sutherland?" asked the young man eagerly. "Why shouldn't I take a spin up there and give them a little excitement?"

"Oh, that would be wonderful of you!" said the mother warmly. "I just know Vanna would appreciate that so much! You see we were all so worried about Gloria, or Vanna wouldn't have left just now. We couldn't persuade Gloria to return. She shrinks so, poor child, from meeting the world again, and keeps putting it off from day to day. That's really why Vanna went up. I've been so hoping she would be able to get Gloria to be sensible about it and come home, but in the last letter Vanna seemed to think it was impossible to move her just yet."

"I might even be able to persuade them to come home with me," said the young man loftily, as if when he undertook a matter it was sure to go through.

"Oh, I would be so grateful if you could do that!" said Vanna's mother with a dewy look of gratitude around her eyes. "I have been so sorry for Vanna. I know she will be just too pleased to see you coming! And I'm sure it will be good for Gloria, too. But, may I ask you, please, not to say anything to Mr. Sutherland about it? He is so harassed with business just now, those foreign finance matters you know, and he takes strange notions."

"You mean against me?" asked the man of the world with a slow smile.

"Well, I wouldn't exactly like to say that," said Mrs. Sutherland, "but somewhere of course he has heard some of the rumors you were speaking about, and it isn't always easy to disabuse his mind of a thing he has once heard. But of course it will all pass away and be forgotten in a few days. And it's so kind of you to think of going to see the girls."

There was a sinister glitter of satisfaction in Zane's eyes as he left the Sutherland mansion and drove away turning over his plans in his mind. It would suit him very well if he could put Mr. Sutherland in a position where he could no longer use his influence against him.

And so Emory Zane had arranged his affairs and taken his way in his big cream-colored car up to Afton.

Vanna was on the front piazza in the hammock reading when he came, and her greeting was not especially joyous. She and Gloria had planned to go to the woods in a few minutes and bring back some lovely maiden-hair ferns they had discovered in a clump by the roadside a few days before. John Hastings had dug up and mellowed the spot at the shady end of the porch where they wanted to put them and they were eager to get them planted. And now this arrival was an interruption. If they were hindered very

long they would have to wait until another day for the
ferns because they were due to go to MacRaes' at
five o'clock to practise some music for a meeting that
evening over at Quiet Valley and they mustn't be late
for the rehearsal.

So Vanna arose from the hammock and came
slowly down the steps to meet her caller, with no very
eager smile on her face. For one thing the car with
its noisy trumpets and gaudy fittings struck a wrong
note in this quiet country town, and she suddenly felt
that it was out of place. She cast a quick anxious
glance down across the road to the MacRae house.
What would Lindsey, sweet quiet Lindsey, think of
her caller? Murray, she knew, had gone into Ripley on
business. He was coming back with Robert Carroll
at five for the practise. Vanna hoped she could get
rid of her caller before that.

"Of all things!" said Vanna lazily when she knew
that she must speak. "Where in the world did you
come from?"

"Straight from your home, darling!" said Emory
Zane coming up the walk and taking Vanna's hand in
his for a close clasp, then stooping he bent over with
courtly manner to kiss her fingers.

"Don't be silly!" said Vanna sharply, snatching
her hand away, and aware of the color that spread
over her annoyed face. This sort of thing didn't belong up here, and she wondered why she had such a
strong desire to give the man a good sharp slap on his
handsome supercilious face. She wondered why she
had ever been intrigued by him.

"I've brought you a package from your mother!"
he said, handing out a suit box which Vanna at once
suspected contained clothing that her mother thought
more suitable for entertaining millionaires than that
she had brought with her.

"Oh, that was kind of you!" she said, trying to
keep the annoyance out of her voice. "I hope you
didn't have to go far out of your way. I am afraid
you did, for I can't imagine your being interested so far
out of the world as this. There really is nothing up here

that you would care for, I'm afraid, unless you like views."

"There is always *you*," said the young man in that soft, impressive tone of his that had so often flattered her, and he looked deep into her eyes with a significance that he hoped would bring the lovely color into her face again.

"Oh, that's so kind of you!" said Vanna, quickly slipping into the old mocking tone wherewith she had been used to meet such flatteries at home.

"I found that Roseland was a desert without you, Vanna!" he said, his eyes seeking hers intimately, "and I've come to take you back again. I came just for that! And your sister, too, of course, if she would like to go," he added formally.

Vanna laughed.

"That's quite impossible!" she said gaily. "My sister and I may be up here several weeks yet. She doesn't feel at all happy about going home, and it's doing her a lot of good here. But it certainly was kind of you to think of us and we're just as grateful as if it were possible for us to go. Won't you come up and sit on the porch a few minutes before you start on?"

"But I'm not starting on," said Emory Zane with that slow lazy smile that was so sure of itself, and that sinister glitter in his handsome eyes that had often fascinated her. She wondered, now, why it had. "I'm not starting on anywhere until you go with me. I don't care what your sister does, but you've got to go back with me. Your mother wants you. She sent very insistent messages to that effect. She needs you very much right away! And—" he looked deep into her eyes again —"*I* need you, *darling!* Isn't it enough that I left everything else and came up here after you? Don't I deserve the right to take you home?"

Vanna sat down stiffly in a porch rocker and looked at him, realized that the last thing she wanted to do in life was to go back home in company with this man, and yet felt a kind of spell of his presence coming over her, a mysterious influence that in the past she had played with, and been pleased to have sway her, but that now had something unpleasant, something almost frightening in it.

They argued for nearly half an hour, Vanna trying to keep her gay mocking tone and yet answer firmly, but the man was persistent. He did not for an instant waver in his intention to take her with him.

Then she grew grave and almost sharp with him, and he looked at her in amused silence for a moment before he spoke. She began to hope that at last she had convinced him that she did not want to go with him.

"Well," he said finally, as if he had given in to her decision. "If you won't go home you won't I suppose, but at least you owe it to me to go out a little while with me after I have come so far for you. Come, get your hat, and a wrap of some sort, for it may be cool in the evening, and we'll take a ride over these mountains and find some nice place to dine and dance for a while."

"No," said Vanna almost crossly, "I can't do that either. I have an engagement this evening to play. I have promised and they are depending on me. I couldn't miss it."

"What time do you play?" asked Zane, glancing at his watch.

"Eight o'clock!" said Vanna. "But we have a rehearsal at five and I must be there."

"Forget the rehearsal," smiled the man of the world. "Let the others do the rehearsing, you don't need it. We can get back here by eight and that's enough. Now, come, let's get started if we have to get back so soon."

"No," said Vanna again much disturbed in her mind, "I *have* to be back for that rehearsal!"

"Oh, well!" said Zane with a half offended manner. "Have it your own way of course. Only I should suppose you owed me one evening to myself, after all that has passed between us!"

Vanna had a quick frightened wonder what he meant by that, but she was too anxious to get that flary car away from the front door before any of the

MacRaes should see it, to worry over a trifling remark.

"You'll surely get me back by half past four?" she asked, searching his face suspiciously.

"We'd better go at once, before you cut the time to nothing," he laughed.

So Vanna, much perturbed, rushed upstairs to her anxious sister who had not failed to recognize the car and the hated voice of the man she despised as a friend for her sister.

"I've got to go out for a little while with Emory Zane," Vanna explained hurriedly as she smoothed her hair and hunted for a hat. "I'm sorry to stand you up on the trip for the ferns but it seems this is the only way I can get rid of him. He came up here to try and take us both home, but of course I told him that was impossible. He says Mother sent him."

"Oh, Vanna!" wailed Gloria in a troubled voice. "You'll be late for the rehearsal! I know you will! And it means so much to Robert Carroll to sing that special song to-night! It just belongs with what Murray is going to say. He was telling me about it last night."

"Well, I'll not be late for the rehearsal. I made that a special proviso. I'm only going to get rid of him later, that's all. Please don't make a fuss. I'll get back as quick as I can. Four thirty at the latest I told him."

"You can't trust him," said Gloria sorrowfully. "I'm sure you can't trust a word he says."

"If I can't I'll know the reason why!" said Vanna indignantly. "I'll be back, and don't you worry! You know when I say I will I mean it!"

"Yes, I know *you*," said Gloria, "but you don't seem to know what you're up against."

"Now, Glory, for pity's sake don't hold me up any longer. The quicker I go the quicker I'll get back!"

"Maybe!" said Gloria cryptically.

She refused to go down and meet Emory Zane. In fact Vanna didn't urge her much. She stood at the window and watched the loverlike way in which Emory Zane put her sister into his sporty car, watched them go blaring down the road toward Ripley with the triple horns playing an ostentatious blast, saw the hired man from down the road pause in his labor and look after them wonderingly, surely identifying Vanna. Now there would be more talk, and perhaps another visit from Joan! Gloria sighed deeply and turned away from the window feeling as if she would like to cry. Did Vanna really care for that slippery snake of a man? Could she admire him after knowing these two wonderful men up here in the mountains?

And then Gloria sat down suddenly and realized that she at least would never again be able to admire the kind of men she had known all her life, Stan's kind, the kind that went in her set at home. That was not going to be a happy outlook for herself, to be dissatisfied with all the men in her world. But her world was spoiled for her anyway, so what difference did it make? And it was good to at least know there were men like Murray and Robert somewhere in the universe; even if they were not for her. She would cherish the days that she could spend in their company, and lay by pleasant memories, even if they were not to be a part of her future.

But oh, what should she do about Vanna, supposing she was late? Supposing she did not come at all? Her heart quaked with terrible premonition. Could Vanna be so lost to all that was fine that she could engage herself to Zane? Could she really care for him after knowing fineness and nobility? Or hadn't she seen it? Had she just been passing the time away and half laughing still at their lack of sophistication?

Now it happened that that very afternoon Murray had gone to Ripley on an errand and had stopped on the way back for a few minutes' chat with Robert. They had been sitting on the porch talking of their work, and planning their program for a meeting they were holding in Quiet Valley that evening.

After a little silence Murray spoke.

"How about Vanna, Bob? Does she know the

Lord? I haven't been able to make her out. She seems interested and yet she says so little. Have you had any opportunity to find out?"

"I've had opportunity," said Robert sadly, "just had a talk with her yesterday, but I haven't met with much response. We've talked, that is I've talked and she has listened respectfully, but has said almost nothing. A smile, a kind of wistful questioning look. That's about all. Perhaps I fancied even that. She has simply been non-committal. No, I'm afraid the answer is no!" and he sighed deeply.

"Yet one might easily take it for granted that she was in thorough sympathy. She has seemed interested in the work."

"Yes, politely so!" said Robert. "How about Gloria? Is she saved?"

"Not yet, I'm afraid," said Murray. "Sometimes I think she isn't 'far from the kingdom'. She's fascinated with the study of the Bible, but I don't know how much of the spiritual truth has reached her. She doesn't say much either, occasionally asks leading questions that show she has been thinking. Bob, I wonder if you have felt as I've been feeling? I'm almost sure you have—that we have no business as yielded Christians going on with those two girls?"

It seemed as if the words were torn from Murray's heart.

"Bob," he went on, "I've been hearing a voice in my ears for days, 'Be not unequally yoked together with unbelievers! Be not unequally yoked together with unbelievers! Come ye out and be ye separate! Can two walk together except they be agreed!' Bob, I don't know what *you* think, but I've been on my knees before God over this thing and I've come to a fork in the road. There's no question of the way for me. *You* know Bob, there's no path for me but the one *He* chooses, no matter what it may mean to me!"

"I know it, old man, He's been speaking to me too, and of course there's no question of what we must do. I believe that at first our Master purposely threw us together so that the girls might hear the truth, and come face to face with Him through the Word. But they have heard now and I believe our work is over. All we can do is to follow His leading and leave the rest to Him."

There was solemn understanding silence between the friends, then Robert spoke again.

"I've been thinking too," said Robert, "all this afternoon, ever since that handsome car went by with Vanna in it, that after all, no matter if the girls were saved, and no matter how much we are prospered in the future, it isn't at all likely that either you or I would be able to match our fortunes with the fortunes of two such girls as that. They are out of our class, that's all!"

"That's true too," said Murray thoughtfully, "but I'm not thinking so much about that. The only class that really counts is the spirtual class. We're not to go out of that. 'Come ye out . . . be ye separate,' says the Word. The other doesn't really count so much after all, if it be among born-again ones. Money and social prominence are *worldy* separations, not heavenly."

"Think so?" said Carroll. "Perhaps you're right, but it might not be so easy to persuade rich relations to think so."

"Well, I hadn't got so far as that," laughed Murray. "I'm only concerned to be 'in the way' so the Lord can lead me to what He wants me to do, even if it breaks my poor natural human heart."

"They're going to wonder, of course, if we drop them suddenly," mused Robert. "That doesn't seem right either, at least without explanation. And of course there's to-night. That's all arranged for. We'd have to carry that through."

"I know," said Murray, "'but I believe that if we're really willing to follow our Master all the way at any cost that the responsibility of working it all out is up to Him. I can't see how He can do it, but I believe He will!"

Murray's voice rang with confidence.

"Yes, of course He will," responded Robert instantly. "How little faith we have after all, trying to think out God's plans for Him! But our part is to be abiding so closely that we'll hear His slightest whisper, so that we won't hinder the working out of His plans. And may I look to you, friend, to check me up if you see me going on in my stubborn self-will? What is fellowship in Christ for if not for that?"

"Yes, but don't forget it works both ways," answered Murray earnestly. And so the two young men set out on the way of the cross with bleeding hearts, yet full of trust in the love and wisdom of Him who called them to follow Him.

A dozen times that afternoon Gloria went to the window and stared off at the loveliness of the hills, almost hoping to see the big cream-colored car returning. But it was lost in the distance, and it wasn't half past four yet anyway. Gloria at last convinced herself that there wasn't a thing she could do about it except to worry, so she sought out a book she had been reading and tried to drown her thoughts in that. But the thoughts ran on in an undertone and distracted her mind, and again she would get up and go to the window.

At last half past four arrived, and no Vanna! She gave up reading entirely and went and plastered herself at the window, her anxious eyes scraching up and down the road, her heart in a quiver. What should she say to the boys if Vanna didn't turn up at five? But of course she would! She had promised, and Vanna always did what she promised. Of course she might have miscalculated the time a little, but she would surely be here by five.

But five o'clock came and no Vanna, and Gloria, distracted beyond measure, went slowly downstairs and out across the road alone. She would come in a minute. She would surely be there very shortly, she told herself, as she opened the MacRae gate and stepped inside. And then Murray came smiling out to meet her, gave her a warm handclasp, and a pleasant searching of the eyes.

"Come, let's sit down here on the porch a minute before the rest come," he said. "We'll look up the verses you were asking about last night. Bob just phoned he would be a few minutes late."

So Gloria, glad to get a few minutes' reprieve from her worry, feeling sure that Vanna would be there before long, sat absorbed in Murray's explanation of what was fast becoming a deeply interesting study to her.

Murray opened the little book to the third chapter of John.

"This was it, wasn't it?" he asked. " 'The wind bloweth where it listest, and thou hearest the sound thereof, but canst not tell whence it cometh, and whither it goeth: so is every one that is born of the spirit.' "

"Yes, I wondered if that was the reason I couldn't 'get' you at first. You were so different from anyone I ever knew."

Murray smiled tenderly.

"Anyone who is born again, born of the spirit," he said, "has a new life, a supernatural life that defies human explanation."

"I would like to be born again," said Gloria wistfully, lifting serious eyes to his. "I heard those young people talk about being saved. I wish I could know that I was saved!"

"You may," he said quickly, a look of surprise and unutterable gladness coming into his eyes. "That's what I have been praying for since I first knew you. But you know there is only one class of people who can be saved," he said gently, to test her.

"Oh!" Gloria's face clouded with disappointment. "I thought the verse said 'whosoever'."

Murray's face held a glory light as she said that.

"Our Lord said that He came not to call the righteous, but sinners to repentance," he said, watching her keenly.

Gloria turned now and looked Murray full in the face and suddenly his meaning flashed over her.

"Oh," she said awesomely, "but *I am* a sinner— a very great sinner!"

Her eyes filled with tears.

"I never knew it till I met you and heard you talk about *Him!*"

Then did Murray, his voice breaking with joy and earnestness, lead his beloved from one precious statement to another in the little book until at last, her own face alight, she said:

"I see it now! I *am* born again! 'He that believeth on Me *hath* everlasting life.'"

But the arrival of Robert Carroll cut short their thanksgiving celebration, for the time, and still there was no sign of Vanna.

"I can't understand why she isn't here," said Gloria with troubled eyes. "She was so sure she would be back. She didn't really want to go, but an acquaintance from home drove through to see her and insisted she should go to ride for a little while."

"Maybe they had tire trouble or something," suggested Murray. "Suppose you play for us till she gets here. Then we'll surprise her by being able to sing much better than she expected. She doesn't really need the practice anyway. We're the ones who need it. It doesn't matter to her if she has never seen the music before of course."

So Gloria sat down at the piano and the singing went on, lovely music, lovely words, enunciated like a message, but her fingers found the notes automatically and her ears scarcely took in the beautiful melody, so wrought up was her mind. A cold deadly fear seemed clutching at her thoughts, gripping her by the throat. She must not give way to it, for if she did she had a superstitious feeling that her fear might come true. She must be calm and not let these two see how troubled she was. Oh, if Vanna would only come!

Every time a car went by on the highway she turned her worried eyes toward the window, but still Vanna did not come, and at last she had to scurry over to get her supper or she would be late for the evening. Oh, wouldn't Vanna come before the evening? Surely, surely she would not miss this appointment in which she had seemed to be so deeply interested!

"Don't you worry," said Murray as he left her at the Sutherland gate, "something has likely come up that she could not help. Maybe engine trouble, that's serious off in the hills away from a mechanic or a telephone. If she doesn't get here we'll carry it through all right. It isn't that we'll miss her so at the piano, but it will necessarily cut out your violin if you have to accompany us. However, there'll be other times. And perhaps she'll come yet. Maybe there is a message from her in the house now. But I won't stop to see. I promised to do something for Mother before I go out this evening, and I must be getting back to it."

But there was no message in the house from Vanna and Gloria's heart went down, down, her fears in a wild tumult which she dared not try to analyze.

"I wouldn't worry so," said Emily, "the audience won't know what they're missing you know, and your sister likely has been detained in some perfectly reasonable way. Besides, an old friend, how could she help going when he had come all this way to see her? And as for accidents, why if there had been an accident we should likely have heard of it by this time. Cars like that aren't very thick in these parts, and there would be plenty about them to identify them, even if they were unconscious and couldn't tell who they were."

But Emily's calm suggestions did not serve to quiet Gloria's troubled heart. Then eight o'clock hurried on, it was time to go to the meeting, and still Vanna had not come! There was nothing to do but go without her.

Gloria noticed that Robert Carroll was exceedingly grave as they talked it over just before leaving the house and took no part in the conversation. Later during the singing it seemed to her that his voice bore a quality that had not been there before, an exceeding sweetness and delicacy like the white burning of a soul that has been, and is going through the fire. She sensed that he felt it keenly that Vanna had not come back for her engagement, and then wondered if that was purely imagination. Oh, surely, surely Vanna would not do this to him willingly! She had seemed so friendly, so wholly interested in what they were all doing, so happy in the company of Carroll and the rest! She could not be going to turn from them to that viper Zane! Could it be that she did not see how much finer these men were than he? Could it be that she would really weigh him against them even for a moment? Was it possible that Vanna was still considering marrying Zane?

Her mind in a tumult, hovering between indignation and fear, she went through her part or rather Vanna's part, of the evenings's program, somehow got through the smiles and appreciation after the meeting, and went out under the quiet stars with the two young men.

She said very little on the way home, letting Murray do most of the talking, with a word now and then from Carroll, who was driving them in his own car this evening.

It was when they reached the house that Murray turned to her and said in a low tone:

"You are worried, more worried than you are letting us know."

"Oh, yes!" said Gloria with a deep drawn breath that sounded almost like a sob. "I am terribly worried. If she isn't home yet I don't know what I shall do! You see I don't trust the man she went with! I didn't want her to go. I don't think she quite trusts him either! But she thought she had to go for a little while because he had come so far! But—I seemed to know it was going to turn out this way! Only Vanna was so sure she could make him bring her back in time. She *wanted* to get back. I'm very sure she did!"

Her tone was excited and her words reached the front seat where Carroll sat seeming not to listen.

"Well," said Murray, "we'll come in and see if there is any word or we can be of service. How about it, Bob?"

"Yes, you go in," said Robert Carroll solemnly. "I'll just sit here."

Gloria hurried in, but there was no word from Vanna, though Emily Hastings said she had sat close to the telephone all the evening. There hadn't been a call.

Murray suggested that they call up the chief operator and get the wire tested out to be sure it was working all right, and they did this, showing that it was in perfect order.

"All right, now," said Murray giving Gloria a compassionate look, "suppose Bob and I scout around and see if we can get any trace of them? Would you like to come along or will you stay here? She might return at any minute now of course."

"I'll stay here, I think. If anything has happened I may be needed," said Gloria shutting her white teeth sharply into her lower lip to keep it from trembling as she followed Murray to the front door.

Murray gave her a quick glance and laid his hand briefly on hers.

"Poor child!" he said softly, with an accent that almost sounded like "Dear" child! Then quickly added: "We have a great God! Remember He's your Father, too, now. I'll be praying."

She looked at him through a glitter of tears.

Just then Emily swung open the sitting room door and came out to the hall and there was no more opportunity to talk. He gave her hand another quick grasp and hurried away, calling back, "We'll telephone of course if we find out anything. In any case we'll telephone occasionally to see if you have had word." Then he was gone and Gloria went up to her room to struggle with her wild fears, and try to learn how to trust her heavenly Father, till at last she dropped upon her knees beside her bed.

XII

Robert Carroll started the car into the darkness. "I wonder if this is the best direction to take?" said Murray looking at his silent companion with a troubled frown. "Perhaps we should have gotten a better description of the car before we started."

"We don't need it," said Carroll briefly. "I saw the car and this is the way they went."

"You saw the car!" exclaimed Murray. "Why didn't you say something about it, old fellow?"

"Well, I didn't see any point in doing so," answered the tall fellow gravely. "I saw it. I'd know what to look for. It's cream-colored, low, stream-lined and fairly screaming with chromium, the most expensive piece of machinery that could be bought I fancy," and he named its make.

Murray gave a low exclamation and sat thoughtful for a minute, then he asked:

"Where were you, Bob? How did you happen to see them?"

"I was just coming out of the meadow lot down at my place. Sam had left the bars down when he drove in and I came over that way to put them up again. I was in overalls!"

Murray gave a whistle and grinned through the darkness.

"Man! That was tough luck! But I don't fancy that would make any difference with her. Perhaps she didn't see you."

"Yes, she saw me," said Carroll grimly. "She waved her hand and called out something. The only word I thought I got was 'back', but they were going at such a pace I wasn't sure, and they were gone almost before they were there. Boy! I hope that man can drive! He was going at a cruel pace, if anything got in the way!"

Murray was silent a long time watching the outline of his friend's face in the dim starlight. At last he spoke:

"I had a wonderful talk with Gloria just before you came this afternoon, Bob. She said she knew she was a sinner and she wanted to be born again!"

"Praise the Lord!" cried Robert, although his heart winced even as he said it.

"I tried purposely to make it hard for her," said Murray, "but I'm sure she understands and is saved."

"Oh, I'm so glad!" said Robert. "Glad most of all for the joy that it brings to our Father and our Saviour in the presence of the angels. But I'm glad for her sake, and for yours, too, old man!"

His voice was husky. "I guess it means happiness for you, and you know I rejoice in that! Even if—Vanna——!"

He broke off, not daring to put into words the possibility that came to him.

After a thoughtful silence Murray spoke again.

"You don't know yet for sure that Vanna deliberately chose not to turn up to-night, Bob. At any rate the path doesn't seem to lead you away from her just yet. You certainly couldn't drop her now when she's lost! Has it struck you, Bob, that it is the Lord now who is throwing us back with the girls? This search to-night was not of our seeking nor planning."

"I guess you're right, Murray," answered Robert slowly. "If my own cup is too bitter,—and I guess it is—it's no more than my Master had." He spoke reverently, with deep feeling. "And, if that's the case let's sing Hallelujah! We oughtn't to be downhearted if we are where the Lord wants us. Now, here's the crossroads. Which way would you say a man like that would have taken?"

"Well, if he's a stranger hereabouts and it was daylight he would have chosen the way to the right because it is beautiful, but if he's anxious to lure her back home he would have gone to the left, and civilization."

"We'll take a chance on the way to the left then. He didn't look much to me like a man who was noticing the beauties of nature, if you ask me."

So they turned to the left and drove swiftly through the night with a definite intention of finding out whether that cream-colored car had passed a certain point going south early that afternoon.

It was an hour later that they telephoned back to Gloria. They had heard of the car going north a little before noon, but it had not come back that way, and finding there had been no phone call at Gloria's end of the wire they turned away heavy-burdened.

"We'd better go back the other way, and take the right hand turn," said Robert Carroll, distress sounding in his voice. "I don't know just how we are going to proceed with this search or what we can do when we find anybody, but I feel we should go on."

On they went into the night, penetrating roads that they knew well, even visiting several places tucked away in seclusion among the hills where a man would be likely to take a girl to dinner, questionable places from their own point of view, but they searched carefully for a cream-colored car, and in several instances went inside and studied the patrons from a shadowed vantage point. If Matilda Coulter could only have got a spotlight on these two she certainly would have made the countryside ring with tales of that night. But these two were wise and heaven-led, and kept well out of notice. And so went on their fruitless search. No cream-colored car could be found, and no trace of it.

"That car would have gone far in a short time!" mused Murray at last when they came away from the farthest outpost in the direction they had taken.

"Yes," said Robert despondently. "There's nothing in this direction now for more than fifty miles, I doubt whether it's worth our while to go on this way. You know, they may have taken the round-about way home, up over the mountain, and so approached Afton from above. In that case there would be good excuse for their being so late, for there are many turnings where a stranger might lose his way."

"Well, shall we take the cut across near Shillingsworth? That would bring us around near the house, and there's no public phone around here. She may be back by this time. It's an hour and a half since we phoned."

In silence the two took the long lonely ride over high hills and across the top of a mountain, coming around at last through little sleeping Afton, to the one house in the town where lights burned steadily over the whole lower part of the house.

Gloria met them at the door. She had been watching at the window of her dark room, listening for a car, and was down before they reached the house. Her face was very white, and her eyes large and dark and frightened. They did not need to ask if the wanderer had returned yet. Her face told the story.

"You are to come in and have some coffee," she said huskily and they knew that there were tears in her voice.

"I have been thinking," she said as she handed them the cups of fragrant coffee, "I suppose I am very foolish to worry so. At home we would think nothing of it if Vanna stayed out much later than this. In our set a group will go from one night club to another, eating, drinking and dancing, and come home at dawn, perhaps, or even later."

She studied the faces of the two young men before her. In her vigil she had known she must tell them this. They had a right to know what she and Vanna had been accustomed to. She expected them to be shocked, to turn away as if they had had enough. Deep searching of her soul had told her what a difference lay between her life and the life these young men had led.

But surprisingly they looked as if they had understood this.

"Yes,—of course,—" said Murray, his eyes down on his cup.

"I had thought of that," said Robert almost sorrowfully. "You should not be—unduly—frightened!"

He was trying to cheer her, and she saw he was deeply moved himself.

"I would not be worried," she said, trying to brighten for their sakes, "only Vanna knows how such late hours would be regarded here, and I'm quite sure she would want to let me know if she had been unavoidably detained. That's why I thought of an accident —with such a reckless driver!"

"There are no precipices, or dangerous pieces of road hereabouts," said Robert. "I am sure we would have heard if there had been a big smashup anywhere near us. I did quite a little telephoning, and made enquiries at a place where such things are known. None has been reported in this locality."

"I really feel that man is at the bottom of this," said Gloria, letting the worry come into her voice again. "I know he is determined to have his way, and I know he is a heavy drinker at times."

Robert Carroll's face hardened, and his lips set in thin determined lines.

"But it is of no use for you two to stay out any longer now," went on Gloria. "I'm quite sure of that. You can't do anything till morning, and by that time we surely will get some word. You'd better get some rest. Besides, you've made a thorough search of all the roads near here. What more could you do till daylight and people were up to be questioned?"

"We couldn't," said Murray, "except hang around and go out to meet them, and I fancy if they are coming home and have just lost their way or had a blowout they wouldn't really welcome us."

"No," said Gloria, "I don't suppose Mr. Zane would, and that wouldn't make it any easier for Vanna.

So, now won't you both go home and go to bed? I can't tell you how grateful I am for what you have done, and I'm just going to trust that everything will be all right and they'll come back before long now. I'm sure Vanna will insist—unless of course there has been an accident!"

"Wait, Bob, I've had a thought," said Murray, "isn't there a train from anywhere coming through Ripley after midnight?"

Robert shook his head.

"Only a way train, a freight. It comes from up the state. They would hardly have connected with that I think. But we'll start out again as soon as dawn comes."

"Then why not stay here with me?" said Murray.

Robert considered a moment, then shook his head.

"No," he said, "there's another phone call I'd like to make before I start out, and I'd better use my own wire. It's a private one and these up here are all party lines. We don't want to broadcast this thing I take it."

"Oh, no!" said Gloria sharply, and thought of her cousin Joan and her aunt Miranda.

"All right, let's go! We ought to get two hours of sleep before dawn." He looked at his watch.

"Well, then perhaps I'd better go with you, Bob," said Murray, "save you the trip up in the morning."

"No," said Robert giving a quick look toward Gloria. "You may be needed here."

"Well, you can take our car of course," said Gloria, "and save his coming back."

So it was arranged, the young men took their departure again, and Gloria was left to her terrible vigil at her dark window.

XIII

When Vanna got into the luxurious car and was sped away into the glorious sunshiny day her heart sank. She distinctly did not want to go. She felt that she might be losing something interesting by being away even for an hour, and the company of this man who was so insistent upon taking her away to visit with himself had ceased to be interesting to her. The question of a possible closer relationship between herself and him which she had been considering when she came up had drifted completely out of her mind, and now that it was brought to view again she wondered why she had ever been uncertain about it.

Moreover, a vague premonition hovered over her and would not let her forget her sister's warning. Well, of course, that was silly, but what if something should happen, some accident, and she be late at the meeting after all their preparation? How disappointed they would all be! How disappointed she would be herself!

She knew that to-night the meeting was of especial moment to Robert Carroll. He had planned it long for this special region, he had worked and prayed for it, he had made several trips to remote districts to get some prodigal sons who never heard a message to promise to come, and he had told her about some of them. She would feel personally disloyal to him and his plans if she failed him to-night, especially in that solo that he sang with so much feeling, that was intended to come at the close of Murray MacRae's address. She loved to play that accompaniment for him because while she was doing it she had a strange ecstatic feeling that she was working with him, helping him to do a great thing that in some mysterious way affected destinies.

"You're not listening!" said Emory Zane looking down at her with a haughty frown. "You act to me as if you had left your real self behind."

She came back to the present with a start. Of course, it was foolish to think of not getting back in time. She would insist on that, and of course now she had come she must be polite and talk, so she roused herself and threw him a careless little smile.

"Oh, yes, I'm listening," she said, "I was just thinking about some of the things I have left undone in running away like this right in the middle of the day."

"What on earth could you possibly have to do up here that would matter in the least?" he sneered amusedly. "I should think you would be entirely fed up on this place. That's why I came up here, to set you free, but I don't seem to get much thanks for it."

"Oh," laughed Vanna decorously, "that was very kind of you of course, but I'm really having a lovely time up here and don't in the least need to be pitied. I'm quite in love with this part of the world."

Suddenly as they swept along she saw the cornfield in the distance where she had planted a whole row of corn and her heart gave an unexpected little leap as if she had sighted something precious. And was that one of the men walking toward the fence? The color flew into her cheeks. Why, that was Robert Carroll! And he would see her go by! He would wonder! This noisy car! This world-weary face beside her. She would have to explain them when she got back. She had a desperate longing to stop a minute, to have just a word with Robert Carroll, to look into his eyes and let him read in hers that this trip was not her wish, to get an assurance from his eyes that he would understand. But the worst about that costly car in which she was travelling was that it was seen at a distance and it shot by before one could draw breath. Before the thought had really formed in her mind of asking Zane to stop, before even she was quite sure that it was really Robert standing there by the bars, she was upon him.

She gave a little gasp, and waved her hand with a bit of a frantic motion, calling as loudly as she could:

"I'll be back in time!" and then saw him far in the distance behind her.

When the ghastly feeling that settled down upon her had somewhat subsided she found Zane looking at her in curious amusement.

"What possible interest could you have in a common laborer that you should make a demonstration like that?" sneered her escort. "Is he one of the farm hands on your father's place? I should say you were being rather condescending to him!"

Vanna drew a deep breath and tried to put down the awful feeling of indignation that seemed to be choking her, tried to summon a laugh.

"No," she said, a little lilt coming in her voice in spite of herself, "he isn't anybody's farm hand. He's a graduate of two colleges, and that's his own land back there! He's a gentleman!"

"Dressed like that?" said Zane lifting supercilious eyebrows. "In the words of the small street urchins, 'Oh, yeah?'"

"One doesn't do farm work in a frock coat," said Vanna sharply.

"Neither does a gentleman put on overalls," said Zane contemptuously.

"Perhaps your definition of a gentleman and mine would differ," said Vanna, now thoroughly angry. Let's change the subject. We haven't but a short time to ride, let's enjoy this lovely day and this lovely car."

"I'm not so sure that we have but a short time to ride," said the man with a sinister glitter in his dark eyes. "Has your desire to be back so soon anything to do with that country lumpkin back there? If it has I certainly don't intend to let him win out."

"You are making me very angry!" said Vanna haughtily. "If you are going on to talk this way I shall have to demand that you let me out and I'll walk back."

"And suppose I didn't stop?" asked the smooth voice.

"Well, then I might have to jump out anyway!" said Vanna, "only that would be rather messy for us both, wouldn't it?" She was very angry now, but she did not want him to see it and she was trying desperately to give an amusing turn to the conversation.

"Come," she went on glancing at her wrist watch, "we've got an hour to ride and then we must turn back. Two hours is positively all that I can spare you this afternoon. Please let's make it as pleasant as possible."

"Assuredly!" said the smooth voice giving her another narrow, vexed glance. But immediately his manner changed and he began to talk pleasantly.

"See that wooded hillside over there? Those are pines. They are really lovely, aren't they? But you should see the Black Forest as I have seen it," and he was off into a reminiscence of some of his foreign adventures.

He could talk most fascinatingly when he chose. Just now he chose. It was his marvellous gift of conversation that had first interested Vanna in him. He knew how to describe an Italian sky, or an adventure on a snow clad mountain, or a perilous voyage at sea, or the depths of a treacherous jungle, till one forgot all else in listening.

Vanna was charmed into forgetting her own present peculiar form of tortured uneasiness, and listening, regained some degree of her first respect for the man, and interst in his charms. There was a mysterious lure in his glance when he was like this, and Vanna felt more respect for her own first judgment of him, more of her initial confidence.

For an hour this went on until he had her thoroughly in sympathy with his mood, until her eyes began to respond to his expression with a merry interest, and she was laughing and answering in a natural way.

Then suddenly, in just an hour, as if the alarm had been set in her mind and had gone off with a whirr, she roused to the fact that it was time to turn back.

"Well, this has been lovely," she said heartily. "I've enjoyed your descriptions so much. It is wonderful to hear such experiences from one who has passed through them. But now, I'm sorry, the hour is up and I shall have to ask you to turn back."

But the speed of the great car did not lessen one iota. In fact it fairly seemed to take warning and leap forward to greater speed and she felt the wind whipping her cheeks.

Her heart began to beat very fast now. She knew she was going to get angry again. She was not used to such high-handed ways. She cast a furtive glance at his side face and saw that it had hardened into cold stubbornness with that haughty sneer lying in wait about his lips like a wild snarling animal waiting to leap upon one's dearest wish.

"Please!" she said gently, looking at him with the calmness of a lady claiming his gallantry.

But the car went flying on.

At last he broke the silence.

"You didn't imagine that I really would bring you back in an hour did you? You didn't suppose I would take the trouble to come all this way up after you for a few minutes' ride, or a call, did you?"

"I'm sorry," she said coldly. "You didn't let me know you were coming or I would have forbidden you. I certainly did not expect you, I have made an engagement that I must in honor keep."

"An engagement with a country lout!" sneered the

man amusedly, and then it was as if the lion lying in wait about his lips sprang out and clawed about her heart.

The car leaped forward up steep inclines now, climbing a mountain with vast views in every direction, and the sun a great red ball of majesty sinking down the opal sky. Farther and farther from home now, and her watch fairly flying, the sun sinking lower and lower.

"I understood that you promised me you would get me back for my appointment at five o'clock." She spoke through the breathless rushing silence.

"No, I didn't promise. Think back and see what I did say. I said have it your own way. But I knew when I got you into my car it would be my way, not yours!"

"Oh!" said Vanna in a very small voice and sat thinking that over for a time. She wondered. Was that the way he had treated his wives when they were once in his power? Well, here was one who would never again be in his power if she could help it. But could she? Was he somehow by this ride planning to get her in his power in such a way that she would have to yield to his wishes? She shuddered and sat trying to think what to do.

This was no time for mere anger. Anger would get her nowhere she was sure. The furtive glances she cast his way told her that he was playing a favorite game now, and that he would play his own part skillfully and firmly. She need not hope to win by using her usual weapons of hauteur and reserve. He had preempted those for himself.

"Just what do you expect to gain by acting this way?" she asked him at last, trying to make her tone quite calm and commonplace, although she had much ado to keep her voice steady.

"I expect to make you have a delightful evening when you come to yourself and give up your childishness."

After considering this for several minutes, she asked:

"And you don't think that possibly you'll end up by making me hate you?"

He laughed at that.

"Hate is akin to love, you know. Many a woman has come to the greatest love of her life through hate."

A great wave of helplessness came sickeningly over her at that, and she suddenly felt like putting her head down and weeping. Oh, if she had only listened to Gloria! And now she began to wonder why in the world she came with this man. Why did she not send him on his way at once, just as she would have done with anybody at home if she had another engagement? Why had she ever been such a fool as to think of him for a moment as a possible friend?

After a long time she said through shut teeth that had suddenly taken to chattering as if she were cold:

"Then I shall certainly endeavor not to hate you!"

He laughed again, and looked at her. Was she coming around?

"You are getting facetious!" he said. "I think you will soon be recovering. A woman likes to find her master."

A still coldness settled down over Vanna's heart, and something warned her that she must go very carefully. This was no ordinary man. This was a man of the world, experienced, sophisticated to the last degree! She could not hope to pit her feeble girl strength against his malignant will. She recalled certain things she had recently been hearing concerning Satan as the prince of the power of the air, and shuddered again as she caught another glimpse of his handsome and now hateful face. Then she knew that she was frightened. Terribly frightened! And her first thought was of Robert Carroll. If she only had some kind of a broadcasting instrument whereby she could send him a message, an S.O.S. How quickly he would come for her. He would save her she was sure.

But she had only her mind. Was it possible for one mind to reach another across the space of miles? She had heard much talk of thought transference. Was it true? If she concentrated her mind on thinking of him and calling for his help, could he hear? For several consecutive minutes she sat, her eyes cast down, trying to send her mind across the great spaces to where she had seen him last: "Robert! Robert Carroll! Come and help me! Help! Help! Help!"

But her overwrought mind kept jerking back to the present and thinking how impossible it was for Robert Carroll to hear! That might be all very well for a theory, but she knew too little about it to put it to any practical use now in her need.

But there was Robert Carroll's God! He would call upon his God if he were in trouble. If she only had a right to call upon Robert Carroll's God!

"Oh, God!" her heart cried groping through the twilight pearliness, up through the gay colored clouds overhead, "Oh, God, find some way to help me for Robert Carroll's sake who loves You!" her heart kept saying it over and over.

The sun had gone down sharply, and left the mountains in a dark purply haze, laying their piny-plumed cheeks against the breast of the sky, and all the air was luminous with lovely light.

Down in the valleys off in the distance there were little nestling villages with dots of lighted windows beginning to show against the valley dusk, and the stern image by her side went driving madly on, never taking his eyes off the wheel, the miles leaping by with maddening haste. She looked at the speedometer and was alarmed at the pace they were making. She watched the road leap away and wished she dared jump out and dash back out of this man's sight as the road was doing! At last she summoned voice again to speak:

"Would you mind telling me your plans?"

Her voice was sweetly steady now as if she were entirely in accord with his purposes.

"Not at all," he said briskly, quite ready to forgive her if she would be reasonable. "We are going to a place I've heard of where we can get a fine dinner, and plenty to drink, and where they have a good orchestra and we can dance, and then we are going to sit down and have a talk in which we shall come to an understanding. After that we will make our plans."

"Your plans, you mean?"

"Yes, if you want to put it that way." He smiled that supercilious smile again, "But I'm expecting by that time that they will be your plans also. I'm not without some worldly experience you know." The smile he gave her now made her desire never to see his hateful face again.

She struggled with her feelings. She did not easily yield to anyone who tried to coerce her. But she knew this man to be more than her match this time. He had her in his power. She must wait. She must think.

In silence the night settled down about them. She said nothing more and he said nothing. The way ran through the darkness of deep forest land, and then wound down, farther and farther, into pitch dark valleys and up again, but still more and more down, and less and less up. She wished she had noted the mileage when they started. How far were they from Afton?

Five o'clock had passed long since. Six o'clock, and seven had come and gone. They would be on their way to meeting now, and what would they think of her? "Oh, God, for Robert Carroll's sake——"

It was after eight o'clock, if she could judge by her weariness, when having skirted the edge of a fairly large town they drove up a hillside into a sharp turn among the trees and stopped before a heavily curtained, dimly-lighted house, where a number of cars were parked along the side of the drive. The place did not look attractive. It filled her with distrust. Would she find someone to help her in this place, or some way of escape?

It was too late now to get back for the meeting of course. That must be well under way, and what did they think of her, a deserter? But it was possibly not too late to get back before midnight. Or was it? She tried in her weary mind to calculate the hours they had been on the way in that fast flying car. But she must be on the alert and take any chance that offered.

"Come! This is the place!" said her escort and

there was actually pleasant anticipation in his voice.

She followed him silently, hating every step she took, wondering if perhaps this was the way God was taking to cure her of her insane interest in this terrible man? Wondering if it was her punishment for insisting on going to ride with him against Gloria's earnest plea?

He seated her for a moment in a sort of reception room and went to speak to a waiter. Her glance went hurrying around the room for possible escape, but she dared not attempt it yet. If she tried to dart out the door with Zane standing over there in full sight of her a word from him would have a dozen men at once after her. She had no hope of escape that way. She must bide her time.

He came back to her in a moment and she forced a haughty little smile, a smile that seemed to say to him that she was here now, could not help herself, and she would make the best of it. Perhaps that was the way he read it for he smiled down at her as if nothing had happened between them.

"Yes, this is the place," he said, "I was sure I was on the right road. Now, dinner is ready at once. I'm going to look over the tables and see which is best. The dressing room is through that door and up some stairs to your right. Would you like to go and powder your nose before we eat?"

Silently acquiescing she went toward the door to which he had pointed. It led to a short lighted stairway. She could hear voices up there. As she closed the door behind her she felt a tiny draught of air blowing across her hot cheeks and drawing a deep breath she turned toward it and discovered a door, unlatched, that led outside. Someone had forgotten to fasten it. She pushed it softly and stepped through, out to a stone doorstep with lilac bushes sheltering it on either side in great thick clumps. Instinct led her to slip behind one of these and there she stood with her heart beating wildly. What should she do now? She could not stay here. He would inevitably discover her, and that right quickly.

Should she dare to run out to the car and drive

away in it? But she remembered seeing him lock the car and put the key in his pocket. Her heart sank. No hope of getting away that way. And even if she could she would soon be caught. He would send out word to the police in every direction that she had stolen his car. She could not hope to get away with that.

But how should she get away? She could not walk all the distance to that village they had passed.

Then up the driveway with two bright lights streaming ahead, and noisy clatter, came a delivery truck, thrashing past her hiding place and coming to a halt near to the regions of the kitchen. Her resolve was taken at once.

She waited till the delivery boy swung down with his basket and went noisily into the kitchen. Then she flew like some shadowy bird of the night across the drive and put herself on the other side of his truck, standing in the shadow waiting for his return, trying to remember how much money she had along with her. How thankful she was that her father had brought them up to carry money enough along for an emergency. It had been a habit with her always. But she couldn't remember how much she had. There had been so little need for money in Afton.

But there was no time to calculate. The delivery boy was coming back with his empty basket and his hands full of cake that some one in the kitchen had given him. Now was her time.

"Could you take me back to the village with you?" she spoke out of the shadow. "I'll give you five dollars if you will."

The boy's jaws paused in their chewing for a second as he surveyed her white face and delicate dress, then he shifted his cake to his cheek and said jovially, "Five bucks? Sure, sister. Hop in!"

He reached down a sticky hand and pulled her up to the seat then whirled his truck noisily about as if it had been a toy, and stepped on the gas.

Vanna shrank back into the shadow of the truck as they shot past the hooded windows and doors. It was all silent. No one was after her yet. Zane would not have discovered her absence so soon. He would wait perhaps a few minutes before making an alarm, or sending some attendant up to the dressing room for her.

She sat breathless as they thundered down the road, almost laughing hysterically at the contrast between this and her ride up to this place.

She found herself clinging to the seat frantically, expecting momently to be thrown out as the truck bumped wildly down the dark hills, and over the humpy road that she had not noticed on her way up because of the resilient springs and soft upholstery. Here was a seamier side of life than even living on a farm and doing one's own work. Or was this perhaps a part of farm life? Would one perhaps have to ride on trucks sometimes? Well, better far a truck and peace in the heart, than luxury, terror, anger, hate.

"What train you lowing ta take?" the truck driver asked when the last mouthful of cake had disappeared, and he had wiped his mouth with the back of his hand, and his hand on the leg of his trousers, and turned to look her over.

"Why, I'm not sure just the exact time it goes," said Vanna, "that's why I am in such a hurry. I haven't any timetable. You don't happen to know about the trains, do you?"

"Well, there's a train around nine thirty ur ten goes through ta Portland, but it's a way train, an' powerful slow. I guess you could make that. It generally takes me ten ur fifteen minutes ta make this run."

He lit a cheap cigarette, took a puff or two, and leaning back gave her a friendly side glance.

"You work up ta that place?"

Vanna caught her breath and was about to make a haughty negative reply when she realized a vantage.

"No," she said with a slight drawl of indifference, "I didn't like the looks of things."

"Don't blame ya!" said the lad approvingly. "It's a tough joint. Wouldn't want my sister ta stay in a dump like that, though times are hard an' ya can't be too choosy of course. Come far?"

"Well, not so far," said Vanna. "It's this side of Portland," she added, "in the country. I can't thank you enough for taking me to the train. I just couldn't see staying there all night."

"Don't blame ya a bit. Well, I'm glad to help ya out."

The boy wasn't much older than Brandon she decided and she looked at him thankfully, and wondered what attitude he would take, just supposing Emory Zane should come on after her and demand that the boy give her up, saying she was his wife, or sister? She felt convinced now that he would stop at nothing to carry out his purposes. She recalled vague stories she had heard of his putting his last wife in the insane asylum, and since her experience of the afternoon and the look on his face when he had declined to take her back she could easily believe them true. She shivered a little, and drew farther back in her corner of the seat. If Zane should hold them up how much help could she hope to get from this boy?

"You cold?" asked the lad suddenly. "I got a piece of burlap back here in the truck that come over a crate of oranges. It's fairly clean ef ya want it round yer shoulders."

He reached back in spite of her protest that she was all right, and brought it forward, shaking it out and laying it clumsily about her shoulders.

"It gets awful chilly sometimes of an evening coming down in these valleys," said the boy. "See them wreaths of fog! Ain't them purty? They look just like feathers sometimes, and then again it gets so thick I can't see a foot ahead of me when I'm bringin' the truck down the mountain in the dark!"

Vanna, in momently fear of being followed, found herself nevertheless greatly entertained by this simple lad's conversation, found it even a comfort to pose as a country girl seeking work. Well, if she heard Zane's car following she would just throw herself on the mercy of this boy, tell him she had run away from a man whom she feared, and perhaps he would stand by her and hide her somewhere.

But the ·moments went by and Emory Zane did not arrive. The village in the valley drew nearer and nearer, till as they entered it they saw far on the upper road the lights of a powerful car shooting alone above the valley. Could that be the cream-colored car? Once it shot out into view with a strange glitter and Vanna was sure, and deeply thankful in her heart, that if it was Zane's car it had taken the high road and she was safely sheltered in the valley.

And so, Vanna Sutherland, daughter of a multimillionaire, rode thankfully up to the little country valley station in a delivery truck, wearing burlap about her shoulders to keep her warm.

But when she got out her purse to pay the truck driver his promised fee he protested, the coveted "five bucks" almost in his grasp.

"Say, I hate to take this! You sure c'n spare it? I'd hate ta rob ya. You've had a rotten deal, goin' ta a place like that fer work. You ain't their kind, anybody c'n see, and ya know I ain't out nuthin' bringing ya down. I druther hev company than not, and it didn't cost me a cent. You better keep that five bucks. You'll need it likely."

But when Vanna insisted he allowed his wistful eyes to linger on the bill again, and his eager hand to grasp it.

"Well, ef you insist—!" he drawled with a grin, "course I *kin* use it," and he stuffed it nonchalantly into his pocket, leaving Vanna to reflect on the gallantry of a mere truck driver. Also the position to which a multimillionaire's daughter could be reduced by circumstances.

XIV

Vanna had no difficulty in making the train. It was late. Later than usual. The truck driver before he left her discovered that fact for her from the loungers who usually made the platform their evening rendezvous.

They were sitting in a row on the edge of the platform with their feet comfortably settled on the nearest rail in earnest converse, and they looked up interested as she alighted from the truck.

Vanna drifted quickly around to the other side of the station and sought for haven within, but found to her dismay that the station, though lighted dimly was locked. She stood leaning dismally against the wall, first on one foot, then on the other, till she spied an empty strawberry crate and sank thankfully down upon it. Vanna, garbed in burlap sitting on a strawberry crate! She laughed softly to herself at the irony of it all, and realized that all her trouble was of her own making.

Just before the freight rambled in like a lazy old bum to whom time meant nothing at all, the young truck driver returned and put her in the caboose. She had to walk the track for about the distance of half a city block before she reached even this haven, and when the boy swung her up the steep steps that seemed like a ladder let down from the skies, she looked about her in dismay. Was that what a caboose was like inside? And that hard seat was all the provision there was for stray travelers like herself!

But nobody apologized and she slipped into the only obvious seat and waited, hours more it seemed, while the train lingered on a sidetrack, shifted back and forth with many a bump and jerk, and outside men up and down the track shouted advice to one another, such things as "Lettur go!" and "Awwright, hold her!" It seemed to the weary frightened brain of Vanna that they were talking about her, and she shrank as far as she could within her burlap drapery, behind a group of dirty tattered bunting flags, of red and green.

At her feet was a clutter of smelly, smoking lanterns, also red and green. She was cold and hungry and downhearted. She was still nervous lest Emory Zane would somehow find her before she got started on this terrible railroad journey. If he should find her he would somehow get control of her again. The thought had become an obsession.

Then the train would seemingly start on its reluctant way, amble along to another brief location, and return to be shunted back and forth.

But finally men seemed to be embarking. The young truck driver returned and spoke a good word for Vanna to the questionable looking man who seemed to be conducting affairs.

"Look after this dame for me, wontya, Ted? She's all right and she's been havin' a rocky time of it."

Then to Vanna who had tried to smile at the forbidding looking conductor he called, as he swung off the now moving train:

"So long, sister! Hope ya get through awwright. Give all the folks my regards!"

With a grin he threw a package of Lifesavers into her lap and disappeared into the darkness. Vanna felt as if she were bereft of her last friend.

She put her head back against the hard window frame that jutted behind her seat and closed her eyes. At least she was off and that was something for which to be thankful. Not even the most zealous of followers could expect to find her at this hour of the night seated in the crude surroundings of a freight caboose. It was terrible but it was safe, at least safe from Emory Zane.

The freight train clattered on with much the same sound and comfort that one might have in a spring wagon. Vanna ached from head to foot, and was cold in spite of her burlap wrap. She was faint from hunger now, too. Presently she thought of her Life-savers and ate them slowly one by one, reflecting on the kindness of a boy's heart.

There was ample time for reflection during that long train ride and Vanna went over her past life up to date and made a number of resolves about the future. She sat face to face with herself and saw that Emory Zane would never have dared go as far as he had that afternoon if she had not encouraged him back at home. Why did she do it? Why was she such a fool?

Then she fell to thinking of her friends in Afton. Would she ever be able to hold up her head among them again? What should she tell them? The whole truth, how she had been detained against her will? What would they think of her choice of friends, of her being willing to go out with a man like Zane?

Question after question beat its way through her weary mind as the train bumped on lazily through the night. Now and then it would come to a jerking halt, and wait till she could hear the treetoads singing, and the crickets in the grass by the tracks, and now and then a marsh frog giving a lazy, sleepy croak. She looked out into the night and saw dark outlines of houses, a scattering handful here and there. Then the train would slat itself into action again and move on a little farther.

Three times they stopped at small towns and shuttled up and down the side tracks, making terrible collisions with a car they were picking up that shattered the little nerve Vanna had left. Then when she had almost given up hope they moved on again.

She dared not look at her watch. She knew the

hour was a frightful one for a woman alone to be returning to Afton. At home it would not have been such a dreadful thing, easily explainable, but she had been in the country long enough to get custom-wise, and her distress was great. She began to strain her eyes out into the darkness to watch for names on stations that she seldom could distinguish till after they were past. She finally ventured to question the grumpy conductor when he returned on one of his infrequent trips to the caboose to get another kind of lantern or flag for use in his mysterious machinations outside.

He assured her briefly that he would tell her when they reached Ripley, and he condescended to tell her the fare and accept it from her silently, almost as if it were a favor to take it.

And then at last, Ripley!

"This train don't usually stop at Ripley without there's freight," volunteered the conductor annoyedly, "but we'll let ya off all righty!"

He helped her down from an immense height when they at last came to an uncertain stop, and she found herself sliding down a bank of cinders to unknown depths of blackness below.

"You'd best stick up here ta the track," he called back to her from the height of the last step of the caboose, "it's better walking up here in the dark. There's the station right down there a piece. You just foller on after the train."

She looked up in dismay from her slippery position, and saw him with his red lantern in his hand, the knotted blue handkerchief about his neck. His gruff countenance in the weird lantern light seemed almost like some seasoned old angel who had been sent down to drop her on the earth from a great height.

There she stood and watched him slip away into the night, herself slipping slowly, down, down, an inch at a time, and struggling to keep her balance. The train seemed to be going away from her so much faster than it had travelled while she was on it! It had gone around a curve now with one last wicked leer from the red lantern at the back, and she was

alone! Alone in what seemed a vast crater of darkness.
But presently when the clatter of the train died away
the earth about her resolved itself into natural night
sounds again. The tree toads in the distance, the crickets near at hand, the chug of a bull frog plunking into
water. Water! There must be a pond or a swamp nearby and if she should inadvertently fall into it what
terrible fate might not be hers. She turned in fright
and scrambled toilsomely up the cinder steep back to
the track as she had been advised, whimpering softly
as she went.

But once firmly standing on the track she found
herself trembling. How long would it be perhaps before another train would come rushing along? And
where would she go, what would she do then? Yet
there was nothing to do but walk that track till she
came to something, and she had much ado to do that.
Ties were not laid with pleasant calculation for a lady's
walk in the dark, and she often missed her footing.
Once she fell and ground the cinders into her hands
and knees, then picked herself up quickly with a frightened look behind and before for that possible train that
might come along on this single track railroad.

She peered into the darkness ahead, and to either
side. They had told her that this was Ripley, but she
could see nothing that could be either Ripley or any
other town. On and on she stumbled from tie to tie,
and sometimes the ties were far apart and sometimes
too near together, and then down she would go again.

The little crickets cricked on, the bull frogs and
the tree toads sang their night song regardless of her
strait, and ahead there were only dark shapes, like
black shadows.

But at last she saw to one side something like a
shed, and now the steep bank sloped gently, till finally
the track was on a level with the general earth and
a plank loomed out of the darkness before her unsteady
feet.

She groped her way across the platform and felt
the door. Yes, that would seem to be a station door,
but it was all dark within. In all her experience of

railroad stations she had not known that one would be closed and dark with no one around to direct. A railroad station had always seemed to be the place to go. She had counted on finding a telephone to call up friends, and a place to wait until they came for her, and there was nothing but darkness!

A little way down the platform there was a tiny flickering uncertain light. A common lantern on a pole, lighting a sign of some sort. She hastened to it and found the faded name of "RIPLEY" being illumined to the lonely night. Why would the night wish to know that this was Ripley? The chimney to the lantern was cracked and a light breeze stole in now and then and wavered the flame till it was almost extinguished. But she managed to make out the lettering and so was glad to be sure at last that she was in Ripley. Well, that was something for which to be thankful.

She peered down at her little wrist watch but the flickering lantern did not give light enough to identify the trifling hands of the trinket. Well, it didn't matter much what time it was. The night had been years long already. And yet there was no trace of dawn in the sky.

She shivered and drew her burlap closer about her shoulders. She went around the end of the station and stood facing what ought to be the town of Ripley as she remembered it from her brief acquaintance in it, but there seemed to be no town, only blank darkness with occasionally a blacker shape looming.

The moon had withdrawn and the stars. A chilly wind was blowing up. There ought to be the road toward Afton, going up a hill, but hill and clouds and sky were all one.

Over there should be a drug store and they would have a telephone. But there was no light anywhere. Every house sound asleep! They would think she was crazy if she attempted to rouse anyone and ask help, or a chance to telephone. She could not forget Matilda Coulter and her field glasses. It suddenly came home to her what a heinous offense this all-night absence of hers would be considered in this old-fashioned town,

and she shrank inexpressibly from meeting any such
fire of criticism as there would surely be if this escapade
of hers should become known. She shrank also from
putting her two friends, Robert and Murray into a
trying situation. They would surely come in for part
of any gossip because they had been so closely associated with her and her sister during the last few
weeks. Meetings everywhere! It would be what Robert
would call a "bad witness." She shut her lips firmly.
Never, for her sake, should he have to go through
anything like that. This was her own affair. She must
get herself out of it the best way she could! Perhaps
it would soon be dawn. She must get back to Afton
before that happened, get inside the house where no
one could see her. A sudden panic seized her. How
long would it take to walk?

She had thought vaguely of a taxi. She had come
in a taxi when she first arrived. But the place was as
bare of taxis as it was of lights. There was nothing
but her two feet to carry her back. And there was
always the fear that Zane might have followed her in
that car that was a wizard for flight, and that he might
overtake her before she reached safety.

She stepped down from the platform, and set her
foot firmly on the road. She must cross the highway
here. Yes, here was a sidewalk. There to the left was
the drug store. She could catch the luminous glow in
one of the red bottles that stood inside the window.
Only a glow, a glimmer, and then it was all gone again.
On the right was the post office. Yes, the sidewalk
turned here. Farther on it would stop and one had to
walk in the road. Then it was still a long way ahead
to Robert's cornfield.

She hurried on, walking on the grass at the side
rather than the pavement, not daring to let her footsteps be heard lest someone should put an inquisitive
head out of a window.

It seemed a curious silent village, like a dead
place. Not even the cry of a sick child to break the stillness. Overhead a bird stirred in the branches and ut-
tered a sleepy chirp. The sound of it made her heart

stand still. Off in the distance the hoot of an owl fairly frightened her. How silly she was! She had never been afraid before.

All along the way were little soft stirrings and whisperings of leaves and night creatures. Beyond the village when she stepped into the road there were the crickets again, and soft gray moths flying about her. One struck her in the face and left her trembling. She began to cry softly, she was so very tired and hungry. Vanna Sutherland crying! And she was almost home, too, almost out of her trouble.

Or was she? She had yet to explain. She shivered and tried to think how she was going to do it, but her mind wouldn't work.

"Oh, God," she whispered, "Oh, Robert's God! Won't you help me? I'm so very tired!"

It was only five miles. She ought not to mind walking that even if she was tired and hungry and a little afraid, for she had done it on the golf course hundreds of times. But the way seemed interminable, and she wasn't just sure she was on the right road either. If it only wasn't so terribly dark!

She tried to brace herself by the memory of whose daughter she was! Of all the proud tales of bravery that belonged in her family. Of the grandmother whom she had never seen and the long line of pioneer puritan ancestors. She tried to take proud steps forward telling herself she was not afraid. She, Vanna Sutherland, had always been able to dominate any situation and she would still do it. A little thing like having to walk a lonely road five miles in the dark was nothing! Then she remembered that she had not been able to dominate Emory Zane that afternoon, and perhaps back of that there was something wrong, some reason why she had failed. She searched around in her mind and found shame lying there. She was ashamed, that was it. It wasn't just that she had to walk through a woods at the dead of night alone. It wasn't that she was tired and hungry and angry. It was that she had done the thing that had brought her into this strait. As she looked back now she knew in her deepest heart that she had known all the time that with her standards, merely her own worldly standards that she had worked out by herself, she never should have had anything to do with Emory Zane. She knew it was playing with fire, and she had knowingly gone on and played, sure that she could control the fire before there would be any danger.

It wasn't anything the world would count as wrong that she had done, just silly prideful things that did not savor of the finest and best,—and she had been learning of late to count these more important than any earthly values. But she felt the sin of her human pride keenly now in this awful night alone, and she hated to think of having to face the truth in the clear glance of Robert Carroll. Oh, it didn't matter whether she told him about it in words or not, he would know. He had eyes that could see, and she dreaded to find that hurt disappointed look in them when she met him. It would be there. It would surely be there. It was something, she imagined, like the eyes of God at the judgment, in lesser degree perhaps.

Suddenly out of the darkness of the sky a shiver of lightning rent across the sky, and a low rumble of thunder followed. Was she going to have to face a thunder storm with all the rest?

She hurried on breathless. The lightning had showed looming darkness ahead, and another flash showed it still more clearly. That was woods, and she must pass there. Perhaps she would be caught in the storm under those tall trees, and trees she knew were dangerous in an electric storm.

She put her head down and began to run, and the lightning came up like some great bright monster and slithered across the sky above her, chasing her into covert.

She gained the woods and the thunder rolled ominously. She stumbled on breathlessly to get out from under the trees before the storm would break, and when she came to the open road again she staggered to the side of the road and sat down to rest. It seemed as though she could not go on another step. One heel had torn loose from her silly little shoe, and every step onward was painful. Presently the shoe itself came off as she hurried on again, and was lost in the darkness. She felt around in the road for it sobbing softly, though she was hardly aware of it, but it evaded her. Even when another long sheet of lightning lit up the sky again her eyes searched in vain for the shoe. She must go on without it!

She hurried forward, the stones hurting her unclad foot. She reached down and took off the other shoe, but that only put both feet at the mercy of the stones. She went back a step or two to try to find the lost shoe again, but saw so sign of it, and the thunder sounded nearer now, long low rumbles. The wind was blowing fiercely and the trees were twisting and writhing like human forms against the hurtling battled clouds whenever the lightning came to show them. Strange that such a storm should come up after such a glorious sunset! Yet the night had been ages long. Perhaps it wasn't the same night. Perhaps she was delirious somewhere in a hospital, and not really walking stocking-footed in a strange dark road at night. Miles she had come. Would she never get there? "God! God! Robert's God! Robert Carroll loves You, God! He believes You can do anything!"

She was talking out loud to herself. There were large cold drops falling now, far apart and very sharp as they splashed into her face. They looked like diamonds as the lightning played with them intermittently. She drew the burlap over her head and crouched as she ran breathlessly on.

She must be coming to Robert Carroll's cornfield pretty soon. That wasn't so far beyond the woods she remembered. What if she should be struck by lightning, fall somewhere near his gateway, and in the morning somebody would find her lying there dead! What terrible things could be said. What unspeakable things could happen! Perhaps Robert or somebody else could be charged with murder, and she not there to prove it wasn't so——!

Wild insane thoughts these were. She recognized

it even as they flashed through her tired brain. But crazy or not she must get away from here. Not a breath must ever touch Robert on her account. Yes, there was his gateway up ahead, and beyond was the top of this little rise in the road. When she reached the top it would be down hill for a little and not such hard going. Her feet were paining her terribly, and there was a cut in the sole of one stocking that put her foot right out on the ground. But what matter! Many people had to go barefoot, why not she? She tried to be stoical but only succeeded in giving a little sad sob.

And then, almost opposite that gate that she was hurrying away from so fast, a light suddenly stabbed her in the eyes, two great red eyes of light, that picked her out in the road and made every line of her sad young figure, every thread of her burlap attire, every nerve in her body it seemed, visible to the world. She stood petrified for an instant just where it had caught her. Then suddenly she sprang into action.

That was a car! That might be Emory Zane. He had come back and been to the house, and not finding her had come out to search again! Well, he might have more human kindness in his nature than she had given him credit for, but he should not find her if she could help it. Never willingly would she look upon his hateful face again. She would rather never get home than have him take her there.

She darted to the right, away from Robert Carroll's gateway, straight into the shadow, creeping stealthily through the darkness, edging herself hurriedly into a great clump of elderberry bushes taller than her head, and drawing the burlap about her, even over her face. She stood so in the driving rain and waited breathless.

"Oh, God! Robert's God!" she prayed, and held her breath to listen!

XV

Robert Carroll had had no very definite plan when he left the Sutherland house and insisted to his friend Murray that he must go home, except that he wanted to get by himself and pray. He had a vague feeling that there still might be something further he could do that night to find the girl who had grown so dear to him.

But he had wanted to be alone, to look into the face of God and listen to his heavenly Father speaking through this sorrow that had come. He wanted to be alone when he took from his Father's hand the cup of bitterness that seemed to be his. His heart was crying out for his beloved in spite of himself and he knew that he must be alone and quiet in order to have it stilled, and that it might be centered again in Christ.

One question kept recurring to him. Why had he been given this great burden for her soul if the Lord did not desire to use him in her salvation? Well, that was something the Lord only could deal with. He could not force her to accept Christ, and if she did not he knew his way was clear before him.

As he drove along now he began to pray that no matter how much it meant of crucifixion to himself, Vanna herself might be saved.

"Just that, dear Lord," he prayed, "and show me

beyond the shadow of a doubt what to do. But, oh, dear Lord, bring her back home safely!"

It was then he topped the hill and his lights shot out their two long bright rays and picked her out as she stood in the road, frightened, weeping, ready to drop.

He knew her at once and his heart leaped up. God had answered a part of his prayer at least. It startled him to have the answer come so quickly even though he was used to receiving startling answers to his prayers.

His car shot forward and came to a stop just where he had seen her standing. He looked all about and strained his eyes but he could see no sign of her. Had it been a mirage, a sort of vision? He was overwrought he knew and weary beyond expression. Such things had been known, visions that were purely imagination.

But this had been so plain! He could not just go on and drive into his own gateway, ignore it utterly. He must be *sure*.

He stepped out and stood on the running board of his car shading his eyes, but there was nothing stirring anywhere except the raindrops falling sharp aslant and pattering on the maple leaves of the trees with which the road was lined.

Vanna had been terrified beyond degree when the car slowed up and stopped opposite her. Her tired brain was sure it was Emory Zane. By the time she had sunk to her knees on the wet ground she was shaking with fear.

"Oh, God," her heart cried out, "if you won't help me for Robert's sake, do it for Jesus' sake! Robert says He died for me. I'm not worth it, but I'll try to be!"

"Vanna!" called Robert softly. "Vanna!" his voice growing clearer. "Oh, Vanna! Where are you?"

There was anguish in his tone and Vanna's spirit leaped up to answer the cry. It was Robert! He was hunting for her!

"Here! Here!" she sobbed, limping out from her

bushes, stumbling over the ditch by the roadside, scrambling and falling into the road.

He was beside her in an instant, stooping to pick her up.

"Oh, my darling!" he said as he lifted her tenderly. "My darling! My precious love!"

He put his face down to hers that was wet with tears and rain, and there in the rain for just an instant he held her close and she lay breathless in wonder. It seemed as if a little sanctuary had suddenly enclosed them, shutting out the elements, shutting them in together.

Then he came to himself and rushed her to the car, pulling off her dripping hat and wet burlap and casting them into the back of the car, taking off his own coat and wrapping it about her.

"Thank God I have found you!" he said. It was as if his soul were talking to itself and he did not know that he was speaking aloud.

Then Vanna summoned voice:

"I spoke to your God," she said awesomely. "I asked Him to help me for Jesus' sake, because I thought if He died for me He must care enough, and then right away you were here!"

Robert turned as if electrified.

"You prayed that?" he said in wonder, his voice shaking.

"Yes," she answered almost sadly, "but I didn't deserve to have Him answer me. That's no way to come to Him, just in terror. Oh, I'm a mess! I don't know why you bothered to come and save me!"

Vanna was crying now.

Robert reached out hungry arms and drew her close to his heart.

"My darling! My precious love!" he murmured with his lips against hers. He was trembling with joy. "I came for the same reason our Saviour came, because I love you!"

"Oh," cried Vanna, "I never knew there was love like this!"

"I knew there was *love*," he said as he looked

down at her face against his breast. "I had it in my own heart, but tell me, do you think you could ever care for me?"

"Care!" lilted Vanna. "My heart turned right over the first time I saw you from the window!"

Then he had to draw her close to him again and set his seal once more upon her lips.

"But, darling! You are cold! Your teeth are chattering!" he said in horror. "What have I been thinking of? Just my own selfish happiness! I must get you home at once!"

"I'm all r-r-right!" she chattered trying to control the chills that shook her.

"And you are crying, dear! How careless I have been!"

"No, I'm laughing!" gurgled Vanna through her tears. "I'm s-s-sorry I'm s-s-such a b-b-baby! But it's s-s-so g-g-good to know you l-l-love me!"

"Precious!" he said reaching for her hands. "But, your hands are like ice. And what is this wet thing you are holding so carefully? Your purse? And what's the other? Let me have it. I must warm your hands. Why, it's *a shoe!*"

"Yes," giggled Vanna. "I lost the heel to the other one, and then I lost the other one itself in the dark, but I couldn't get on very well with only one shoe so I took it off!"

"Oh, my dear!" he said in a hurt tone, feeling down for her wet feet. "Why, child, your feet are sopping wet and you're practically barefoot. Your stockings are in rags. Here, let me rub your feet!"

He took the cold feet and held them in his big warm hands.

"This is terrible!" he said. "We must get you right back to the house where you can get warmed quickly or you will be having pneumonia. I have been all kinds of a fool to waste precious time."

"It wasn't wasted," said Vanna snuggling close to him. "I'd rather have pneumonia than miss this."

"Well, we won't miss anything," he said with deep tenderness in his voice, "but it's my job now to look out for you and I'm getting you home at once. I wish we had a robe to wrap around you, but how about tucking your feet under you? I'll drive as fast as I can and it won't be long. Perhaps there is something in the car to help."

He searched and found a duster in one of the pockets of the car and wrapped her feet up in it. "At least it's dry if it's not very immaculate," he said. "And I'll find that other shoe in the morning before anybody spies it and makes up a tale for the neighborhood about it! Where was it you lost it? Over there where you fell?"

Vanna began to giggle.

"No," she said, "it was just after I passed through the woods. I think it was on the other side of the road in the ditch. I felt around everywhere and didn't get it. But maybe I'm mistaken about where it was. I was so frightened and tired I guess I was confused."

"Well, I'll locate it. Leave this one in the car so I can match them up. Is the heel near the slipper?"

"No, I lost that before I entered the woods."

"All right, now, let's go!"

He slipped back behind the wheel, drew her close to him again with the coat buttoned under her chin.

"It's just come over me," he said as he looked down at her, and felt her hands to see if they were getting warm. "I'm just realizing who it is that I've been daring to make love to. An heiress! And I only a poor farmer with nothing to his name but a little land and an old farmhouse! I ought to be horsewhipped, I know, but somehow I can't help being very happy!"

"I'm learning to cook," said Vanna with an hysterical little giggle. "Emily taught me how to make an apple pie day before yesterday."

"You precious child! As if I'd let you cook!"

"Well, you'd better," said Vanna. "I want to be a real farmer's wife! I'm not going to be cheated out of my share!"

That made another embrace necessary, but it was

a hasty one for he knew he ought to get her home. So he tucked her up again and put his foot on the starter.

"What a selfish brute I am," he grinned down at her, "keeping you here so long just to enjoy you and realize that you are mine—and *His!*" he added softly as he started the car.

"Do you think He will take me for His? I'm no good at all," wailed Vanna, like a little child.

"He took me, dear, and I wasn't even as good as that. It's Christ's righteousness that He looks at, not our own."

Vanna sighed with relief and joy.

"But your poor sister is waiting there for news!" he suddenly exclaimed. "We must hurry!" and he made the car leap forward. "You poor, cold little darling!"

"Oh, I'm warm now," said Vanna nestling close to his shoulder. "But you're all wet where my hair has touched your shirt sleeve, see! It will be you that will catch cold——!"

He then did what he had so many times deplored in other young men driving along the road with a girl, kept one arm about her. However, they were not being troubled with traffic. Not a car had passed, not a soul was abroad, and the storm swept on furiously with rending thunder and sharp bright lightning, but it did not bother them. The road was straight now to Afton, and all too soon for them they arrived.

"But I haven't told you a thing about how it all happened!" said Vanna suddenly as she saw the brightly lighted house. "I ought to have explained at once. I am so ashamed!"

"Never mind explanations now," said the lover, stopping his car. "We want to get you in to the warmth quickly!" and he lifted her out and bore her swiftly through the rain, up the steps to the open door where Gloria waited, the light from the hall making a halo of her hair. Across the street Murray was hurrying, slinging on his coat as he ran, not bothering to wait for an umbrella. Vanna caught a glimpse of it all as she was borne along. There came to her a new sense of the pain and anxiety through which they had all been passing for her sake, and an overwhelming shame came over her.

Robert laid her down on the big old couch in the living room, and drew the couch out in front of the fireplace.

"She is very cold and wet," he said breathlessly, "have you got some hot coffee or something? She must be warmed and dried at once." He knelt beside the couch and busied himself pulling off the wet stockings and rubbing Vanna's cold feet.

Emily appeared coming down the stairs in dressing gown and slippers, her hair straggling about her shoulders. She brought blankets and a pillow. She spread the blankets before the fire.

"Is she hurt?" she asked anxiously. "Was there an accident?"

"No, I think not," said Robert still rubbing away at the little white foot. "I really—haven't had time—" he cast a twinkling look at Vanna, then finished boldly, "haven't had time to ask her yet. I found her walking on the road, *walking* up from Ripley! She was out in all the storm, and she lost one of her shoes. It was hard going."

"I'm all right, really," said Vanna trying to rouse herself from the lethargy that the warmth and brightness brought over her. Now that she was safe she realized that she was terribly tired. It was enough for her just to lie still and watch Robert's face. Robert, who loved her! Amazing fact! Was it really true?

"Get that wet coat off of her," commanded Emily capably, holding the blanket perilously near to the blaze. "Where is Murray? Didn't I see him coming in? Murray!" as he appeared at the door, his face still just a bit anxious, "please bring in another armful of wood. John will be down in a minute I think, but we don't want this fire to die down. Bob, pull that coat off and hang it by the kitchen range to dry. You're all wet yourself, do you know it?"

"It doesn't matter about me," said Robert gaily.

"Well, you two men run out in the kitchen anyway then," said Emily laughing. "I want to get this wet dress off of her. Then I'll roll her in a hot blanket and you can all come back. My goodness! Take this wet hat with you, too, and call to John to bring some turkish towels down. Her hair is sopping wet!"

Lying comfortably rolled in hot blankets at last, her hair rubbed dry and beginning to curl up again in lovely ringlets, Vanna looked up to see a small procession entering the room. Gloria, her face still white and anxious, and Murray, bearing a tray containing a bowl of hot soup, Robert hard behind putting a final turn to the stopper of a hot water bottle, and John bringing up the rear with a basin of warm water, soap and a towel.

Vanna caught a sight of them and began to laugh and then to cry.

"Oh, to think I've kicked up such a fuss as this in the m-m-middle of the n-n-night!" she gurgled out. "I'm so as-s-shamed!"

Robert hurried to put the hot water bottle to her feet and tuck her up warmly.

"Darling!" said Gloria rushing to her side, and down upon her knees beside her sister. "We're just so glad to have you here to make a fuss. It isn't a fuss, it's a celebration! We've been so worried!"

"They also serve who only stand and wait!" said Murray in mock solemnity. Murray was happy for he saw the utter peace and joy in his friend's face. "Will you have your soup now, Madam, or wait until it's cold?"

"What in thunder am I to do with this basin, Emily?" asked John sleepily, eyeing the group indulgently.

It was Robert who seized the basin and the soft linen rag and soap, and quite capably washed Vanna's muddy face and hands and dried them while the others stood around and laughed, and seemed to think there was nothing strange about it.

"You see I fell down in a mud puddle!" exclaimed

Vanna giggling embarrassedly. But Robert went straight ahead with the business in hand as if it had always been his right to look after Vanna's needs. Emily gave him a quick significant look, and caught a wink in John's left eye, but the other two did not seem to notice, and Vanna subsided into the comfort that was gradually stealing over her tired body.

Murray drew up a low stool for Gloria, and held the tray while she fed her sister.

"You know I'm really able to feed myself," laughed Vanna, "but this is all so nice, and I'm perfectly starved!"

"Lie still!" commanded Gloria, the spoon poised carefully. "Just lie still and rest, darling."

"By the way," said John from the doorway, "you haven't told us a thing yet. Was there an accident? There isn't anybody else out on the roadside unconscious or anything that we ought to go out and search for is there?"

"No!" said Vanna sharply. "But he wouldn't deserve searching for if there was!"

"Darling, never mind," said Gloria, "you needn't tell us anything to-night! You're here, that's enough! Don't think about anything else!"

"But I *must!*" said Vanna. "I've got to explain. I wouldn't want to wake up to that, untold, in the morning you know. I want to get it off my mind."

"Don't bother!" said Murray indulgently. "You needn't *ever* explain if you don't want to. We all trust you, don't we, Bob?"

Robert grinned, sitting down on his heels before the fire and holding one wet shirt sleeve out to dry.

"But I must tell," said Vanna determinedly.

"Better let her get it off her mind," said John lazily, leaning against the doorway and drawing his sleepy wife within his arm. "Besides, if there's a duel ahead of us or anything we'd better be prepared. Go ahead, Vanna!"

"Don't bother, darling!" whispered Glory. "I'll tell them in the morning."

"No, Glory," said her sister, "I feel better now, and I'm so ashamed about the whole thing I don't know what to do! Holding up the evening's program, and making all this fuss in the middle of the night!"

"It isn't night any longer," said John Hastings with a wink at the rest. "There's a streak of dawn in the sky, and besides, we're all enjoying the celebration, only I want to know what it's a swellabration of, please."

"Shut up, John!" said his wife laughing, "you're only prolonging the agony!"

"We got by with the singing all right," said Murray soothingly. "Didn't we, Gloria? And you're not to think of that part again. If anything happened that was unpleasant and you want us to go out and lick somebody Bob and I are ready any time, and we'll take John along to make sure. How about it, John?"

"Sure thing!" said John.

And then Vanna looked around on the queerly attired group: Gloria in her butterfly kimono, Emily in a gray flannel wrapper, Robert in his shirt sleeves, Murray collarless with uncombed hair, and John in a bathrobe, and thought how dear they all were, and nearly choked over the spoonful of soup that Gloria had just put in her mouth.

"Hush! I've got to tell," she said when she had recovered speech. "The whole thing was my fault. I shouldn't have gone at all. I knew that man wasn't considered an angel. I knew he drank heavily. But he had come all the way up from home to see me, wanting to take me back again, and I couldn't seem to get rid of him easily. It was a compromise, this going out to ride with him for a couple of hours, and he promised he would get me back by five o'clock. I shouldn't have trusted him, of course. I knew he wasn't always trustworthy, at least people said so. It was just my pride, I guess. I thought I could make him do what I told him to. But when we got out on the highway an hour from here and I tried to make him turn back he pleasantly but absolutely refused. He made me very angry, and I tried to show him I was offended but that didn't work at all. He told me he was going to take me to a place he knew for dinner but he went on and on until it grew dark and late before we got there. I was frightened and angry, but I didn't know what to do. He drove like mad, sixty and seventy-five miles an hour sometimes. I couldn't jump out."

"Oh!" said Gloria hiding her face in her hands and shuddering, "I've been visioning some such thing all the evening!"

Vanna put her hand out and rested it on Gloria's golden head.

"Poor kid!" she said softly. "You warned me! I ought to have listened to you!"

"Was there an accident? Did you go over a cliff or anything?" asked Emily excitedly.

"No," said Vanna, "we stopped quietly enough and went into this road house for dinner, but while he was ordering the table I slipped away and found an outside door. There was a delivery truck just starting back to a town. I didn't know what town, I don't know the name yet, I didn't ask. I begged the driver to take me back with him, told him I wanted to catch a train. I offered him five dollars and he took me willingly enough."

"Oh, I'm so glad you had some money with you!" sighed Gloria. "I found your bag up in the drawer with money in it and I didn't know whether you had more or not."

"Yes, fortunately I had enough, but not much over after I paid my fare. But, Glory, when the train came —it was late, of course, and I sat on a strawberry crate to wait for it—but when it came it was a way freight, and I had to ride in the caboose! That was an experience! I'll tell about it to-morrow."

"A caboose!" said Murray indignantly and cast a startled look at Robert. "I certainly would enjoy hunting up that fellow Zane and giving him his."

"The truck driver thought I was a village girl who had tried for a job at the road house and got turned down," went on Vanna. "He bought me a roll of Lifesavers and introduced me to the individual who ran the train. He looked like a tramp but he turned out to be fairly polite. After we had bumped around for hours and shifted from one side track to another he finally dumped me on a side hill of cinders from the considerable height of the bottom step and advised me to crawl back to the track and follow the train till I found the station. He said that would be Ripley, and I found after considerable labor and time that he was right!"

They were all laughing now as she continued her humorous recital, but there was a mistiness in their eyes, as they watched her tenderly.

"Well, that's about all except the rescue," continued Vanna thoughtfully, her eyes turning toward Robert with a strange sweet light. "I found after a time that it must be Ripley I was in, and I felt my way across the road, but the drug store seemed to have retired from active business and there were no lights anywhere. Remembering certain relatives of mine and their dislike of gossip I naturally refrained from waking any honest Ripleyites and asking them to telephone my friends. I wasn't sure I was on the right road but I started out to find out, and then the storm came up and I lost the heel off one slipper, and then I lost the slipper itself, and had to take off the other one to keep my balance in the dark. When I saw the lights of a car I was afraid it was Emory Zane." Vanna was serious now. "So I hid in the bushes and tried to pray. I thought that was what you all would do. Then, when the car stopped I was terrified and I *had* to depend on God for myself then. I never had any use for people who came to God out of fear, but I guess He took me, so my pride doesn't matter any more."

There was a hush over the little party now till Murray spoke suddenly to Robert:

"Boy! It's a good thing you went home instead of staying with me!"

"And I guess that's about all there is to tell—tonight—isn't it, Robert?"

Vanna's eyes sought Robert's, and he gave her a rare smile.

"All that's going to be told to-night, lady," said Robert rising alertly, "for now I'm going to carry you up to your bed, and you're going to get a much needed sleep. Murray, you bring that hot water bag! Gloria, you and Emily get her tucked up as quick as you can, and see that she sleeps till noon at least to-morrow, and longer if you can manage it!"

Stooping, the tall fellow gathered Vanna as if she had been a child, and trailing a superfluous blanket in his wake, carried her lightly upstairs and laid her on her bed. Gloria and the rest were coming on behind, Murray bringing up the rear with the hot water bag and pillow.

So in a few minutes Vanna lay upon her own soft bed, with silence sweet about her, for the storm had slackened, and a sense of forgiveness and well being upon her soul such as she never remembered to have felt before.

Presently as the house sank away to a belated rest, she thought of Robert's arms about her, and his lips against hers. It was enough to give her peace and deep, deep joy.

The future, like a door open into another day, was there inviting her thought, but she would not glance that way now. Her heart was at rest, such rest as she had not hoped ever to know. There might be perplexing questions, adjustments, unpleasant discussions to pass through ere her love could come to its consummation, there certainly would have to be changed standards, concessions, sacrifices, and perhaps a certain kind of suffering that she did not yet understand, but it was enough now that Robert Carroll loved her and she loved him.

Perhaps, too, she vaguely saw in their love for one another, a seal, a shadow, a picture of another deeper, higher love that ran beneath and above it all. A something settled forever between her soul and Robert's God, something that she did not yet understand, but a something that cast out fear and gave her soul a sense of being cleansed and made fit in spite of sins and mistakes, and indifference of the past. Yet she sensed that she must walk softly all the rest of her days if she would hope to keep this deep underlying delight in her heart.

XVI

The storm had cleared away and the sun shot up all golden next morning as if the night before had been a sweet still time of rest.

Of course they all slept later than usual but habit is a queer thing, and the sunlight in a big quiet room a wonderful alarm clock.

Gloria awoke first and lay quiet thinking how happy she was that Vanna was safely back, wasting a few minutes of anger against the man who had made all the trouble for them. Yet, she reflected, it had been a good thing. Vanna had openly confessed herself in the wrong, her account last night had made it plain that she was pretty well disillusioned about Emory Zane, and best of all, it seemed that Vanna had entered on the new life along with herself.

She lay awhile listening to the quiet morning sounds of creatures waking to the light, calling for their needs, unaccustomedly delayed by sleepy keepers. She heard Emily and John go downstairs, identified the flutter of wings and cackles of satisfaction a bit later as the poultry were being fed. Then her mind went back to Emory Zane again. What had become of him? Had he had to spend the night in hunting for Vanna?

Surely he was gentleman enough to feel some anx-

iety about her. He would be responsible for her, even
though she had willfully deserted him! It wasn't con-
ceivable that he would just go on and do nothing about
it. Even though he might be very angry no man in
decency could just ignore it. How did he think she
would have gotten home? How did he know that she
had money with her? How did he know but that some
terrible thing had happened to her? And he would be
responsible!

They would undoubtedly hear from him some
time during the morning. It was strange he hadn't telephoned! She glanced at the little traveling clock on her
bedside table and saw that it was not so early but that
he might have ventured.

Or perhaps he would drive back to find out if
she were at home, hunting for her all along the way,
hoping to overtake her before she reached her friends.

And when he arrived what should she do? Could
she prevent his seeing Vanna? She decided that she
would make it her business to do that. He seemed to
have some strange baleful influence over Vanna, and
she would protect her!

She did not know that Vanna now was protected
by a new love that utterly shut out such as Emory
Zane forever from her life. So she lay and planned
and worried, and finally stole out of bed, dressing silently, and went downstairs. She was determined to
get Murray, or perhaps both Murray and Robert Carroll to hang around the house during the morning so
that she need not meet Emory Zane single-handed.
Not that she expected he would dare do anything high-
handed. But just the idea of him was horrible to her.
She wanted Emory Zane if he came at all to find that
they were not two unprotected girls alone at his mercy.
He would undoubtedly use smooth words. He was glib
and had a rich vocabulary, a telling way with him,
and eyes that could lure and deceive. As she thought
of it more and more Gloria boiled with wrath at the
way he had treated her sister.

So when the telephone finally did ring Gloria was
ready for it, and out on the front porch sat Murray

MacRae ready to give her moral or physical support, of whichever kind she should stand in need.

The voice that came over the wire was unmistakably Emory Zane, haughty, demanding, insolent. He wished to speak with Miss Vanna Sutherland. How sure he was that she had reached home!

"Who is calling?" asked Gloria in a chilly voice.

"Emory Zane speaking," came the answer in a smug tone.

"Wait a moment." Gloria stepped back from the instrument and laid down the receiver. Should she let Vanna know, or should she carry it through herself?

She went slowly, thoughtfully out on the porch where Murray sat. They had been talking the matter over in low tones, and she had told him what she knew of Zane.

"He is on the phone," she said when she reached him, "ought I to let Vanna know? What shall I say to him?"

Murray looked at her and answered, after an instant's thought:

"I guess she will have to know, won't she? After all she will be the one who will have the ultimate word."

Gloria hurried upstairs and peeked quietly into the room but saw at once that her sister was awake.

"Is that Emory Zane on the telephone?" she asked sharply.

"Yes," said Gloria, "he wants to talk with you. Shall I tell him you are not able?"

"No," said Vanna with a decisive lifting of her chin, "you can tell him I do not wish to speak with him, now, or at any other time."

Gloria drew a long breath of relief and turning sped downstairs. She did not wish to give her sister time to qualify that message. She did not know that Vanna would never qualify that message now.

She hurried to the instrument.

"This is Gloria Sutherland!" she announced crisply. "My sister does not wish to speak with you."

There was an instant's silence and then the man's voice spoke in angry tones.

"Is Vanna there? Is she in the room with you? Tell her to come to the phone at once! I have something important to tell her."

"My sister does not wish to speak with you, Mr. Zane!" repeated Gloria calmly.

"Look here, Gloria——" said the man irritably.

"Miss Sutherland, please," said Gloria freezingly, "I am not Gloria to you."

"Well, Miss Sutherland, then, if you must have it," said the impatient voice, "will you kindly tell your sister that I must speak with her at once? There is an explanation due her of course, and I can give it, a message from your mother she does not understand yet——"

"My sister does not wish to speak to you either now or at any other time!" said Gloria decisively.

"How unfair to refuse a man the opportunity to explain——!"

"There is no possible explanation for what you have done, Mr. Zane," Gloria's voice was final.

"You to be the judge, of course," sneered the angry man. "Have I got to drive over there to get my rights?"

"It would not do you any good to drive over," said Gloria sweetly. "My sister will not see you if you come!" and she hung up the receiver.

"That's fine," said Murray eagerly as she turned back to the porch. "I couldn't help hearing what you said of course, and now I think the best thing we can do is take Vanna away somewhere so if he comes he won't find anybody at home. We'll just give the tip to the Hastings and they needn't go to the door unless they choose. I'd rather horsewhip him of course," he added with a grin, "but perhaps silence and absence will do just as well and save trouble for everybody, for if I once—if *we*—for I know Bob would want to be in on it—if we once began on him there wouldn't be much left to tell the tale. But I suppose it would be better to clear out and leave him to a higher Judge. Suppose you ask Vanna if it will suit her to go, and I'll call up Bob. We ought to get away from here in ten minutes to make sure we don't run into him. Can you make it?"

Gloria hurried upstairs and found her sister nearly dressed. She listened to the plan eagerly.

"That will be grand!" she said. "I don't ever want to see that man again. Oh, you don't know. Some time I'll tell you all he said! Not now. I don't want to spoil the day!" and there was such a light in Vanna's eyes as she spoke that Gloria eyed her with surprised delight and hurried down to tell Murray they would be ready.

Emily was interested at once.

"He won't get anything out of me," she said with a firm setting of her lips. "But here, Vanna's had no breakfast. I'll bring her a glass of milk, and fix a sandwich she can eat on the way. Then you can find a nice place to get dinner along the way. When you come back tell the boys to take the back pasture road. If the coast is clear I'll hang a sheet out the back chamber window. If he is hanging around waiting, or coming back again I'll put out a red blanket. Then you can go away again if necessary and come back later. If it gets dark I'll put a light in that back window when it's all right. Now run along and have a good time. It's a lovely day, and for pity's sake, if anything happens to make you late, call up. We don't want an excitement two nights running."

Fifteen minutes later in the big comfortable Sutherland car they were driving over a back mud road that led across the mountain, a winding way that a stranger would never find, and the haste and excitement of their departure gave a thrill to the expedition that made it all the pleasanter.

The day was perfect, and the four friends, after the experiences of the night before, felt as if their comradeship was all the closer and more precious. Also there was an undertone of deep joy in all their hearts which showed now and then as they spoke of the meetings, and especially of the meeting the night before. There was a spirit of accord and sympathy that had not been before, a greater freedom in the way the

young men spoke of spiritual things, an evident looking to the girls for interest. They spoke of one young
boy who had made a decision for Christ the night
before, and Vanna astonished them by saying: "Oh,
I'm so glad! He was the one you had been praying
for, wasn't he, Robert?"

Gloria who had been present the night before
and watched the struggle of the new convert before he
actually surrendered, and who had been deeply impressed, looked at her sister in amazement. Was this
Vanna, talking like that?

They drove on the mountain top a good deal of
the time till they reached a height where they could
look off in the distance to the blue sea.

"Some day we'll drive over to the shore," said
Murray. "It's not such a long drive if you start at
daylight. You can make it before noon, picnic on the
shore, take a swim, then come home by moonlight!"
and he smiled at Gloria.

"That would be wonderful!" said both the girls in
chorus.

"How Brand would love it up here!" said Vanna
suddenly. "Poor Brand! He's having a tough time of
it this summer. His best friend has gone to Europe
and Dad wouldn't let him go along. He thought he
was too young for that sort of thing without the family.
Mother's worried a lot about his being home this
summer, wanted to send him to a camp, but he thinks
he's too old for that and so he is staying home running
around with all sorts, and I don't believe it's being
any too good for him."

"We must get him up here!" said Robert. "Would
he come?"

"I think he'd love it!" said Gloria. "We haven't
seen much of Brand these last four years, he's been
off at military school, and I feel as if he was almost
a stranger."

"We'll have to see what we can do about getting
him up here," said Robert with a glance at Vanna
that brought the glad light to her eyes, and the color
to her cheeks. How wonderful it was going to be to

have someone who was always interested in what was dear to her!

They found a pleasant place to take dinner, in a little wayside village, a big white house labeled "TEA ROOM."

After lunch they started back home another way.

"We'll show them the falls, shall we Murray?" said Robert.

So they presently penetrated a deep sweet wood and parked their car away from the road in a thicket.

The ground was paved with pine needles, and when they had gone to the brow of the hill where the way sloped down, and an opening in the wood gave vision of rocks and a waterfall below they stood to look and admire and exclaim.

"You have to go down the hill to get the full beauty of the falls," said Murray. "Shall we go, Gloria?"

"Oh, yes," said Gloria.

"I believe I'm lazy," said Vanna. "Would you mind if I just sat down here and watched awhile?"

"I'm lazy too," smiled Robert dropping down by her side. "We can see all the falls we need right from here, children. You go on down and enjoy yourselves."

So Murray slid his arm within Gloria's, sliding his hand along to hold her hand firmly, and support her elbow, and close together they went gaily on down the slippery way until the plumy pines hid them from view. The two sitting at the top of the hill watched and smiled, and drew nearer together.

"Darling, isn't it all wonderful!" said Robert, looking at Vanna earnestly. "You're not sorry, are you?"

"Sorry?" said Vanna turning a gorgeous look upon her lover. "Do I look sorry?" Then she buried her glowing face in the shoulder he offered.

"I've been wondering," said Robert, reaching out for Vanna's hand and gathering it close in his, "how soon are we supposed to tell our wonderful news to the world? Isn't it up to me to go down and see your father right away? I've been quaking at the thought, for what will he think of my presumption?"

"Father's not hard to meet," smiled Vanna, "and he's quite simple in his requirements. Mother's the hard one to please, but she generally succumbs to the inevitable. But, I've been thinking, Dad ought to be up here pretty soon. He promised me when I came that he would get away as soon as he could. We might keep it to ourselves till he comes. Or maybe I'll just tell Gloria? What do you think?"

"And Murray? Or would you rather not?"

"Oh, yes, of course, Murray!"

And while they sat leaning against a great tree trunk heaped over with pine needles discussing their precious secret, Gloria and Murray passed out of sight, down where the water was falling musically among the rocks, and moss and ferns grew everywhere, fringing the pool.

They found a mossy bank where hemlocks draped the entrance and sat down close together, looking up to the blue overhead, looking across to the waterfall that plunged over the great smooth rocks, listening to the drip of the water and the note of a far bird.

"This would be a lovely place to read the rest of that chapter you began on yesterday," suggested Gloria resting her elbows on her knees and her chin in her hands.

Murray swept her a covert endearing glance and pulled his Testament out of his pocket. Soon they were deep into the greatest book in the world. Shoulder to shoulder they sat, their heads bent together, almost touching, the brown head and the gold with glints of sun upon them, touching them, each holding a side of the book, fingers glancing and touching now and again when the pages were turned, a thrill of wonder passing from one to the other, till finally a tender silence fell with only the tinkling of the water and the drowsy song of distant birds for a background of their thoughts, thoughts that had been busy with great questions of eternal values.

Their hands were still holding the book, close together, and there was sweet awareness of the contact, as if some power beyond their own volition was bringing their souls in closer touch. Gloria sat still and held her breath at the sweetness of the moment, not daring to move lest she break the dear spell, lest she should make him think she shrank from his touch, of which he seemed not perhaps to have noticed. Dear, this was, preciously dear, something delicately beautiful that she had not known before. She was afraid to stir, to think, lest it would be gone, and she wanted to hide it deep in her memory when a barren time might come.

But then he turned his gaze which had been out across the valley to the dim blue hills of the distance, and looked tenderly into her eyes, deeply, intimately.

"Isn't it sweet," he said, "to read His word together this way?"

"Oh, it is!" she answered him, a lovely light in her eyes.

He kept his look on her with that reverent intimate loving gaze, and slowly, softly without seeming scarcely to move, his hand beside hers stole about her hand. The thrill of that clasp brought the sweet color into her face, and a light into her eyes he had never seen there before. Then as he still looked deep into her eyes they two seemed to be drawn together by some invisible bond till their lips met.

"I love you, Gloria!" he whispered putting his other arm about her and drawing her close to his breast. "Oh, I love you, my dear! My dear!"

The little book was between them now, her hand in his, holding it. It seemed a lovely omen. She smiled as she lifted her lips to answer his kiss once more, and for a little while they forgot everything else but their two selves.

But presently Murray slipped the book back into his pocket and set their hands both free, and taking her face in his hands lifted it and kissed her eyelids, and the lovely spot on her forehead where the gold hair curled away in little rings.

"But you haven't told me whether you can ever love me," he said suddenly, holding her face back tiptilted so he could look deep into her eyes again.

"Oh, you know I do!" she whispered and reached her lips to his again.

"My beautiful!" he murmured, drawing her close again.

Suddenly Gloria raised her head and her hand stole back into his.

"Murray," she said softly, "this is so sweet I can't bear to break in upon it with a word, but——"

"What is it, sweet?" he answered tenderly, a note of apprehension breaking into his voice. "Have I been too soon? Have I jumped in where angels fear to tread? Don't be afraid to tell me, dear! I would rather know the truth."

"No, no, it is nothing like that," she said bringing her other hand up to stroke his cheek softly. "No, I am glad, glad, glad! So glad you love me and I love you. But there is something about me that you ought to know. I should have told you before, only—I never dreamed there would be any reason why it should matter. I didn't dream of this wonderful thing coming."

"Don't tell me anything unless you want to, dearest!" he said gravely.

"But I want to," said Gloria seriously, "and besides you would be sure to hear it sooner or later. I'd rather tell you myself."

"Perhaps I know it already, dear!"

She gave him a startled look.

"You didn't know that I was to have been married a few days after I came up here, did you?"

Murray took her hand gravely and held it as he bowed his head.

"Yes, I had heard that. Mother told me when I arrived. Mrs. Weatherby told her."

"Oh!" breathed Gloria with relief. "But did she tell you the rest? Did you know that—my—fiance and a dancing girl were shot together in a night club in New York? Shot by the lover of the girl he was with?"

Murray nodded again and regarded her sadly, studying her face keenly, almost anxiously.

"You knew all that and yet you were kind to

me!" she said almost wonderingly. "You, to whom all
that mess must have been awful! It must have made
you see what kind of a life I had lived that I was
going to marry a man like that!"

"It made me see how much you must need my
Lord Jesus!" he said, lifting her hand reverently and
laying his lips on the tips of her fingers. "It sent me to
my knees for you. I began to pray for you that first
night I came, even before I had seen you. Oh, how
my heart ached for you! And now that you have told
me this I can see that perhaps I ought not to have
told you of my love yet. It is so soon since you have
lost one you must have loved——"

"Don't!" she said closing her eyes and drooping
her head. "I don't even think I ever loved him now,
though I thought I did. I thought I was crazy about
him. But he killed all that in me by what he did. It
was as if everything had been nullified and I was left
there alone having to appear to be broken-hearted
when I was only shocked and disgusted. It was as if
everything I had counted dear had been taken away
from me, cut out like a putrefaction. I might not even
have dear memories to comfort me. He had made me
loathe all the memories because I felt they never really
had been mine!"

"Poor darling!" he said tightening the pressure of
his arm about her.

"Oh, it was never anything like this!" she said,
suddenly putting her face down in his neck and beginning to cry. "This is like heaven! I did not know
there could be such love as this, such peace and rest!"

"My precious sweetheart!" he said laying his lips
on her bright hair.

"And the most beautiful part of it all is," she said,
raising her face for a moment all wet with her glad
tears and wreathed in smiles like a rainbow, "you've
shown me how to have rest and peace in my heart!"

It was then the passing shadow which her reference to her former engagement had brought to his eyes
fled away entirely.

"That is the best of all that you have said, dear-

est!" he said and his voice sounded like a hallelujah.
"I don't know what your parents are going to say
when I tell them that I want to make you my wife.
But I'm convinced that our God is with us, and that
He has given you to me as a lifemate. I pray that I
may be able always to make you happy and at rest
and peace. My love, my precious Gloria!"

They came back up the hill at last to the others,
his hand under her arm helping her up the slippery
steep, and she felt as if she were walking among
beautiful clouds.

They made their way slowly home as the twilight
came softly down, taking the meadow road as they
were told, and finding a light burning steadily in the
upper back window for them. So they came laughing
gaily in.

"Is he gone?" asked Gloria peering around the
corner of the doorway into the living room.

"Quite gone," laughed Emily. "I think he is on
his way to a dinner and then home. He spoke about
stopping in Boston."

"What time did he come?"

"Why, about a half hour after you left," said
Emily, "that is, the first time. I told him you were out.
I wasn't sure when you'd be back."

"The *first* time!" said Vanna. "Did he come more
than once?"

"Three times," said John Hastings grinning from
the kitchen door. "The first time he sat in his car sulk-
ing, and when we didn't ask him for dinner he went
away and said he'd be back. Then he came again at
three o'clock and Emily served him a glass of spring
water and said she hadn't heard anything from you."

"Then he went off again and said he'd be back
at five," put in Emily, "and I put out the County
newspaper and the Bible and told him to sit on the
porch and make himself comfortable. Of course it was
possible you might be home for supper at five-thirty.
He waited till almost six and then he knocked on the
door and asked if there wasn't some place he could
telephone to you, but I said you didn't say where you

were going when you went off with a party of friends. Of course, I said, you had relatives around the state and you might have stopped off there, but I couldn't tell him how to get there."

"I am so sorry that you had to bother," said Vanna.

"Oh, it was fun," said Emily. "When it began to get so late he got up and came into the kitchen where I was frying apples to ask me questions. He said you had got offended at something last night and had left him, and he was worried about you. He wanted to know had you really come home, or didn't we know where you were? Because if you were lost he must hunt you. I looked surprised at him and said Oh, no, you got home all right. You caught a train and one of your friends went down in a car and met you, and that seemed to make him furiously mad, so he turned around and walked out to the porch, and called back to me to tell you he would wait now until he heard from you before he came again."

Vanna laughed happily.

"Well, he'll wait a long time," she said with a glad look at Robert.

Then they sat down to the hearty supper that Emily had waiting for them.

XVII

The next evening just as they were coming in from prayer meeting there came a telephone call from Mrs. Sutherland. Vanna went to answer it.

"Emory Zane surely can't have got home yet, can he?" she said to her sister as she went toward the phone.

Gloria flashed an understanding look.

"He might have phoned her from wherever he was," she said. "Is it Mother calling? Well, don't be too much upset. Ask for Dad if she gets imperative."

But Vanna came back from the upper hall where the telephone was located with a troubled look in her eyes.

"Mother says Dad is very sick and we must start home right away to-morrow morning. They brought him home unconscious from the office and he's in a raging fever. They have a trained nurse and two doctors. She says Dad keeps asking if you are all right, Glory."

Gloria gave her sister a stricken look.

"You don't think this is something that Emory Zane is trying to put across do you?" she asked anxiously.

Vanna shook her head.

"No, Mother didn't mention him. I doubt if he's

been back. She said we'd better drive down if we
could get somebody reliable to come with us who
could drive part of the way as she couldn't spare the
chauffeur now to come after the car. But if we couldn't
get an escort we were to come on the train and leave
the car anyway. She said we needn't worry. The doctor
said there was no immediate danger, but it was better
for us to be at home as soon as we conveniently could.
She made me promise we wouldn't fly. She's terribly
afraid of flying you know."

"Well, I think we ought to go at once!" said Gloria rising excitedly. "Do you know if there is a train
yet to-night? That would be the fastest, wouldn't it? If
Dad is sick I want to get to him as soon as possible,
especially since he has asked for me."

"The only night train has gone," said Murray.
"There's nothing now till ten to-morrow morning. Our
fastest train leaves Ripley at six in the evening. That
makes good connections. The day train is slow and
uncertain. I believe you could make better time driving.
Of course Bob and I would go with you. How far is
it? Bob, haven't you got a road map in the car?"

"I have one," said Gloria.

"If we start at daylight," said Robert, lifting his
eyes from the map and looking at Vanna, "we ought to
make it by evening, and that's as well or better than
you can do by train. If you want to start within an
hour and travel all night, why that's so much to the
good."

Vanna looked at Gloria, and Gloria looked at
Murray.

"It would be awfully hard on you boys," she said,
"but I do wish we could start right away."

"It won't be hard on us," said Murray. "We can
take turns sleeping. I'm only wondering if you girls
won't stand the trip better with a good sleep before
you start."

"I'd rather be on the way," said Gloria drawing
a quick sorrowful little breath that sounded all a-trem-
ble.

"Then we'll go!" said Murray. "How about it, Bob, don't you say so?"

"Of course," said Robert looking at his watch, "how soon can you girls be ready?"

"In less than an hour," said Vanna quickly. "We've only suitcases to pack you know."

"I'll put you up a lunch," said Emily. "That helps a lot when you have to keep awake at night."

"It sure does," said Murray cheerily.

"Are you sure the neighborhood won't be scandalized at our starting off at night with two young men?" asked Gloria, looking toward Emily and John.

"Of course not," said Emily, "not in a case of emergency like this anyway, and if they did let them be. But of course there's no need in their knowing. Leave that to me. I'll fix it. Run along and get your things together. Boys, you go home and get your baggage. I'll have some hot coffee for you to start on."

So, just a few minutes before midnight the big Sutherland car silently slipped out the driveway, down the mountain road to Ripley and out into the world, with Murray driving. The girls in the back seat agreed to sleep at least till daylight. The two young men were to take turns driving.

But curled into comfortable positions in the luxurious back seat, neither one of the girls found it easy to go to sleep, though their eyes were closed. Gloria kept going over the way step by step since she left her home, burdened, shamed, distracted, her life broken. And now she was going back with the burden gone from her heart, the shame lifted by a new joy, and life all made new. She was going back into the life she had left so hurriedly and so frantically. There would be the room where the wedding dress hung and all her trousseau, and those colorful bridesmaids' dresses! Would Mother have done anything with them yet? She hadn't thought of them since! And the wedding presents too. Stacks and stacks of them! What had been done about them? But their horror had gone. They meant nothing to her now. She was no longer a heathen widow to be burned on a funeral pyre with a husband who had not thought it worth while to be true to her even until they were married.

Poor Stan. She could feel sorry for him now. He never had half a chance with a family like that and an upbringing like that! Still, no one was without excuse. But he didn't know the Lord. She wished she might have told him. Only if she had known the Lord herself she never would have engaged herself to him. She saw that now.

Yes, she was going back to the old house, and the old friends, but not to her old life, thank God! She had found something new. Even if Murray hadn't told her he loved her, and filled her life with a new interest and wonder, she knew she would never have gone back to the old life. Murray had given her a taste of better things. She would have gone searching for them the rest of her days, even if she never saw Murray again, she told herself. Then she opened her eyes a tiny crack and watched Murray through the fringes as he sat there gravely talking, the dear outline of his head and shoulders against the luminous sky where the moon was about to rise.

And Vanna just frankly arranged herself so she could watch her Robert, and hugged herself to think he was hers. Soon she meant to own him before her world, just as soon as Father was better. Father had a right to know first. She must not, if possible, battle with her mother about anything like that until Father was thoroughly out of danger. She would probably have to tell Gloria though. Gloria would be in sympathy.

Then she fell to wondering about her sister's affairs. Did Gloria realize what adoring glances Murray MacRae cast in her direction? Poor Murray! Of course Gloria wouldn't think she could look at anybody for a long time. It hadn't probably occurred to her that she might be hurting Murray. Perhaps it was a good thing for Murray that the summer had come to so abrupt an end. And yet,—who could tell? Dear Gloria! And

Murray was delightful. He was a dear! Next to Robert he was the finest young man she had ever met.

And just that minute Gloria, in her corner, was feeling sorry for Robert, and wondering whether Vanna had promised to write to him.

Then she fell to worrying about her father once more, her heart gripped with fear about him. If he should die! Oh, if he should die! Dear Dad! And he had been brought up to go to church and hear prayer and Bible reading. Did he know the Lord? She feared not. She had never heard him talk about being saved. Dared she say something to him sometime? Oh, if she could only take Murray up to see him when he got better! Ah, there was going to be much to worry about unless she learned to trust and pray the way Murray did.

And then there was Nance! Poor Nance! She would be another problem! Gloria wondered if she could ever get a bit of the word of God across to Nance who needed it so sorely.

But about that time both of the girls went soundly asleep.

Some time in the night the two in the front seat changed places according to schedule, and once, when Robert was driving and Murray had dozed off they passed through a mountain resort and Robert saw among a line of cars parked in front of a brilliantly lighted hotel, a long cream-colored car bright with chromium, but he shot on ahead and said nothing about it, tenderly glad that it was he and not that other man who was taking Vanna to her home to-night.

At daybreak the girls roused cheerfully and distributed sandwiches and hot coffee from Emily's thermos bottle, and three hours later they stopped for a regular breakfast at a hotel.

There Gloria telephoned home, having to talk to the nurse because her mother was not yet up. The nurse said her father was doing as well as could be expected. He was a very sick man, but the doctor felt that he had a good chance to recover. He was still delirious and probably would be so for several days until the fever broke, but they were hoping for the best.

Gloria went back a little comforted, and brave to go on with the journey. At least she did not have to have that continual fear that her father would be gone before they got home, which fear had haunted her the night before. Then she looked into Murray MacRae's eyes and knew that he would be continually praying with her for her father's life, yes, and for his salvation! What a thought! To belong to a man who was great with God!

The girls insisted on taking their turns at driving during the day, but they were not allowed to stay at it long, and there was continual pressure brought to bear upon them both to rest.

"We can rest afterward," Robert said. "We shall have nothing to do when we get home without you there."

"Nothing to do but plant corn and preach!" mocked Vanna tenderly, and then let her eyes linger on Robert's face with her heart all out there written for him to read. It was hard to think of those two carrying on and she and Gloria not there to help!

"We'd like to cry, you know, but we won't," grinned Robert, as he saw the look in Vanna's eyes. "Better days may come later, bless the Lord!"

And Gloria, who was sitting just then in the back seat with Murray, stole her hand out and crept it into Murray's, quite out of sight of the rest, and he held it hard and fast. Gloria was having to wink very hard to keep the tears back now that she had thought of Murray going back to Afton without her. Why did one have to be separated from loved ones? She had never felt this especially before! In her old world one didn't care much. One went and came and didn't feel much at all. But all things were different now, and besides, she had never before loved anyone as she loved Murray.

They arrived at home a little after nine o'clock in the evening having been delayed by three detours and the traffic of a couple of cities through which they had passed.

The butler opened the door for them and seemed relieved that they had come. He said their mother had retired with a bad headache and had given orders that she should not be disturbed. He said he believed that Mr. Sutherland was no worse, and a moment later the nurse came down and confirmed the word, Mr. Sutherland was about the same. They did not look for an immediate change.

Murray and Robert had come in with them to learn how the sick man was, and lingered a few minutes to speak last words.

Brandon came in looking glum and unhappy, like a stray cat, and was introduced against his will to the two strangers. He lingered watching them furtively.

"Why don't you come on up and visit me for a while when your father gets better," said Robert, turning his winning smile toward the lad. "I've got a farm I'm playing with and I could use another man. In between there's hunting and fishing. Murray here shot a bear last winter, and we have deer in plenty, and wild birds. Like to shoot?"

"I sure do!" said the boy eagerly, his face lighting. "Sure I'll come! Any time you invite me I'll come, as soon as Dad gets better. I'm sick ta death of sticking around here all summer!"

"I can offer a tennis court and a mother who makes gingerbread and cookies," laughed Murray. "I might rake up a girl or two if I tried."

"No girls!" said Brand with a frown. "I'm sick ta death of girls! They spoil everything!"

Brand's sisters laughed amusedly. They knew he was pleased with their two men and they were glad.

The girls had told the chauffeur to be ready to take Murray and Robert in to the city, but Brandon insisted that he would take them himself in his own car, and he did, driving them to their hotel and going in for quite a visit and a midnight supper with them. He came home loud in his praise of them.

"They are white men," he said, frowning at his sisters as if they had scorned them.

Murray and Robert each called up the girls next morning, which greatly lifted the gloom in which they had been plunged. The young men gave blessed Bible verses for the girls' comfort, and they promised to keep in touch by letter and telephone, and be ready to come whenever or whatever the need should be. They promised to pray, moreover, and the tone of their voices was as good as a morning draught of joy. Each came away from the telephone with sparkling eyes and more cheerful countenances.

"You don't seem so very much depressed," said Gloria's mother later in the day when she arose with the shadow of her headache still hanging over her spirit.

"No," said Gloria with a wistful smile. "Did you want me to be, Mother dear?"

Her mother watched her for a minute with a puzzled frown.

"You always were a queer child!" she said. "I'm sure I don't know what to make of you," and she sighed deeply. "You're hopelessly like your father!"

"But you love him a lot, don't you, Mother?" said the girl with a yearning tenderness.

"Why, certainly," said her mother, brushing away a moisture in her eyes and speaking crossly to hide her emotion. She was cold by nature and it annoyed her to be caught showing any tenderness. It wasn't good form in these days.

"That reminds me, Vanna," she said quickly as her other daughter entered the room, "Emory Zane told me he was going up to call on you sometime this summer. What a pity he hadn't got there in time to bring you home. I'm sure he would have been so glad. He has been kindness itself, stopping every day or two to ask after you."

Vanna and Gloria exchanged significant looks.

"He did come, Mother," said Gloria with a stern expression on her usually gentle face. "He came and took Vanna to ride one day and treated her outrageously. He promised to bring her back in time for an engagement she had to play, and then he refused absolutely to turn around, and took her miles and miles away and she had an awful time getting home. If it hadn't been for a kind neighbor who finally met her near home I don't know what might have happened to her."

"But I don't understand," said the mother, "how did Vanna happen to have to get home by herself?"

"Because I ran away from him," said Vanna haughtily. "He was no gentleman, Mother. He refused to take me back. He insisted that I should stay at a road house and dance, and—I was *afraid* of him, Mother. You don't know what he is!"

"How absurd!" said the mother. "Have you been listening to some of those ridiculous tales about the poor man too? Your father has got hold of them and nothing will get them out of his head. But it is just ridiculous. And I'm ashamed of you Vanna! It certainly wasn't polite of you when a man had come all that way to take you for a drive that you should childishly run away from him!"

"No, Mother, it wasn't polite," said Vanna, "and I never mean to be polite to him again. I don't think he'll ever try to come here any more, but if he does I shall not see him. I want that thoroughly understood."

"Vanna! How absurd! You can't be a spiteful child! You don't realize that he is not a boy to be treated like the rest of your boy friends. He is a man of the world, a man of fortune and culture, and you cannot afford to throw away a friendship like that. He is more than ready I feel sure to put himself and his fortune at your feet, and these days there are not so many men with fortunes going begging. I want you to understand that ladies do not behave in such childish ways."

Vanna shut her lips hard together, and then she spoke.

"I'm sorry, Mother, for your sake, but I'm done

with Emory Zane forever!" and Vanna went quietly out of the room and closed the door.

"I cannot think what has come over your sister!" said Mrs. Sutherland to Gloria.

"If you had lived through the night of storm and worry while we waited for her return, you would understand, Mother. You just don't understand, that's all!"

"Yes! So you too have caught the germ of rebellion! Well, I thought when I heard your father had taken you up to that forsaken farm country that trouble would come, and it will probably be a long time before we get you back to normal again. Wild, strange doings! Planting corn in the mud!" and her mother arose with dignity and walked from the room.

Gloria went and stood by the window looking out over the lovely stretch of lawn, bordered now with glowing summer flowers, and felt exceedingly lost and lonely. By and by she went upstairs to find her sister, but Vanna was writing a letter already to Robert, and did not see the loneliness in Gloria's eyes. So Gloria sat down and wrote a letter to Murray, and by lunch time her fortitude was restored. Also both Murray and Robert called up again that evening from New York where they had been all day on business, and that helped a great deal.

But by the time another forty-eight hours had passed both Vanna and Gloria had enough to keep both hands and hearts busy, for the morning papers came out with the announcement that the fine old firm of Sutherland and Brainerd had gone bankrupt, and that Brainerd the friend of years had committed suicide! They had found him in his palatial library with his pistol by his side and a bullet through his brain. He left a note behind him saying that the failure had been all his fault and he could not face the shame of it.

The girls read it with blanched faces and looked at one another.

"Oh, Vanna!" said Gloria. "If you and I had not

learned to know the Lord how could we stand all
this!"

"Isn't that the truth, Glory!" answered Vanna.

But then came their mother wildly downstairs in
her dressing gown, her hair still in its combs, frantic
tears on her face that looked old and haggard without
its smart make-up.

"Now, Vanna, you'll *have* to marry Emory Zane!
You'll *have* to, you know, to save Daddy's business!
You wouldn't let a little freak stand between you and
saving the business would you? Why, Vanna, how
are we to live without money?"

"Mother, how would marrying Emory Zane save
Father's business?"

"Well, it would!" said her mother with emphasis.
"Your father has been under a heavy strain for a
long time financially. That's why he had to come home.
It was all the fault of those foreign agents, something
about the dollar or the price of gold, or else it wasn't,
I forget. Anyway your father was almost distracted,
and I happened to mention it to Mr. Zane one evening
when he was here and he very kindly offered to help.
He said he wouldn't let any price hinder him from
helping your father if it came to that. He spoke as if
things were all but settled between you and himself,
Vanna. He said that it was all in the family, and things
like that——!"

"But, Mother," said Vanna in distress, "how could
you discuss Father's affairs with a stranger? You know
that Father would not like that!"

"Your father might not like it at first, but the
business had to be saved, didn't it? How could we
live otherwise? Why, Vanna, we might even have to
give up this house."

"There are other houses," said Vanna coolly.

"That is ungrateful, Vanna, after your father has
provided a palatial home for you."

"I'm not ungrateful, Mother. I loved it while we
had it, but I think there might be places where we
could be a lot happier than here. And anyhow, Mother,

now the business is gone, and likely the house is gone too, but if Father gets well it won't matter."

"If your father gets well and finds his business gone he will go all to pieces. He will die. Or else he will do what his partner has done," said the mother now suddenly gone tearful again.

"No, Mother, Father wouldn't do that," said Gloria. "Father wouldn't think that was right. Father isn't a coward! And, Mother, it's up to us to keep him from feeling downhearted. We must just be happy and cheerful and do our best to show him that everything will be all right even if he has lost his money. That isn't the greatest loss in the world."

"Yes," said her mother with a sob, "that's what I'm trying to tell Vanna. She must rise to the occasion and marry Emory Zane who is so deeply devoted to her, and then everything will be all right. He has great holdings abroad and no end of money. The depression hasn't even touched him a tiny bit, and he has practically promised me that he will see your father through. It doesn't matter what the paper says, Emory Zane will straighten everything out. He has promised that he will if Vanna marries him."

"I wouldn't trust him around the corner," said Gloria indignantly. "Vanna shall *never* marry him. I would rather we all died of starvation than have Vanna marry that awful man!"

"Gloria," said her mother, "have you turned against me too? Well, you might at least have a little forethought for your sister. If she doesn't marry Emory Zane, and the money is all gone, she won't ever have a *chance* to marry anyone. Who would want a penniless girl. Have you thought of that?"

Vanna suddenly stood up and looked her mother in the eye, speaking very quietly.

"Mother," she said, "you are wasting breath. I shall never marry Emory Zane! And you needn't worry about my never having a chance to get married, I'm going to marry a farmer! I've been engaged for almost a week, a whole wonderful week, and there's his ring on my hand!" And Vanna held out her slim white hand whereon gleamed a lovely ring, a ruby and a pearl set in quaint antique silver.

Mrs. Sutherland gazed in horrified silence for an instant and then became voluble again.

"Stuff and nonsense!" she said, relapsing into the vernacular of her earlier days. "Wearing an old-fashioned ring like that when you might have some of the crown jewels if you wanted them!"

"But I don't want them," said Vanna with a royal smile, "and I love my farmer man! I'd rather be dead than marry the man you want. I'm going to marry Robert Carroll!"

Vanna walked out of the room and left her mother weeping, but Gloria rushed after her sister and threw her arms about her.

"I'm so glad, so glad, Vanna dear!" she whispered. "And I'm going to marry Murray, only don't tell Mother yet for she would think I was indecent so soon after Stan's death!"

"No," said Vanna, smiling, "we won't tell Mother yet, poor dear. She's got enough to do to contend with me for awhile, and, oh, Gloria, it's going to hit her hard to have the fortune gone! I don't think Dad would mind so much if Mother would take it bravely, but she never will!"

"No," said Gloria, "I'm afraid she never will! It's going to be a hard time for awhile, isn't it, Vanna? But, oh, if Father will only get well it won't matter so much!"

But before night Robert and Murray arrived by plane. They had seen the news and had come on to see if there was any way they could help, and the girls realized that their heavenly Father had not left them without earthly human comfort as well as heavenly.

XVIII

The days that followed were full of anxiety and distress, and the newfound faith of the two sisters was tried to the utmost. Their father continued to be critically ill, sometimes seemingly at the point of death, and their mother took to her bed, plunged into deepest distress. They could not rouse her to take a hopeful view of things. It almost seemed at times that she was grieving as much or more over the loss of the fortune than over her husband's critical condition, almost as if sick as he was she was blaming him for not getting up and doing something about it.

Gloria and Vanna slipped in often to their father's bedside, one at a time, and sometimes when the nurse let Gloria stay in her place a few minutes she would kneel softly and pray for her father. Both the girls learned to depend much upon prayer in those hard days.

Things downtown in the office were in chaos. Underlings came and went and sought to get advice, but there was nobody to give advice and the course of the law went on its inexorable way. They were going to lose everything of course. The girls had quietly accepted that as a fact at the first, and it was not troubling them. They scarcely realized what it would mean, they had so many worse things to face just now.

Then one day came Nance, a frightfully haggard, strangely old Nance. Her eyes were sunken deep and had a wild glitter, her voice was harsh, her expression bitter. She looked at Gloria in amazement.

"You're fresh as a rose!" she said enviously. "Maybe you didn't care as much as I thought you did!"

Gloria gave her a sweet look and folded her in her arms.

"You poor dear!" she said softly, "you've been walking down a fiery path since I went away, haven't you?"

Nancy Asher accepted the affection stoically, blinking away a mist in her hard eyes that Gloria's tone had brought.

"It hasn't been easy," she said harshly, "but at that it was only my parents, my brother. I didn't lose a bridegroom. And you with such wonderful prospects! All gone to smash! Wedding presents returned, trousseau put away, wedding dress unworn, and that great gorgeous mansion of yours standing there empty! And yet you seem to have survived it. What's your secret? Tell it to me! I've been thinking of going into the garage and starting a car, or something. I can't go on like this. Father's like a dead man with his great eyes following me around the room, and Mother's entirely crazy. I can't stand it much longer. You, with your father at death's door and your mother sick with worry, can smile. You have a light in your eyes. What's your secret? Have you one?"

"Yes, I have a secret," said Gloria lifting tender eyes, "but maybe you won't understand. *I* wouldn't have a while ago. But I've found Jesus Christ as my Saviour, Nance dear, and my whole life is made over!"

Nancy Asher stared at her bitterly.

"Do you mean to tell me you've gone religious on us? Got a God-complex? My soul! How did you get that way?"

"I have been studying the Bible, Nancy," answered Gloria, "and I've been finding out God's secrets. I've been learning that this life down here on earth is only a little part of the wonderful whole. It doesn't matter so much about what kind of house I have here, there's a mansion preparing for me in heaven. I've learned too that it is sweeter to let God have His way in your heart than to have your own way!"

Nance stared again.

"No, I don't understand you at all," she said. "It sounds batty to me. You're out of my class! I think I'll go home!" and she marched out of the room and stalked sadly away.

But she came again several times, and though she asked no more questions she watched Gloria's sweet serenity and sighed.

The letters that came from Maine or New York, as the case might be, were great sources of comfort to the two girls now, and the not infrequent telephone calls that brought beloved voices near. The two made a little circle of their own, and sometimes during those hardest days when the life of the precious father hung in the balance, they would go together to a quiet place where they would not be disturbed and kneeling hand in hand would pray quietly.

And then one morning the fever was gone, and their father, though mortally weak, opened his eyes and smiled at Gloria when she slipped in to look at him. He said afterwards that he felt it was Gloria's smile and the look of peace in her eyes as much as anything else that brought him back to earth again and made it seem possible for him to live and go on.

Slowly he crept back to a semblance of strength again, and one day when Gloria and Vanna had come in with some late roses from the garden, to bid him good morning, he made them sit down and began to ask questions.

"You're not to talk about business yet," said Vanna smiling but firm. "The doctor positively forbids it."

"All right," he said pleasantly, "but there's something I've got to say. I know that everything is lost. That won't be any news to me. That's what put me on this bed of course, though I hoped I'd pull through somehow and be able to stand by when the crash came.

I know it must have come now. I've seen the shadow of it in your eyes sometimes, and it was written all over your poor mother's face when she came in to see me yesterday, but I just want you to know this. You two girls are provided for, whatever else goes. Gloria has her house of course in her own name. I saw to that when it was built, and it's all paid for too. It ought to bring a good price if she wants to sell it. There's the same amount of money put away safely in trust for you, Vanna, when you want to marry, or build. It can't be touched. Then there's only the old farm at Afton left. They won't touch that. It isn't worth enough. We can live there of course, only it will be hard on your dear mother! But at least it will be a roof over our heads till I can do something! Unless of course Gloria wants us all to live in her house."

"Oh, no, Father dear!" said Gloria with a shiver. "Never! I'll tell you what I will do with my house, sell it and give you the money. I couldn't keep a cent while you were in debt."

"Nor I," said Vanna quickly. "It all goes back to you, for debts or living or whatever you say. And we'll make Mother love Afton. We love it, Father dear, and she must learn to. She will, you'll see. We'll go up there and have a grand time! And now, you're not to say another word about business to-day!"

"You precious children!" smiled the father. "Well, we'll see about it when I get up. It's wonderful of you to take things this way!"

During the days that followed both the girls had sweet converse with their father, and because of the intimate talks they had had on their trip to Afton Gloria found she could speak more and more freely to him about her experiences after he left her, shyly telling him of the preacher who came to his old church and gave such a thrilling gospel that she had taken to studying the Bible.

He listened to her thoughtfully always, and let her bring her Bible and read it when she suggested that. He even asked her questions about what she had learned, until there came to be a lovely fellowship between them, an understanding of the change in her life.

And one morning when there was no chance of anybody coming to interrupt, she told him that she had found a young man with standards such as he approved, and that they loved each other.

"Do you think it is wrong, Daddy," she said shyly, "for me to love someone so soon after Stan's death?"

"Certainly not!" said her father heartily. "I'd be glad for you to be happy. There is no virtue in mourning, especially after a man who was never meant to be your mate. But who is this young man? I'd like to meet him before I pass judgment, I don't intend to have you make two mistakes of the same sort. I'll have to look him over before I'll give my consent. You're too precious! What's his name?"

"His name is Murray MacRae," said Gloria, her cheeks in a lovely glow of color, "and he's the man who taught me to read the Bible!"

"Oh!" said her father with a look of relief. "But, MacRae! I wonder—— There was a Lawrence Mac-Rae! A most unusual young man. They lived across the road——!"

"Murray is Lawrence's younger brother," said Gloria, "and from what he tells me of Lawrence I think he is a good deal like him."

"I want to see him!" said the father. "I can't be easy until I see him! Has Mother seen him? Does she know?"

"No," said Gloria, "I wanted you to know first. I suppose Mother will object. He isn't exactly what you would call rich, though he's got a good business position."

"Poor Mother!" said the sick man. "I'm afraid life has been rather disappointing for her!"

"I'd like to know why?" said Vanna coming softly in. "Mother's had *you* all these years, and this gorgeous house for a long time, and everything she's wanted. It will be hard for her to stop having it, of course, but life is that way, and she must know it."

"Well, I'd like not to have disappointed her," said

the man drawing a deep sigh, "but maybe we can weather it back again somehow if things brighten up."

"I've just been telling Dad about Murray," Gloria spoke to her sister, hoping to turn her father's attention and take that hurt look out of his eyes.

"Oh, have you? And shall I tell about my man, too? Dad, I'm going to marry a farmer! Will you like that? He's a peach. You can't help liking him."

"You, too, little Vanna!" said her father turning loving eyes to his other daughter. "Why, I hadn't realized you were grown up yet. And you think you can be a farmer's wife? You think you have any idea what that means? Your grandmother——!"

"Yes, I know about my grandmother, and I'm going to try to be just like her. So is Glory. We've learned to cook, Dad. We can make Johnny cake and hash and apple pie, and on a pinch we can help in the fields. We've planted corn!"

Their father grinned.

"And you think that constitutes a farmer's wife? Well, you're all right, but first show me the man. *He's* got to be all right or he can't have you."

"He's Robert Carroll," said Vanna proudly. "He belongs to the old Carroll family, Charles Carroll of Carrollton was one of his ancestors."

"That sounds good," said the father, "but I repeat, I'd like to see the young man before I give my decision. The young *men*, I should say," he added, smiling at Vanna. "I have all respect for your selections of course, but I'm not trusting too much to your judgment. This time I'm going to see for myself."

So two voices lilted over the telephone to two happy young men, summoning them to inspection, and that night they started, driving down in Murray's new car, and stopping on the way in New York for a bit of business.

Two days later they were admitted to audience in the sick room where Mr. Sutherland waited anxiously to greet them. After a few minutes Gloria and Vanna slipped out of the room and left them together.

A little while later, as the girls hovered about the halls, too excited to sit still, awaiting a summons from their father, they saw their mother come out of her room dressed impressively in black satin.

Mrs. Sutherland had been told of the arrival of the two young men, although nobody had as yet dared to tell her that one of them belonged to Gloria. Twice before when they had come, being described as the two neighbors who had driven them home the first time, she had declined to see them, and she had made no remark that day when Vanna had informed her that her fiance was coming. But here she was dressed up and obviously heading toward their father's door.

Precipitately they scuttled ahead of her and opened the door before she should get there, having a vague idea of thus preventing trouble.

"Had we better get them down to the library before she comes?" whispered Vanna with her hand on the door knob, looking back to be sure her mother was coming. "It may be hard on Dad."

"No, just let's leave it to work out," said Gloria serenely.

"That sounds like Murray," murmured Vanna as she swung the door quietly open and stepped inside, noticing with another backward look that her mother had paused in the hall to adjust her collar.

"Well, I like them both!" announced the father as Vanna closed the door carefully. "I can't tell which I like the most! I'm just wondering if you girls are good enough, that's all! I never hoped to find such sensible sons-in-law in this wicked world!" There was a broad smile on his face and a happy light in his eyes, and it was just at this instant that Mrs. Sutherland chose to open the door noiselessly and sweep in.

The girls were so happy over their father's whole-hearted approval that they had for the instant forgotten her approach, and they stood startled for an instant, scarcely knowing what to do.

It was Murray who filled in the silence by stepping forward to Gloria's side and saying:

"And this is your mother, isn't it, Gloria? I have wanted so much to know her!"

Mrs. Sutherland turned an astonished look at the good looking young man, and forgot to impress him with her jeweled lorgnette as she had planned. She suddenly became all graciousness, spoke to each of them, looked from one to the other a moment and said: "Which is *the one?*"

"Both of us is the one, dear madam, if you please," said Murray, bowing low. "I belong to Gloria, and Robert here is Vanna's property!" He swept a twinkle at Gloria's frightened eyes. Hadn't she told him that her mother didn't know about her yet?

But beyond a catch of her breath the good lady was a sport. She never by so much as the flicker of an eyelash let it be known that this was news. Her husband was watching her and his eyes grew bright as they used to be in days long gone by, and he thought how handsome Adelaide still was. Maybe she wouldn't take it so hard after all.

There was a pleasant little stir getting them all seated and then Mrs. Sutherland, taking command, looked toward her husband.

"I asked the nurse if we might have tea up here with you," she said. "She said we might if we didn't stay too long. Does that suit you?"

"It certainly does," said the father heartily. "I feel more like myself than I have for months! These two new sons of mine are a great tonic, and it's so good to think we are getting these girls so nicely off our hands, isn't it Mother!"

The two girls gasped, and then gazed at their lovers in a daze of happiness, and gazed at their mother in speechless astonishment.

"Didn't I tell you the Lord would work it all out?" whispered Gloria to her sister under cover of the talk.

"You're getting more like Murray every day," answered Vanna. "I hope I can be like Robert some day, but I doubt if I'll ever be good enough."

It was a happy time with nothing to mar it, and

not one reference to lost fortunes. Mother was a thoroughbred when it came to a public appearance.

Afterward, when the boys had gone, promising to come down again in a week or so Mrs. Sutherland turned from the window where she had watched Murray's new car drive away, and said to the girls with a new kind of satisfaction in her tone:

"Well, for country people they certainly have good manners, and that is more than can be said of a great many young people to-day!" and she opened a note they had brought her from Brandon and read it with a smile. The daughters perceived that Mother was in process of a transformation of standards to suit the inevitable.

Brand's letter was characteristic:

Dear Mater:
    Sorry I couldn't get down but I had to stick to the job while Bob is gone. It's great up here. We saw a bear the other day and I killed a snake. Hope you soon come. This beats Roseland all to smithereens. See you subse.
                    Yours,
                        Brand.

Mr. Sutherland got well quickly after that. Every morning saw marked improvement.

"It's my new sons-in-law," he said when the girls told him how well he looked, and his wife, standing in the doorway seconding the congratulations, smiled complacently. After all, she reflected, it wasn't every day you could get two such good looking young men for your daughters when you were in a depression and your money was all gone.

After that things moved rapidly. Men came to see Mr. Sutherland from the office, and he learned the worst, including the tragic death of his partner. That set him back a little but not for long. He was eager to get things wound up and adjusted. The attitude of both girls about their money, and also of the two young men who were to marry them, materially assisted in the final adjustments.

Gloria's house was snapped up by a young couple who were soon to marry and it brought a good sum. There were several bids for the big mansion, for there were a few who had envied afar, and still had money to spend.

The packing was not a lengthy matter. Mrs. Sutherland was at last made to understand that a house and its furnishings meant a house *and its furnishings* and not just a few old things left behind that one didn't care to take along. Only her own personal belongings she was to take. And she took the medicine bravely, even surrendering most of her jewels, keeping only those her husband had bought her when he first began to have money, which touched him very much when he discovered it.

"What made her do it?" he asked Vanna wonderingly when they were discussing it. "She didn't have to, you know. They were hers."

"Well, I think she's trying to go the whole length," said Vanna. "She wants everything to be in keeping. She was, mourning because Glory and I wouldn't have a lot of jewels as she had, and I told her that it would not be good taste up in the country to wear jewels, and I think she saw. She always wants to be in harmony with her surroundings."

"If you ask me," said Gloria, having come in without their seeing her, "I think Mother is falling in love with Dad all over again, and I think she wants to please him. She says the money from her jewels and laces is to live on up in the country."

For answer the father smiled a slow sweet smile, and a light came in his eyes that reminded the girls of the lights in their own lovers' eyes.

A few days later, in the midst of the confusion which even the packing of a few personal possessions can make in any house, Mrs. Sutherland paused as her daughters entered the room, radiant as they always were nowadays.

"It's such a pity," she said, "if you two girls are really going to get married, that you can't do it before we leave this lovely house. It is so adapted to a wedding, and a double wedding especially. It would be something to remember. We could have movies taken of it, and there's the lily pond and the outdoor garden —, it would be so lovely!"

"But, Mother, we couldn't afford to have movies taken, and we haven't any money for a wedding such as there would have to be in this house. You know that!"

"Of course! I forgot!" sighed the parent tearfully. "But I don't see how you're going to get together a trousseau up there in the country. You'd have to keep running down to New York continually, and that would be expensive. The wedding dress and all. Of course Gloria wouldn't want to use the same wedding dress even if I hadn't sold it."

"But, Mother, we're not going to have a trousseau," said Vanna quickly, with a troubled glance toward her sister, "and we aren't going to buy any wedding dresses. We couldn't, we haven't the money!"

"But Vanna! You *have* to have a wedding dress! What would you be married in?"

"We both have white organdies," said Vanna, "that we haven't had on yet. And Gloria is going to wear Great-Grandmother Sutherland's wedding veil for hers. I'm counting on borrowing yours for myself!" Vanna grinned.

"Of course. But *white organdy?*"

"It's being done," said Vanna briskly.

"But where would we get a caterer?" wailed the poor woman as her last trouble.

"Why, they don't use caterers up in the country." It was Vanna again, talking eagerly. "Mother, we're having only a few friends and we're making our own refreshments, Glory and I. Homemade ice cream, coffee, darling little rolled sandwiches with chicken filling and little frosted cakes. We're not going to be married anyway until next Spring, we arranged that the last time the boys were here. We want to get you settled and feeling at home in the ancestral house before we fly away, even though it's only down the street and across the road at first. But we're going to have a long winter to learn how to cook and run our houses. We're going to practice on you and Dad. And at Christmas we're going to have the most gorgeous time! Now, Mother, do smile! Father is just coming up to the house and he mustn't see you look gloomy!"

The mother drew a long breath and managed a watery smile in one corner of her mouth.

"It's Gloria I feel so for," she sighed, "leaving that wonderful house. It's really a miniature mansion, and built just as she had planned. And you too, Vanna, this mansion that Father and I had hoped would always be in the family!"

"I don't mind a bit, Mother," lilted Gloria, "I like a farm house just as well. Wait till you see Father's house in Afton. And besides, you know, I'm having another mansion built for me that I'll live in sometime!"

"What do you mean, Gloria, is Murray planning to build?"

"Not Murray, Mother, we'll live in apartments when we're in New York and across the road when we're up in Afton. I'm speaking of my Father's house! *Our* Father's house!" and she quoted reverently:

" 'In my Father's house are many mansions! If it were not so I would have told you. I go to prepare a place for you! And if I go and prepare a place for you I will come again and receive you unto myself, that where I am, there ye may be also.' "

Heartwarming Books
of
Faith and Inspiration

☐ 12674	**POSITIVE PRAYERS FOR POWER-FILLED LIVING** Robert H. Schuller	$1.95
☐ 13269	**THE GOSPEL ACCORDING TO PEANUTS** Robert L. Short	$1.75
☐ 13266	**HOW CAN I FIND YOU, GOD?** Marjorie Holmes	$1.95
☐ 10947	**THE FINDING OF JASPER HOLT** Grace Livingston Hill	$1.50
☐ 12483	**THE BIBLE AS HISTORY** Werner Keller	$2.95
☐ 12218	**THE GREATEST MIRACLE IN THE WORLD** Og Mandino	$1.95
☐ 12009	**THE GREATEST SALESMAN IN THE WORLD** Og Mandino	$1.95
☐ 12330	**I'VE GOT TO TALK TO SOMEBODY, GOD** Marjorie Holmes	$1.95
☐ 12853	**THE GIFT OF INNER HEALING** Ruth Carter Stapleton	$1.95
☐ 12444	**BORN AGAIN** Charles Colson	$2.50
☐ 13436	**SHROUD** Robert Wilcox	$2.50
☐ 13366	**A GRIEF OBSERVED** C. S. Lewis	$2.25
☐ 13077	**TWO FROM GALILEE** Marjorie Holmes	$2.25
☐ 12717	**LIGHTHOUSE** Eugenia Price	$1.95
☐ 12835	**NEW MOON RISING** Eugenia Price	$1.95
☐ 13003	**THE LATE GREAT PLANET EARTH** Hal Lindsey	$2.25
☐ 11140	**REFLECTIONS ON LIFE AFTER LIFE** Dr. Raymond Moody	$1.95

Buy them at your local bookstore or use this handy coupon for ordering

Novels of Enduring Romance and Inspiration by

GRACE LIVINGSTON HILL

Bantam Book Catalog

Here's your up-to-the-minute listing of over 1,400 titles by your favorite authors.

This illustrated, large format catalog gives a description of each title. For your convenience, it is divided into categories in fiction and non-fiction—gothics, science fiction, westerns, mysteries, cookbooks, mysticism and occult, biographies, history, family living, health, psychology, art.

So don't delay—take advantage of this special opportunity to increase your reading pleasure.

Just send us your name and address and 50¢ (to help defray postage and handling costs).

BANTAM BOOKS, INC.
Dept. FC, 414 East Golf Road, Des Plaines, Ill. 60016

Mr./Mrs./Miss_____
(please print)

Address_____

City_____State_____Zip_____

Do you know someone who enjoys books? Just give us their names and addresses and we'll send them a catalog too!

_____

Mr./Mrs./Miss_____

Address_____

City_____State_____Zip_____

_____

Mr./Mrs./Miss_____

Address_____

City_____State_____Zip_____

FC—9/78